TALES OF THE EMPEROR

ALSO BY JACK WINTER

STAGE PLAYS

The Evil Eye (1961)
And They'll Make Peace (1962)
Before Compiègne (1963)
The Mechanic (1964)
The Death of Woyzeck (1965)
Hey Rube! (1966)
The Golem of Venice (1967)
Party Day (1969)
The Centre (1971)
Waiting (1972)
Mr. Pickwick (1972)
Letters from the Earth (1973)
Ten Lost Years (1974)
You Can't Get Here from There (1975)
Summer Seventy-Six (1975)
Family Matters (1988)
Ravers (2005)
Caboose to Moose Jaw (2009)

BOOKS

The Island (poetry, 1973)
Misplaced Persons (poetry, 1995)
The Ballad of Bladud (poetry, 1999)
Nomad's Land (poetry, 2000)
The Tallis Bag (literary memoir, 2012)
My TWP Plays: A Collection Including Ten Lost Years
    (annotated anthology of five plays, 2013)

TALES OF THE
EMPEROR

JACK WINTER

TALONBOOKS

Talonbooks
278 East First Avenue, Vancouver, British Columbia, Canada V5T 1A6
www.talonbooks.com

First printing: 2015

Typeset in Garamond
Printed and bound in Canada on 100% post-consumer recycled paper
Interior and cover design by Typesmith
Cover photograph by Mike Locke via Flickr Creative Commons 2.0

Talonbooks gratefully acknowledges the financial support of the Canada Council for the Arts, the Government of Canada through the Canada Book Fund, and the Province of British Columbia through the British Columbia Arts Council and the Book Publishing Tax Credit.

LIBRARY AND ARCHIVES CANADA CATALOGUING IN PUBLICATION

Winter, Jack, 1936–, author
    Tales of the emperor : fiction / Jack Winter.

Issued in print and electronic formats.
ISBN 978-0-88922-944-0 (PBK).—ISBN 978-0-88922-945-7 (EBOOK)

    1. Qin shi huang, Emperor of China, 259 B.C.–210 B.C.—Fiction.
I. Title.

PS8545.I73T34 2015   C813'.54   C2015-904124-4
                                               C2015-904125-2

...for Jackie for Jackie for Jackie...

AUTHOR'S NOTE ON NAMES

Tales of the Emperor is a novel loosely based on ancient archives, notably *Records of the Grand Historian* by Ssu-Ma Ch'ien. That wonderful collection (c. 90 B.C.) is, by the standards of modern historians, largely imagined.

Readers familiar with Hanyu Pinyin, the phonetic system developed in the 1950s for transcribing Mandarin pronunciations of Chinese characters into the Latin alphabet, will find my spelling of proper names (c. 1949!) antiquated, a reader-friendly plus in my estimation, perhaps not in theirs.

For them, here are some principal names along with the Hanyu Pinyin equivalents:

Ssu-Ma Ch'ien / Sima Qian

Li Ssu / Lǐ Sī

Master Ching / Jing Ke

Kao / Gao

Fei-tzu / Feizi

Tao-chou / Táo Chǒu

Wang Chien (General Wang) / Wáng Jián

Lu Pu-wei (Lu Wei) / Lü Bùwéi

Chao Kao / Zhao Gao

Chen She / Chén Shé

Kao Tsu / Gaozu

Others, like Madam Ng, Lipless Wang, Jovial Peng, Lady Shang, Peh Yi, Ffut, Gerrhi, are invented and require no transliteration.

By the way, the Hanyu Pinyin proper name of the real First Emperor (260–210 B.C.) is Qin Shī Huángdi. I prefer his more familiar citation, Ch'in, since that is the root of the name he gave to the empire he founded and the modern nation he bequeathed. In *Tales of the Emperor* the matter is entirely academic (i.e., non-academic?) since his historical name is never used.

CONTENTS

IV. FROM COLD MOUNTAIN (poems of Kao) : The musician-assassin, now only a deaf poet, contemplates the First Emperor and the empire from the perspective of a frigid hermitage.

A modern conception of a stone relief from the Wu Liang Tomb in Shantung (c. 150 A.D.) depicting the attempted assassination of the First Emperor (c. 227 B.C.). The potential assassin (Master Ching) is being restrained by a courtier (perhaps the advisor, Li Ssu?), but already has thrown his dagger at the First Emperor who, with one sleeve torn off, cowers behind a pillar that has been pierced by the weapon. Other petroglyphics include a severed head in a box, a soldier entering too late, another (or, perhaps, Master Ching's accomplice, Kao?) flat on his backside.

I

DISCOVERING THE FIRST EMPEROR

The First Emperor took over a state founded on doctrinaire legalist principles, a universal mandarinate bureaucracy, and a cultural tradition of inventing the past that is called "writing history." Even the Great Wall already was in place and only required a joining of its segments in the First Emperor's name. Correctly perceiving that a perfect state requires no governing, the First Emperor dedicated himself to preparing its death and his own. He brought about public works and literary monuments such as the Imperial Tomb and the Imperial Archive, then withdrew his body into the one and his spirit into the other and removed the keys to both. So successful was the endeavour of the First Emperor and all who served him that he and they and the empire that contained them lay two thousand years without a trace until the recent excavations at Mount Li. Even then nothing more would have emerged had everyone been content with vast ceramic armies and traces of rivers of mercury. In this our modern era of revised revolutions and dying empires no one was, and excavations have resumed. Today archaeologists and other tourists stand at the threshold of the tomb itself. When they enter, these are the relics they will not find.

WRITING HISTORY

The tale of the uncovering is too well known to require innovation. Excavating a domestic earth-closet in a field seldom used because of its reputation for vapours, a family of farmers struck something at a depth of seven snakes. What they found destroyed them. The testimony of one of their number survives.

"At first we saw the bottom of an upside-down pot. Then, as we dug further, we saw it was the top of a head. Then, a whole head. Thinking it a rarity that could be sold at market to one who values such things, we took a hammer to it and broke it off. When we carried it home and washed it and saw its face, its fierceness and its sorrow, everyone refused to touch it again. We thought it was a juju. We were frightened the juju would punish us for breaking off its head, so we summoned the village priest. Thus began all of our misfortunes.

"The priest summoned the schoolmaster, the schoolmaster the magistrate, the magistrate the mayor, the mayor the constabulary, and so on and on until at last the governor himself summoned the army and serious excavations began. In no time at all more than eight thousand clay warriors — one headless — were uncovered and washed down and marvelled at. Then the tomb itself was broken into and the First Emperor was revealed. By that time all the land around our village had been uprooted and made valueless for planting or for pasture, and our village itself was levelled to make way for exhibition halls and gift shops.

"My family and everyone else's were forced to move to another village, where we were expected to pay for the construction of our own new homes with government compensation that was siphoned off by officials before it reached us. Meanwhile we slept on stones and lived on air, and we gained the reputation among the native villagers of being ne'er-do-wells and idlers, too proud to work, too filthy to befriend, and not to be trusted. There was employment for us when at last the excavation was filled in again, a task our new neighbours feared to undertake, but it ended when the reburial of the First Emperor was complete. We were forbidden to move back to the site of our former village to prevent the temptation to dig again.

"Of our original number, I alone remain to tell the tale. It is a tale of bottomless misfortune. Besides the animosity of our old neighbours and the contempt of our new, my family suffered more than anyone else's its share of unmerited calamity. My father died of a skin disease that began in his digging hand and caused his body to rot away. My brother developed a heart complaint brought on by digging and disappointment, and did not want to be a burden to my mother and me and hanged himself. My sisters, who had done nothing more than carry away pailfuls of rubble, married beneath themselves to escape our curse and never were heard from again. Even a distant cousin in a remote province ran mad and butchered his cows before they had calved. All of which caused my mother to expire of shame at an advanced age but before I was ready to lose her. For my family's achievement, our village was awarded ten exemptions from tax that were eradicated when our village was.

"Worst of all, not one of my family was named or honoured as the locator of the site. The former mayor of our vanished village sits there today under a banner that describes him as the man who did it. For the one or two tourists who continue to visit to see what cannot be seen, he autographs bad replicas of the original decapitated head although he never in his life wielded a shovel or a hammer and only concerned himself with earth-closets when using one and had to be taught to sign his name.

"This much is certain. It is a mistake to place an earth-closet upon a warrior's head. Would that my family had been content to shit elsewhere."

The method of writing history is to know the past by entering it and, thus, to discover the present. In a mosaic of tales, some no more than fragments, others chapter-length, strivings are examined, accomplishments are measured, tittle-tattle is enlarged, and the reader is led through the remains of an imagined time with a contemporary meaning. Inevitably, questions remain.

What was it that was seen in the brief glimpse of the First Emperor before the apparatus of his tomb was reassembled and the accumulation of Mount Li was impacted upon it?

Was it the First Emperor who was seen? For the family who found the clay head, what else could account for the dimension of the devastation visited upon them? For others, misfortune has to be attributed elsewhere, and whether it was the First Emperor who was revealed means nothing.

Who can guess the date of the next uncovering? The chronometrics of a future age are by no means certain. Perhaps a year then will be no more than a fraction of our current calculation, perhaps greater? Perhaps it will be other than lunar-based, and immeasurable by any astrologic standard other than its own? Perhaps two thousand such years will consist of no more than a geologic moment or a meteorologic season or a hiatus of cultural trauma such as that which follows the death of anyone's emperor and the discovery that his dynasty did not outlive him?

There are those among us who will memorialize the First Emperor in other ways than excavating. With an impregnation, perhaps, to mark the morn of his renaissance, with a massacre on the eve of his decease ... with the honorary debasement of the coinage of his foes, the tumbling of their towers alleging a confederacy, the incorporation of their continents into the grandeur of our land mass, the absorption of their mores into the folkways of our own ... with a decorative monogram, a commemorative medallion, a heraldic device, an ancestral masque, a genealogical tableau, a painted cave invoking the First Emperor's profundity, a mountain crested to commemorate his potence ... with predestinatory omens, talismanic prophecies, animistic hallucinations, demonic inhabitations, spectral visitations, astral emanations, a star cluster imagined in the profile of his brow, a galaxy invested with the provenance of his reign, an improved earth-closet with his name upon the lid.

Mere chinoiseries? Perhaps. Is there a better moment for them?

II

THE ASSASSINATION OF
THE FIRST EMPEROR

Many wish to reach the First Emperor, one may say all men wish it. There are as many ways to reach him as there are those who desire to do it. One may reach the First Emperor upon the highway of the mind. That is how I have travelled, and how I travel still. Sometimes I succeed. Especially after a night of prayer I have only to close my eyes and he enters like the dawn. He is very beautiful. You must reach him in your way, for he is yours to reach and everyone's.

THE THREE TRAVELLERS

One day three men set out to reach the Emperor: Li Ssu who wished to advise him; Master Ching who wished to assassinate him; a musician named Kao whose companionship was required by Master Ching. Li Ssu departed alone. At a crossroads he met the others and they decided to continue their several quests together. When they reached the imperial throne, Li Ssu showed the Emperor how to thwart the attack of Master Ching. Li Ssu thereby won himself a high post at court. Master Ching was seized and executed, but Kao was punished more severely.

THE RECRUITMENT OF
MASTER CHING
(A SONG OF KAO)

Master Ching and the prince went to a pool of the palace.
Master Ching picked up a tile and threw it at a tortoise.
The prince gave Master Ching balls of gold to throw.
Master Ching concluded, "My prince entertains me royally."

Master Ching and the prince rode on matched white horses.
Master Ching remarked, "What is rarer than matched white horses?"
The prince drew forth his sword and slew the horse he rode on.
Master Ching concluded, "My prince entertains me royally."

Master Ching and the prince watched the princess dance a dance.
Master Ching observed, "The princess has skilful feet."
The prince cut off her feet and gave them to Master Ching.
Master Ching concluded, "My prince entertains me royally."

Master Ching and the prince were afflicted with old age.
Master Ching grew weary of all the court amusements.
The prince went among the people and caught the plague and died.
Master Ching concluded, "My prince entertains me royally."

THE DEPARTURE OF
MASTER CHING

In the matter of my commission to assassinate the Emperor, it is not true that I have procrastinated. Nor that I was awaiting the death of my host, the prince, before departing to fulfill the task he had entrusted. That famous witticism was accomplished by my companion, the musician Kao. Who better than Kao to have jested, for is it not he who shared my sojourn at the court of our delightful prince? Neither did Kao commit procrastination. Accomplice to the assassin of the emperor of the world, is that not a post that requires preparation? Since the Emperor never before has been assassinated, who is qualified to conclude how long is necessary to prepare oneself for the deed? Or that fifteen years is too long? It is appropriate to observe that I merely awaited the convenience of my admired accomplice. After the example of my prince's hospitality to me, his guest, could I have demonstrated less to Kao who was mine?

It is correct to point out that, as his provinces fell one by one and the armies of the Emperor approached the gates of his very palace, my prince became unable any longer to purchase my amusements and, bereft of life and kingdom, he soon would have been required to decline the honour of remaining my host. Such are the vicissitudes of decorum in a state under siege by an unassassinated emperor. Nevertheless, it cannot be disputed that I exploited my prince. Wherein did I exploit him? Why, in omitting to convince him that my commission on his behalf must fail!

THE DEPARTURE OF LI SSU
(A SONG OF KAO)

On a tree no limb is straight. Yet there are arrows.
On a tree no trunk is round. Yet there are wheels.
Li Ssu concluded, "Art is stretching and bending."

In the latrine there are rats. They flee the approach of a dog.
In the granary there are rats. No dog dare approach them.
Li Ssu concluded, "Ability depends on place."

There is a truly hard substance. It is not afraid of grinding.
There is a truly white substance. It is not afraid of dyes.
Li Ssu concluded, "Such an emperor can be advised."

The spoor pursues the hunted. The arrow pursues the spoor.
The chariot pursues the arrow. The carrion bird pursues the chariot.
Li Ssu concluded, "A politician must travel."

THE THOUGHTS OF
LI SSU ALONG THE ROAD

I go to serve the Emperor. To others it will seem that I but use the Emperor to serve myself. That is how it seems to this old assassin riding beside me, but that is because he has not long to live and must come to quick decisions.

I go to serve the Emperor for one reason only. Now is the time for such service, a moment later would be too late, a moment sooner too soon. It does not follow that the Emperor will welcome me. If he did, it would be because he is diminished by the lack of me and is not worth the serving. No indeed, I must manage affairs so as to create the need.

I seek to advise the Emperor. Others seek to reach him with their hands. Such a one is that watchful drunkard riding behind us, but that is because he is a musician and must fondle remarkable events. I seek to advise the Emperor for one reason only. Yesterday the empire was unborn, tomorrow it will be dead, this is the only day to immortalize its dying. For that great task mouths are more useful than hands, advice more necessary than remarkable events.

A single misfortune impedes me. It is said the Emperor has a deaf ear, and it is that ear that is reserved for aliens. Because there is no alternative, my way is clear. I must await the one event so remarkable that it averts the head of the Emperor and turns his good ear toward me.

THE THOUGHTS OF
MASTER CHING ALONG THE ROAD

My assassination of the Emperor must fail. Can you imagine if it did not? It is as if it had already failed. Why, then, am I proceeding to the capital city? Because the details have yet to be settled.

Such is not the case of this young politician riding beside me. He seeks to gain high office. His attempt assumes the life of the Emperor and, since my attempt will fail, it follows that his will succeed. The dimensions of his success, those are the details of his attempt that remain to be settled.

Yet the case of this ambitious young man is not entirely different from mine. Although I seek to end the life of the Emperor, my failure surely will alter his life if only for the instant of his deliverance. In that sense even my attempt will succeed, though not in the way that I nor the son of the prince who dispatched me intend. That way no longer is possible. Even along this endless road the news has reached us that the son of the son of the prince who dispatched me is dead and the last of his state has fallen to the Emperor.

Why, then, do I proceed to the capital city? A journey once begun must be ended. But why there? Why not here? Or at the next meadow or at the last? Why must I ride past meadow and meadow, heartland and morass, toward a task I cannot accomplish? Surely the road is a little to blame. It leads straight to the Emperor, for it is his road. Even were I to turn aside into a byroad and then to another and then to a footpath and then to none, I would find myself on the Emperor's highway, for it gathers all ways to itself in the end. As for stopping, that would require more strength than I can command, enough perhaps to accomplish my commission, and then what would be the need of stopping?

THE THOUGHTS OF
KAO ALONG THE ROAD
(A SONG OF KAO)

Hanging on this lip of time, fully informed, bewildered, are they
    keeping something from me? Do I know too much already?
    What is there to know?
Hanging on this lip of time, fully informed, bewildered, do they
    know what I am thinking? Have they thought of me at all?
Hanging on this lip of time, fully informed, bewildered, does
    knowing make the difference between my work and theirs?
Is there any difference between my work and theirs? Do I care to
    know the difference? Do I care at all?
Hanging on this lip of time, fully informed, bewildered, why have
    I not been consulted?
Are they having consultations? Ear to lip? Lip to ear? Nightly?
    Hourly? If so, where?
Why do they keep secrets from me? Why have I been told so much?
    What am I required to do with what I think I have been told?
Hanging on this lip of time, fully informed, bewildered, pending
    contrary instructions shall I withhold certain measures? Shall
    I undertake the rest?
Hanging on this lip of time, fully informed, bewildered, are they
    keeping something from me? Do I know too much already?
    What is there to know?

THE CHANT OF THE BEARERS

The road to the Emperor is long and hard.
 Long and hard.
The stones on the road are sharp and dry.
 Sharp and dry.
That is why no tigers reach him.
That is why no ill winds reach him.
That is why no devils reach him.
That is why few men try.
 Long and hard.
 Sharp and dry.
 Reach him, reach him, reach him, try.

The walls of the city approach, approach.
 Approach, approach.
The bricks of the walls are red, blood-red.
 Red, blood-red.
Through the chinks in the bricks not a nail can enter.
Through the chinks in the bricks not a thought can enter.
Through the chinks in the bricks only spirits enter
And the walls are stained with the flight of the dead.
 Approach, approach.
 Red, blood-red.
 Enter, enter, enter, the dead.

The streets of the city are endless, endless.
 Endless, endless.
The gates of the palace are endless, endless.
 Endless, endless.
Parks and pavilions, endless, endless.
Towers and forests, endless, endless.
Grottoes and galleries, endless, endless.
Endless, endless, the steps to the throne.
 Endless, endless.
 Endless, endless.
 Endless, endless, endless, the throne.

THE ASSASSINATION

It is well known that history is the study of the paintings of great events. What, then, is to be observed from the famous depiction of the assassination of the Emperor? Why, that the dagger did not reach him! There is the bronze pillar and there is the dagger embedded in it. Behind it, recoiling beyond the border, must be the figure of the Emperor. There beyond the border on the other side must be Master Ching himself in the very act of throwing. These details are too well known to require further recounting, and surely that is the reason no other painting of the event has been permitted to survive. This one is our authority.

What can be concluded from it other than the fact that it was the pillar that was pierced and not the Emperor? Is it correct to conclude even that? After all, the painting records but one moment of the attempt, the instant at which the dagger pierced the pillar. Who is to say what happened later on? Perhaps the dagger was not arrested? If one were to object that the pillar appears to be bronze and this fact alone is sufficient to curtail the flight of any dagger however fiercely thrown, could we not be justified in asking how it was, in that case, that the dagger came to pierce the pillar at all, and to conclude that a dagger sufficiently thrown to pierce a pillar of bronze might pass clear through it, blade, hilt, and tassel? Indeed, it often has been observed that festivals commemorating the event during which rural competitors of every degree of malevolence attempt to pierce bronze pillars with missiles must have had their origin in the curiosity of our folk concerning this very point. Since none in decades of participation has so much as dented the face of a single pillar, little can be concluded beyond the implacability of bronze pillars and the eagerness of our folk to pierce them.

To return to the matter of the assassination, in the next instant after the painting did the dagger gather its velocity and hurl itself still further into the body of the pillar, impelling before it innumerable shards, every one of them a minute dagger, twisting this way to avoid an alloy, that way to exploit a flaw,

parting layer after layer of inner encrustation until splinters and
splinterer, daggerlets and dagger, burst in an orifice of bronze
and hurled themselves at the body of the Emperor, penetrating
him, transfixing? It is difficult to say. For one thing, how could
such an unauthorized calamity accord with the well-known fact
that Li Ssu saved him? For another, like Master Ching and the
Emperor, Li Ssu does not appear in the painting. Are we meant to
conclude, therefore, that Li Ssu rushed into the scene a moment
after the pillar was pierced which is proof that the dagger passed
through it, for why else would the Emperor have required further saving? If that indeed is the case, why has the painter chosen
to represent not the assassination of the Emperor at all but the
moment before it, thereby denying us any authentic history of
the apprehended event?

Or do these omissions suggest that the painting is to be
interpreted symbolically? That Li Ssu is represented as the pillar?
That he, like it, interrupted the dagger that itself is a symbol of
some less direct mode of assault: a suggestion, perhaps, that the
Emperor resign? a campaign for his impeachment? If the pillar
does represent Li Ssu, its interception of a dagger could well
refer to his defence of the Emperor with brazen words. Such
an assault would not have penetrated that defence! Indeed, the
impervious multiloquence of the renowned Li Ssu must have
absorbed every argument of Master Ching, thus protecting the
unassailability of the empty space behind the pillar that then
could be seen to represent the Emperor against the aggression
of the word-assassin Master Ching who, of course, would be
represented by that eruptive empty space in front.

Who, then, or what is the musician Kao? Kao, at least,
might be in the painting. That crumpled pile of fabric lying in
the corner — in a fuller depiction, perhaps, just below the flying
sleeve of the Emperor's robe torn off in his struggle to escape
and adjacent to the box containing the severed head of Master Ching's former host, the prince, offered as a diversionary
tribute — that could be he, flat on the ground like a discarded

garment, protecting his instrument. If so, Kao represents the painting itself, and his posture the vanity of interpreting great events other than by means of the instruments of art.

THE LAST WORDS OF
MASTER CHING

Waiting for my head to fall, I caress my neck and think. We have been a long time together and I for one welcome this opportunity to contemplate the nature of our attachment.

THE ADVICE OF LI SSU REGARDING
SEVERAL MATTERS

Sire, Master Ching could no longer live, and that is why he has been made to die. The musician Kao had heard enough, and that is why he has been deafened. What of me? I comment on these matters, so that is my employment. I am in your presence, so you intend to hear me. You continue to live, so my service to you has begun.

In my case, sire, you will not distinguish by conferring high office. As has been demonstrated, it is unfortunate that you are perceptible. Elevate me and who will defend us both? The same is true of my citizenship. You will permit me to remain an alien so that my presence is not accorded visibility and my advice may emanate from your mouth unimpaired by the reputation of having entered your ear.

Regarding the matter of aliens, punitive banishment retroactive to the sixth generation is gratifying to contemplate and productive to threaten, though you do not wish it accomplished because it has not been. Regarding the matter of the remaining world, you will continue to refrain from absorbing it lest banishment and alienation alike be rendered inconceivable.

Regarding affairs in general, two conclusions are certain. The present situation will not continue. Prediction is impossible.

Regarding the well-known matter of the impending death of the empire, two observations are permissible. Because your assassination has been resisted, the empire is not yet dead. Because the death of the empire remains inevitable, you intend to govern its dying. Clearly, it is upon this latter task, the greatest of your reign because it is the last, that I am intended to concentrate my service.

Here, then, is my first advice. Collect tales! National ballads, political songs, odes of lamentation by the wearied and the slandered, festive hymns on fixed occasions, murderous anecdotes and tomes, imprecations, work cries, gossip, curses, diary dreams and tavern murmurs, sacred jokes and long night ramblings ... excepting only the military, the academic, and other matters related to vanished sentiment, collect them, sire, collect them all! Collect them, and command their collection, and prefer those by whom they are collected! Is it not by attending their tales that one locates the pulse of the people? Is it not by touching the pulse of the people that one perceives the moment of its cessation? Indeed, sire, do not neglect to collect tales! How else are you to know when the empire has died?

THE DEPARTURE OF KAO

Concluding that a deaf musician is only a poet, Kao broke his instrument and retired to Cold Mountain and was heard of again.

III

THE RISE OF THE FIRST EMPEROR

At one stage the First Emperor was inclined to consider the pursuit of others as his destiny. Because it was the destiny of others to pursue anyone in pursuit of his own, no one corrected this misapprehension. Thus were many blessings accomplished, none to the advantage of the First Emperor.

THE LONG RETREAT

How the Emperor rose to prominence is not a tale that can be told. With every step he took, he eradicated the one he had taken. His rise was not so much a succession of steps as an accession of states, each unprecedented. The Emperor did not appear to rise. He appeared to remain stationary while events conferred upon him and history subsided around him. The Emperor did not rise. He unfolded until at last the empire turned and found him at its zenith.

The Emperor permitted none of the documents of his rise to remain, except perhaps the Tale of the Long Retreat. The reasons for the Emperor's having undertaken his epic withdrawal are illegible. So are the events. For instance, it is not certain whether the Emperor was alone during that time or whether, as most seem to believe, he was accompanied by minions. Today virtually every senior official attributes his influence to his having accompanied the Emperor during the Long Retreat. Not all the claims can be true. If they were, the hordes in attendance would have rendered the event not a retreat but a progress. That the Emperor never has discountenanced these claims, nor verified some and thereby discredited the rest, doubtless is due to his reticence to be drawn into unseemly clarification.

The precise course of the Long Retreat is impossible to specify. The terrain was hazardous. One need only compare portraits of the Emperor before and after the Long Retreat to recognize his enormous expenditure of spirit during that unimaginable pilgrimage. But the route of the Emperor, his itinerary, even the duration of his travail … these are impossible to specify for there is scarcely a single mountain hamlet in the entire empire that does not enshrine at least one flagstone scored by the Emperor's very horse, despite the Emperor's suggestion — contained in the Parable of the Flowers, now regrettably lost — that he travelled on foot.

Since so little is known of the Long Retreat, why bother to interpret it? Because the famous Tale of the Long Retreat constitutes the only document of the Emperor's rise he has permitted us to retain. As such, it is infallible. Interpretation of it is not merely warranted, it is commanded.

THE EMPEROR LEAVES HOME

Before he left home to conquer his future, the Emperor killed his parents. This was done according to the ancient protocols, and because the Emperor truly was eager to depart and had chosen the correct moment to do so. The procedure benefited everyone. The Emperor because it freed him to live apart. The Emperor's parents because it protected them from loneliness. Had he had brothers and sisters, it would not have been necessary for the Emperor to kill his parents. The last to leave home would have done it. Because the Emperor was the first and the last, the duty fell to him.

Much time was spent discussing which would be the first to die. The father, of course, offered himself because he had a cowardly nature. The mother urged the Emperor to accept his father's plea, and the Emperor knew she did this so the old man would not have to bear the inconvenience of her death even for a moment. For her loving nature, the Emperor decided to reward her. That is why, although not in accordance with custom, in the family of the Emperor the mother was the first to die.

THE EMPEROR'S SCHOOLING

As a child the Emperor attended a series of tuitional institutions of expanding endeavour and contracting utility. What he learnt there was the practice of tuitional institutions, a knowledge measured by competitive examinations devised and set in accordance with the procedures of each institution, and assessed by an instructor who had never set foot outside it. The process culminated at the academy.

For several years the Emperor thought he would never leave the academy. There seemed no reason to leave, none as compelling as the reason to remain: he seemed always to have been there, and could think of no place other to go.

Indeed, reasoning of the sort current at the academy suggested that the world beyond it was merely a compendium of information that, when acquired, became an apparatus of instruction to impart what it was one had learned. In effect, the world beyond was an extenuation of the place one already was in. As such, the academy presented no need to vacate and every incentive to stay on and, in the way of the academy, to seek out an abject corner in a neglected field of study and to become its propagator and its proponent, its proctor and its prodigy, its professor and, eventually, its professed. Indeed, the Emperor might have elected to remain at the academy, a prisoner of its delights, were it not for the profound misery he detected there.

The delights were many, or many aspects of the one. As a student he was introduced to them by a hoary mentor of decaying gender who, in weekly tutorial sessions, augmented his instruction by placing a hand on the Emperor's thigh, interjecting nostalgic references to "the academic staff" and "the student body" and, after a sip or several from the tutorial tea flask, "the nubility" and "the arsetocracy."

Other than thigh-kneading and innuendo, however, this ambiguous elder made no further encroachment, and seemed content to impart tales of the exploits of his more energetic colleagues which he did with the gusto and the attention to detail of a connoisseur of salacious enterprise. Thus the Emperor was apprised of the intimate commerce between fellow students and their vigorous demanding mentors, the transactions taking place in a room labelled "common." During those encounters the commodity in transaction was a measure of professorial probing ("research") and the currency in circulation was an apportionment of academic accreditation ("grades").

Considering the delicious blend of geographic isolation and temporal insulation ("cultural independence"), the blissful absence of social obligation and public scrutiny ("academic freedom"), the monumental salaries, perpetual pensions, subsidies upon demand, and eternal *emeritus honoraria* ("intellectual property"), no other sector of the community, indeed no sector of any community in the Emperor's experience thitherto or thereafter, was graced with privileges in excess of and pleasures commensurate with those of the academy.

How, then, in the midst of such indulgence transpired such misery? Yet misery prevailed, of that there could be no doubt. Deep into the countenance of every inmate of the academy regardless of age or pretence of age — the young aspiring to be old, the old striving to appear young — misery was etched, a misery of a type peculiar to the academy and, as far as the Emperor could determine, exclusive to it. What in this perfectly contained and self-perpetuating micro-galaxy did an academician have to regret or to repent? Yet regret and repentance there must have been, its repression producing the self-justifying meanness and the aggressive self-loathing characteristic of academic studies. It was a conundrum the Emperor perceived but never resolved.

Despite his admiration for the bravery of those willing to bear, amid such amplitude, such abiding sorrow, the Emperor saw no reason to remain among them and to share it. He accepted graduation and never looked back.

THE EMPEROR AND THE PRINCESS

In the second portion of his first life the Emperor permitted himself to marry at an absurdly early age. By magnifying her virtues, he enabled himself to select a certain princess. By protesting his unworthiness, he encouraged her to win him.

The princess possessed several attractions. She considered herself higher born than the Emperor; since, until he came to reign all matters of birth remained without status, the Emperor accepted this pretension as testimony that she would recognize veritable nobility when it was sired upon her. The princess prized her ability to concentrate her attention in an obsessive manner that led one to mistake the focus of her gaze for insight; as yet possessing little insight himself, the Emperor thought it excessive to expect it in another. The princess considered herself at variance with her parents; since her family quarrels concerned such issues as the vivacity of her lip rouge, the Emperor elected to believe that the princess was determined to separate herself from home regardless of topic, and he decided to consider this wilfulness as a bond between them rather than as an omen of their disjunction.

There were other bonds. There was the matter of the giant willow. Taller than the house of the parents of his betrothed, the first to green in the spring, nightly the Emperor and the princess parted its curtains, crept into the alcove where fists of snow lay clenched about the roots, released bodices and girdles and explicit admonitions, and grappled among the seasonal rubble. These engagements, the Emperor recalled, had been largely a condition of pain, his to enlarge while seeking its encasement, hers to alleviate by accepting its infliction. Each activity involved courage or, at the least, dedicated pursuance. Both seemed doomed by imprecision.

Then one evening, after many hours of hushed commands and complex tumescence, when the participants at last lay apart bruised, clotted, disconsolate, there occurred an alteration in the demeanour of the princess. To relieve the inflammation of her contusions, she edged her backside onto the hillock of snow. As the Emperor watched in limp fascination, she began to rotate herself deeper into the melting mound which exercise she facilitated by raising her legs upwards along the spine of the willow. As the pace of her movements quickened, her legs sank along either side of the tree, and her heels disappeared behind it drawing her torso across the snow closer to the rough bark. To steady her progress the princess's arms reached backward and her hands closed around the Emperor, grasping, grasping, grasping him in the rhythm of her undulations. Together they slithered toward the trunk.

It seemed as if the ancient willow itself were awakening to the game. Just above the Emperor's gaze there was a swaying of branches and a distant sigh of leaves. Nearer the tumult approached until the very shaft of the tree, moist with the juices of its own springtide, pulsated in the clasp of her thighs and the innermost lips of the ultimate chamber parted to reveal the congested countenance of the princess's livid father!

The branches closed, then opened again, then snapped shut with a cracking of limbs. Shrinking together in damp adhesion, the princess and the Emperor heard footsteps retreating through the fallen leaves and a remote ascending wail.

Had the espier amid the foliage chosen to obliterate from his memory the image of his daughter's simultaneous despoilment by willow tree and suitor, and sensibly replaced it with his favourite recollection of her five-year-old self emerging from her bath immaculately breastless, it is doubtful that the bachelorhood of the Emperor would have ended prematurely. But the princess's father resolved to commemorate the incident by forbidding the princess and the Emperor access to one another in this world or the next, and they were left with no alternative. And so they married, and the old man had to content himself with felling the willow.

MADAM NG

Once his marriage was achieved, the Emperor began to search for a wife. He found many. Few were recalcitrant, several instigative, each as indelibly wed as he. Typically, the husband of such a wife — generally a rising official — had demanded matrimony at a time and parenthood at a pace that synchronized with his own ascending destiny. Consequently, the wife of such a husband was required to pursue her bypassed bachelorhood within wedlock. Which incentive also propelled the Emperor.

Such was the case of Madam Ng, with one difference. Because her husband was more than commonly preoccupied with his destiny, that of a rising litigator, it was necessary for Madam Ng to dramatize every aspect of her deportment in order to call herself to his attention. To this end it was essential that she disclose to her husband each of her encounters with the Emperor, but that she moderate the contents of those covert congresses so that she could continue to confess the majority of them.

At the same time, in order to retain the devotion of the Emperor, Madam Ng was required to perfect a maddening blend of sultry reticence and prudent abandon. How else to explain the fact that, although she and the Emperor relieved one another in a variety of geographic and architectural bolt-holes in unprecedented conditions of bodily permutation and haberdashery disarray, they never once, in scores of triweekly encounters, mated?

Naturally there was much talk between them of correspondent need and correlative devotion, of a hostile cosmos polluted with incomprehension, of a transcendent future when each would be released from inhibiting requisites — mates, offspring, domiciles, ascending destinies — and both, at last, would interpenetrate ecstatically and redeem every current humiliation reciprocally inflicted. Yet the truth of the matter was that neither liked the other much. In fact, had various unsolicited advisors of the Emperor eventually tired of pointing out to him the banality of Madam Ng, he might not have been required defiantly to perpetuate the liaison.

As it was, transfiguring her in the philtre of his fantasy, the Emperor clung stubbornly to Madam Ng. As months passed into years, he came to visualize only her while performing the nightly protocols of his own marriage, and the wife of the Emperor, noting that his devotion to her delight accelerated thrice weekly, came to accept the phenomenon as their peculiar connubial rhythm.

The Emperor envied the husband of Madam Ng because that fortunate man was permitted access to the only orifice denied the

Emperor, and was licensed to ignore her except on those fort-
nightly occasions. Madam Ng envied the wife of the Emperor.
"How blessed," she thought, "to be married to a man who weeps!"
The wife of the Emperor envied Madam Ng, or would have had
she known of the existence of her rival. Imagining his wife's distress as if he had perceived it, the Emperor truculently offered
recompense by perpetuating their marriage. Only the husband of
Madam Ng was free of envy and resentment or, rather, was freed
to focus them upon the receding backsides of those litigators who
ascended the ladders of their destinies immediately ahead of him.
The Emperor envied the husband his innocent preoccupation.

Under the impress of these bleak emotions the Emperor
found himself become that most tedious of creatures: a young
man possessed of an incessant, unfocussed, unquenchable rage.
For no reason that was apparent, he anticipated critics, harangued
intimates, and frequently insulted passersby. Injustice due to suppression was his favourite theme, although he was equally voluble
about the repressive powers within. He advised others without
invitation, and tirelessly manufactured opportunities to articu-
late his position on domestic affairs however minuscule and
social affairs however vast. Ignorance did not impede his flu-
ency. Inaccessibility of the enemy was an incentive to his attack,
and he displayed a predilection to abuse those responsible for
the defects of remote history. On one famous occasion as guest
lecturer at a charity home for the elderly, he berated a gathering
of geriatric paupers for the complicity of their generation in the
mercantile inequities of the universe. Fortunately his audience
remained unaware that they were being addressed, and they con-
centrated instead upon the free breakfast that had secured their
attendance. Shortly after this experience, the Emperor withdrew
into a session of self-critical meditation that lasted for several
months. He emerged with his lust for Madam Ng redoubled, and
he concluded that monasticism does not promote clear thinking.
At future lectures, he arranged for breakfast to follow.

Bachelor wives found the anger of the Emperor magnetic. Their enthusiasm had the effect of augmenting the number of his liaisons and multiplying beyond measure the tactical intricacies required to avoid untenable situations. Presently the Emperor's entire waking day was expended in the accomplishment of interlocking timetables designed to avoid a collision of extramarital encounters. Because this schedule edged the infuriating Madam Ng into further inaccessibility, she increasingly invaded the Emperor's fantasies which amplified his rage and, therefore, his seductiveness.

Finally the Emperor became aware of an impediment in his amatory performance. At first he attributed it to satiation, then to exhaustion, then to Madam Ng who, he learned, had taken to entertaining her husband with jocular rumours of the Emperor's complicated adventures. One black night the Emperor heard himself explaining to the torso beside him that his embarrassing temporary incapacity was due to a paroxysm of guilt at this further betrayal of his marital fidelity, only to realize by the hostile silence that he happened to be addressing his wife. At that point the Emperor decided he could no longer evade a more direct pursuit of his destiny.

THE LIPLESS WANG

There is no doubt that, one way or another, the destiny of the Emperor was pursued at a velocity that irritated the ambitious and magnified the malevolence of those already envious. There was, for example, the case of the lipless Wang, a chronicler. Of this auspicious personage little remains even in the minds of those who wish to recall him. Not that Wang sought invisibility. Indeed, the Emperor never again encountered a man so desirous of being seen. At gatherings, amid projects, behind this friendship and that antipathy, within each plot and counterplot, was Wang. Wang was everywhere. Where he was not, he strove to be and generally arrived on time. Yet, for all his amplitude and presence he disappeared before one's very eyes.

Wang did not seek invisibility. He contained it. Consider his face. It is not true he was lipless. Manner made him seem so. A certain suction after utterance as if withdrawing from contact with the words just spoken, and the lips of Wang vanished into a seamless mask. One could not be sure one had seen them. How much more difficult to recall what he had said, and to hold him accountable for it! Even his written words were invisible. Blessed with a talent for skimming the surface off any topic, Wang composed exclusively in borrowed quotations. Since he considered it unprofessional to acknowledge fellow chroniclers, it was possible to read Wang but impossible to know whom one had read.

The Emperor first encountered Wang in the library of the academy where the lipless one was engaged in the theft of obscure manuscripts. Because Wang's circuitry of acquaintance was many times greater than that of the Emperor and included high officials to the exclusion of any others, and despite the Emperor's repeated assurance that he himself was neither such a one nor likely to become other than their scourge, Wang offered to solicit preference on the Emperor's behalf, requiring only that the Emperor advertise his dependence upon Wang and seek to moderate his own achievement.

When the Emperor nevertheless pursued his solitary destiny, Wang was there at every juncture, broadcasting the Emperor's failures by distorting them with praise, commiserating his accomplishments so that the Emperor himself mistook them for defeats, counselling the Emperor to diminish his endeavour and to minimize his expectation and to abandon his hope while trusting Wang to eulogize his despair. And all the while Wang fomented his own destiny by compiling catalogues of the dying utterances of those others upon whom he had bestowed his depressing friendship.

"Collector, collator, cloacal compactor, Lipless Wang, imperial colon." It is said the Emperor himself composed that epitaph, though somewhat in advance of its application.

THE JOVIAL PENG

Of all the associates of the Emperor's rise, the most influential was the least enterprising. One is referring, of course, to the jovial Peng. What a pity no one is certain he existed! If he lived, it is hard to imagine anyone more delightful.

Peng was compact of lethargies. In other respects he overflowed. Peng's bellies, for example, were a matter of controversy. Was it true Peng dated his life like an elm, laying down a ring of new flesh each season, or was that merely the waggish contention of those who were called upon to feed him? While the debate raged, Peng passed his time digesting his latest engorgement and contemplating the prospect of his next, this latter activity accompanied by deep-throated grunts of a positively sexual resonance. Peng, in fact, rarely moved at all, and then only as a result of persuasions, the most potent of which was an invitation to dine. In that event his motion was instantaneous, his direction unerring, his timing exquisite.

The least conspicuous household in the remotest precinct of the empire never scheduled its most unpretentious meal without first dispatching members in every direction to ensure against the approach of Peng. No precaution sufficed and, as like as not, at the moment the last family scout returned to report the absence of any invading bulk, Peng would be there, apologetic at the consequential business that had prevented his more timely arrival, adamant regarding the suspension of the rules of hospitality in his unworthy case, acquiescent to the rescue of his inadvertent host from the loss of a reputation for magnanimity, and benignly settling himself at the table which operation generally required the displacement of three juveniles whose portions Peng would then reluctantly commence to absorb. At the end of each such meal he would recall another engagement that he hoped the protocols of guesthood had not caused him to neglect, and would rumble off hiccupping gently, leaving the household poorer in victuals, no richer in the knowledge of the business Peng had arrived to transact, yet vaguely aggrieved at his precipitate departure.

Peng's trade remained a mystery. Even those like the Emperor to whom Peng referred as "colleagues" and who willingly shared with Peng the fruits of their various labours in which he confessed to have participated a little, found themselves hard put to account for the precise nature of Peng's involvement and incapable of locating his actual piece of work. But pay they did and, as Peng departed delightedly jingling the lesser half he always insisted was more than his due, they somehow regretted their repressed resentment at indulging so transparently amiable a fellow.

For a time the Emperor's relationship with Peng was particularly close. This was the phase of his rise during which the Emperor was determined to pursue his destiny but was not yet able to perceive it. It is said that, in the halcyon days of his companionship with the youthful Emperor, Peng accumulated two belly rolls in a single season and burst his purse. Then he vanished, leaving entire communities to dismantle their apparatus of Peng-evasion and ruefully to ask themselves wherein they had been found wanting in generosity.

It was then the Emperor first was seen to smile. He knew that, when his rise was complete, he would hear of Peng again.

THE EMPEROR IS BETRAYED
BY THE PRINCESS

Sir, you and my wife have made me a gift I cannot reciprocate. Every man should own a betrayal. Some own several, which is excessive. A single is sufficient. Thank you, sir, for mine. In time and time, I wish you yours. Forgive me that, in your present circumstance, I have not the stomach to provide it.

THE EMPEROR DIVORCES
THE PRINCESS

Madam, I divorce you. Had I less to give, it would be yours more heartily.

THE EMPEROR WITHDRAWS TO A PROVINCE OTHER THAN THAT OCCUPIED BY THE PRINCESS

Why in the midst of my rise would I accomplish withdrawal? Why in pursuit of my destiny would I cast myself incoherent and remote among innumerable native sons? Can you understand that I too wish to reach the Emperor despite the fact that I am he? There can be no other explanation for my conduct.

THE EMPEROR'S DAUGHTER

The girl came to resemble the princess. Such things do not happen in a day. Perhaps they do not happen at all. In this case there could be no doubt, a resemblance, a definite resemblance, amounting at moments to an identity, the Emperor noticed it at once. "Her mother infected my life," he thought, "and now she has dispatched her emissary, her toxic flower, touch it and be dead!"

So the Emperor refused to see his daughter, which was not easy to accomplish. He had fought long and hard in many places, the office of his spokesman for one, where he was urged to demand more and to offer less but, instead, only repeated, "Five weeks and one vacation a year and a day and a month cumulative until the child has reached maturity, which is to say, has escaped that terrible woman who only says more possessions! more possessions! no privileges at all without more possessions!"

How could the Emperor now deny his daughter the very benefits he had won on her behalf? It was not easy to accomplish. But when he first noticed the resemblance and assured himself it was not a trick of the light — no, there it was again, that simultaneous employment of the fingers of both hands to brush back the hair from her forehead, who else could have taught her that? who else and why else but to stamp this daughter hers? — it was at that very moment that the Emperor determined to begin to refuse to see his daughter or, rather, to refuse to let her see him.

It always had been thus. Whenever it became necessary to abuse intimates, the Emperor withdrew from them his presence.

From the lipless Wang who betrayed with fraternity, from the aromatic Madam Ng who wooed without heat, from every schoolmaster who profited upon a student, from these and more than he could bear to recall the Emperor had withdrawn his presence. "For such offences," thought the Emperor, "what else is it in my power to remove that cannot be replaced?"

The child, however, would not be relinquished. The further the Emperor withdrew from the vicinity of his daughter, the more closely she embraced him. There was a time the Emperor interposed between them several thousand leagues and an entire new family, only to wake screaming with the dread certainty that his very daughter was standing there before the embers of the night-fire brushing back with the fingers of both hands her glowing hair. The Emperor came to know that, with respect to this daughter, death itself would not be sufficiently remote.

THE EMPEROR'S POSSESSIONS

After their divorce the Emperor visited the princess. Walking through the doorway of their former home was like entering the funnel of a web. Not an aperture, not a cranny, not an obscure corner was empty. Every patch of wall was adorned with a portrait, a landscape, a plate. Every floorboard was cloaked by a rug covered with a mat. Even the ceilings were obscured with hangings, and frames had been constructed to bear residual drapes. What was worse, as he made his way toward the proprietor squatting somewhere near the centre, the Emperor recognized every item!

Nevertheless the Emperor visited the princess again. This time he noticed the mongrel bitch he had raised from a pup, and had cherished for its unfawning whimsicality and its steadfast resistance to training. As he knelt to embrace the animal, the princess informed him of the circumstances of its death and taxidermy. Whoever administered the poison, she pointed out, had calculated the dosage so as not to impair the hide that blended marvellously with several carpets.

Nevertheless the Emperor visited the princess again and again.

One day the Emperor arrived to find the princess's house empty of furnishings. Silently the Emperor moved from room to room observing the emptiness. Then, for the first time in many years, the Emperor addressed the princess.

"There was a time no one gave me pleasure. That also was the time I acquired possessions. Many were amassed by you on my behalf, for you too had no other means of disguising your despair. When our divorce was transpiring, I struggled with you for the possession of our possessions and succeeded in wresting a few out of your many arms. For years this share followed me about, resisting disposal. It was not until I relinquished the last tendrils of hatred that bound me to you that my marital possessions fell from me and vanished. Now I observe that you have emptied your house. At last you too are free of our possessions and I am no longer required."

When the Emperor had gone, the princess ordered the house burned to the ground. Later the Emperor learned that the conflagration had included their daughter.

THE EMPEROR'S GHOSTS

Although the mortals of whom they were the spectral emanations could never have met, the ghosts of the Emperor seemed to know one another. Between mortal acquaintance and spectral propinquity there appeared to operate an inverse correlation. The spirits of his parents, for example, seldom appeared together in the same dream and, when they did, they steadfastly refused to acknowledge one another, whereas the vaporous manifestations of the princess and Madam Ng materialized bosom to bosom for an entire month of nights, and on one occasion engaged in a mutual coupling of such spectacular dexterity that the Emperor consummated upon his current companion before he or she had a chance to wake.

There was a distinction between the ghosts of the Emperor's dreams and those pearl-grey emanations of his sleepless hours before dawn. Whereas the Emperor could warn the ghosts of his dreams that, if they exacted too much pain, he would exorcise them by awakening, he could hardly threaten the ghosts of his dawn with the very sleep they had dissipated, and from them there was no escape. None, that is, but his rising from his bed with the hope that they would not follow.

In time the Emperor became as familiar with his ghosts as he had been with their counterparts in life. He came to prefer his ghosts. They, at least, were without rancour, without hope. There were nights the Emperor required his ghosts and deliberately woke to contemplate them. At such times the mists of dawn would find him gazing into the hearth at last night's ashes, his ghosts a grey corolla around his head. "They are," the Emperor thought, "my first crown."

THE PARABLE OF THE RISE

When he began to climb the pyramid, the Emperor discovered that steps had been cut along the wall or, rather, along the angle of two walls, good stone steps, toe-cap deep, half-a-shin apart, each a perfect pyramid of air wedged into the spine of the great stone pyramid that he climbed, one hand upon the wall on either side, toes inserted, spine bent, rather like a pyramid himself. Halfway up the Emperor looked down but could see no farther than his topmost foot that disappeared into the body of the pyramid. He dared not look up for fear the steps would disappear. And so, forehead upon stone, he climbed.

Then he felt it. Not with the fingers of the hand he could see. But with the fingers of the other. He dared not lift and turn his head. There was no need. He climbed another step and watched the fingers of the hand he saw disappear around the juncture of the walls. The Emperor held the pyramid! Boldly he moved on. Now his hand disappeared, now his arm. Slowly he lowered his torso to the straight spine of the stone. Slowly he raised his head and straightened his fingers and reached up and touched the ground.

IV

FROM COLD MOUNTAIN

(POEMS OF KAO)

I am a bottle. Pour me out, I am empty.
A bottle cannot choose its cup. Do not waste my wine.

ANSWERING QUESTIONS

Why have I come to Cold Mountain? Have I not been here, then,
    as long as the snows?
Someone rolled my world up like a mat, left me standing no
    place else.
Down there I think he's still at work. The valley weeps sometimes.
Poor Emperor, he'll never stand as high as I, all Cold Mountain
    between my feet.

Why have I come to Cold Mountain? Why have you come to ask?
You'll have to speak a little less, both ears are gone.
Why have I come to Cold Mountain? They say the view is good.
I say the tops of clouds look fine when you don't care what's
    underneath.

Why have I come to Cold Mountain? For health? I find less and less.
To be nearer God? A flea in the snow of His beard, I still can't see
    His face.
To be accounted wise? You'd not have sought me if I hadn't come.
Why have I come to Cold Mountain? Do you know of a colder one?

GIVING DIRECTIONS

How can I tell you how to get to Cold Mountain?
Ignore the stars and you're halfway there.
Come by chariot and you're farther off.
Accompany a prince and you'll never start.

Who has the courage to come to Cold Mountain?
Not you, no one, not I.
How can your loved ones help you to find it?
Enable them to throw you out.

The road to Cold Mountain is without a sign.
He who travels it already knows the way.
How can you be certain you've got here?
Should you arrive, I'll move on.

TAKING TEA

I build my fire of bracken boughs, my bed of straw and twine.
I boil and pour my nettle tea, not once expecting wine.

Between my knees the valley lights flicker and are gone.
Above my eaves the cooking fires beyond the clouds burn on.

I never am invited to sup and sleep elsewhere.
I'm too high up for some folk, for some not halfway there.

Here beside me on this ledge where I sip and sit,
The stunted tree has cracked the rock you'd think imprisoned it.

SELF-RULES

Avoid the rhetorical question,
Suppress the sententious reply.
They smother what no one dare mention,
That even a poet can die.

The rhyme that is false is the true one.
The pulse that skips beats marches on.
Each certainty must misconstrue one.
The sun that is setting's not dawn.

Don't give up your hope, just disown it.
What's never been there you'll not miss.
The line that is last, don't postpone it.
All endings are bad. So is this.

DRINKING SONG

There are some things I know I know
And some I know I don't
Like how to make some seedlings grow
And how to guess which won't,

Why babies have their father's frown
And yet their smile's their mother's,
Why boys' colours are black and brown
And girls' are all the others,

And why it takes just one more word
Than all the words you've got
To say precisely what you mean
But less to say what's not.

Of those things certain in my mind
The one I know the best:
If each part of a poem has rhymed,
Why, so will all the rest!

REMEMBERING THE CAPITAL CITY

In the capital city it is forbidden to cultivate
Root vegetables for fear of unearthing unholy remains.
In the capital city passersby contain dreadful forgotten stories.
In the capital city beggar-boys advertise their addictions
And thickening princesses whisper the coordinates of their abodes.

REMEMBERING THE IMPERIAL PALACE

In the imperial palace fires are lit in entrance halls and footmen are
    permitted pockets.
In the imperial palace dogs are voiceless and clocks are keyed
    to harmonize.
In the imperial palace menus are arranged so kitchen odours coalesce.
    The smoke of my cooking pot hangs like fog.
    Do those ice clouds swing from the sky or my brows?
    It's cold way up Cold Mountain. There's no other truth than that.

In the imperial palace wallpaper framing windows is altered
    seasonally.
In the imperial palace peacocks must be discouraged from mating
    with the drapery.
In the imperial palace a courtesan achieves her ecstasy only with the
    tearing of silk.
    Across my roof the branches chatter.
    A bird on a crystal limb drops me a chip of song.
    It's cold way up Cold Mountain. What less is there to say?

And now I hear the imperial palace
Has become a mound where white-haired palace maidens
Slither past on carpet slippers telling old tales of the Emperor.
    It's cold way up Cold Mountain.
    It's so damned cold. No one was meant to live up here.
    Too bad there's no place else.

REMEMBERING THE EMPEROR

I remember his eyes,
I do not know how many
Nor where they resided.
Of dragons there were few.

REMEMBERING MASTER CHING

When my good friend died,
He disappeared utterly
Leaving me his shaving bowl.
I warm it for his sake.

REPLYING TO MASTER CHING

How goes the revolution? The dagger you threw hasn't reached him yet.
Do people still talk of me? As of the last great locust plague and other
     ways to count.
Am I that dead? It takes more and more Cold Mountain to catch me
     a glimpse of you.
Do you follow the old good cause? At a distance but closer than most.
Will things improve? One year's snow looks much like the last.
Whatever became of — Nothing, I say, nothing, that is what he became.

BLAMING MASTER CHING

There was a time you and I and the hog butcher became drunk in
     the marketplace
And afterwards wept together as if there were no one else around.

There was a time you and I and fat Madam Wu reclined in a tangle
Singing songs opposed to things as they are and the ways of all
     the princes.

There was a time we made some sense, you and I,
Watching the sky pour dusk on the valley and spill a little into
     our room.

Who'd have guessed I'd be the one asking the wind:
And if not you, who is there to blame?

BLAMING THE EMPEROR

There is so little to blame him for, birth being the fault of
    others, life the common misfortune.
Of all men born to die, which brings about the death of
    another is more a matter of luck,
Bad on every side. As soon blame Cold Mountain for being
    mountainous but no volcano.
Yet I cannot find it in my heart entirely to relinquish rancour.
    Of every diurnal pleasure, this the affordable one.

WHEN THE ENEMY DIES

When the enemy dies, you're not sure you wanted him dead
With only his own hand at his throat.

When the enemy dies, he dies in the night,
Inglorious as fog, inaccessible.

When the enemy dies,
He dies without you in mind.

RELINQUISHING MASTER CHING

A gentle man does not know he is gentle.
He gently makes us know he is a man.

He takes his wine when we no longer thirst.
He passes friendship round like table bread.

His stillness stills the voices of our children.
His gentle voice is in our every child.

A gentle man makes gentle those about him.
He passes gently from us as one who steps aside.

SCARS

Every man bears a scar somewhere on his body.
Look for it. He has put it there himself.
It is the signature of his nature, his true name.

Every man bears a scar somewhere on his body.
Some bear more than one. Look for one only.
When he received that scar, he did not need another.

Every man bears a scar somewhere on his body.
Such a scar is visible only in his mirror.
If you wish to see a man, look only at his scar.

Every man bears a scar somewhere on his body.
You appear a perfect man. Who can hope to meet you?
You appear a perfect man. Go acquire your scar.

COLD MOUNTAIN SUITE

I

When the first of them came, she brought news of the most recent
    death of the Emperor
From causes unknown on a date unspecified at a location yet to be
    discovered,
Seeking to please me with a gift I could not afford. All in all I'd have
    preferred flowers.
I resumed the long sleep of my life. When she returned, she was no
    longer who she'd been.
This other bore no riches but a mouth as sweet as fallen snow, eyes as
    grey as distant peaks,
Spoke no language I could comprehend, and stayed a day, and sent
    another in her stead,
That other another whose cost as well exceeded value, and so on and
    on to the end of dreams.

You arrived after many convulsions of several epiphanies. You didn't
    seem to be anyone else.
Your hands were empty. Your hands were full. Nothing you offered
    resembled flowers.
I prepared a meal to welcome you, annoyed at your delay.

II

In the first of our years I gathered my good fortune and tested its
    coinage with my teeth.
You awaited my assessment with a smooth brow, nodded, and carried
    on where we'd left off,
Giving our lives to one another, each confident a bargain had
    been struck.
As season followed season and the lips of this year's snow touched the
    hem of the last,
As the voices of men receded and the echo of their intentions died in
    the valleys,
We fed each other hearthstone bread, we bedded where we lay.
    Occurrence was our currency, procedure protocol.
The chair of spools, the chest of pine, the spoon and fork of bone, the
    feathered implement to hand, the ink of charcoal dust,
The hieroglyph engraved on slate by ancient tidal crest in accidental
    craftsmanship of patient happenstance ...
In articles, our artifacts, iconic talismen, we read a canon of our own,
    unexegetical.
As common chore made festival, Cold Mountain seemed less cold.

III

When I left home to seek my home, my mother gave a cactus plant.
    Something else to keep alive.
Oblivious to husbandry it outlived every drought, blooming once
    and dying with no need to bloom again.
When you left all you'd tenanted for what remained of me, we two
    became one stubborn core encased in spines of ice.

Cold Mountain was our amplitude, its prospect our purview.
    We hugged its steeple camber, we huddled in its gut,
Barely noted spring from fall where every month was white, peered
    through folds of that enclosed to what enclosure held.
Beyond rose other mountains, none quite as cold as ours if judging by
    the absence of migrationists from there.
Within lay what we fashioned of what was left behind by those who'd
    been before us and gone before we came.
You'd wandered in the valleys. I'd followed every road. Which led us
    to Cold Mountain as surely as a star.
Once here our tasks were manifest, our destinies ordained. Make
    homeland where you shelter. Make heartland where you lie.
Prepare an orchard in the snow, a bower for grey cat.

IV

Propelled upon the brittle breath of east wind or another, dishevelled
    and distraught she came in her disguise of need,
Permitted you to snare her as she feigned to stagger on, surveyed
    what little comfort she suspected lay within,
Elected the best corner by the sanctum of the fire, awaited our
    eviction and selectively reclined,
Her mild face in her tail, one eyebrow pleasantly arranged, inviting us
    to reconcile and make ourselves at home.
We poorer for the lack of her she came for what's in store, accepting
    all there was of what she let us think we gave.
Declaring reciprocity a fair exchange of kind, frivolity for vigilance,
    grace for gracelessness,
To us she offered sustenance we thought we offered her. She supped
    at dishes she preferred and deigned to be fulfilled.
We hungered at the loss of those who'd fed us and moved on. She
    warmed a broth of recollection, ladled it on call.
We thirsted for attainments, better prospects, rather, some. She
    poured a draught of present tense and supped her portion first,
Sighed westerly into the curve of her postprandial nap.

V

We nearly lost her twice. First to food, the lack of it, then to sudden
    weakness in the hind:
The inability to hunger or to leap, each as essential as any perhaps to cat.
In fact we lost to neither nor even nearly so. From the one you brought
    her back with finger feeds
In laptime folds and then, long after fowl and biscuit, biscuit, milk, milk
    and water, water, fowl,
Normal service had resumed, you weaned the both of you from cure
    with many a lingering backward look.
From the other she nursed herself, making less demand on pushing off,
    contemplating trajectory and destination,
Impetus and altitude, amplitude and attitude of horizontal carry,
    launching pad and landing,
Weighing all and balancing desire against gain with calculating strategy
    no kitten ever would.
Two lives gone then, the rest to play, she lingered with us yet,
    instructing how to cope with appetite and thrust
Where we not she saw loss as illness, why to live with it.

VI

Unwilling to abandon us without the care of kind
When her flame burned so low it took no breath to blow it out,
She authorized and nominated sisters to succeed her
On this or any mountain just as high, however cold,
Discharge of duty, helping lesser species to survive,
Bequeathed in perpetuity to those who follow on.
Not seeking to progress the breed nor winnow weakness out
Mistaking man for cat and so requiring of him more,
They find us as she left us: inscrutable, adored,
Attempting habitation on a pinnacle of ice.

TELLING TALES

An ancient tale told of a man
Or a tale told of an ancient man
Or a tale told by a man in ancient times
Who may himself have been ancient
And likewise his tale or not was this:
Long before there was a time of telling tales
Or tales to tell or men to tell them
No tales worth telling were told
But that was once upon a time.

I often think of the tale not told
By the man not telling
And what I think is this:
The tale of that time is a tale worth telling
In a time when men tell ancient tales
Or ancient men tell tales
Of a time that is ancient or not.

If this were once upon that taleless time,
I'd sleep beside the waterfall to purify my ears.

DRY STONE WALLS

In my native province there is a tradition of building dry stone walls.
Though it is an exacting craft full of intricate devices,
None is too stupid to learn it.
Though the task is heavy, two on one, one on two,
Less than the length of an arm in a day, none is too feeble to perform it.
Preparation is hardly possible. Planning is always wrong.
The nature of the job instructs the doing of it.
Nor is there more than one way.
The slope of the terrain, the consistency of the subsoil,
The disposition of the climate, the temper of the day ...
It is the stone at hand that makes of a wall the only wall to be made.

Though every wall be made anew, none is the first of its stones.
Though every mason works alone, what he builds has stood before.
To discover the wall to be made of these stones, that is the art of
   the builder.

THE POET AND THE PEASANT

The last poet, recluse atop Cold Mountain,
Grown fat because of cold, merry because of fatness,
Wise because of merriment, drunk because of wisdom,
Old because of drunkenness, cold because of age,
Dead with cold and poetry recluse atop Cold Mountain.

> *Once I journeyed into the capital city.*
> *I so esteemed the flavour of the walnut*
> *I wished to bring it to the attention of the Emperor.*
> *Forty years now I haven't gone back.*
> *I have forgotten the road I came by.*

> *In the morning followed out by an old peasant.*
> *She bears the bag into which I toss my poems.*
> *Grey cat follows her.*
> *At night I read my poems to her alone,*
> *Altering any lines she can't understand.*

Three hundred poems none longer than a groan,
Three hundred poems on solitude and cold,
Three hundred poems inscribed on trees and rocks
And the walls of peasant houses,
Three hundred poems remain

And one scroll painting of two old folk
Fat and merry, wise and drunk,
Guffawing in the wilderness.

EPITAPH FOR THE EMPEROR

After the tyrant, the mandarinate.
Too many heads to decapitate.

OUR EPITAPH

Lovers bedward bound so gaily,
Do not pass our ashes palely.
Grasp this urn and shake twice daily.

POEM IS

Signature to validate commerce in a market square gone silent,
Merchants departed, contracts as binding as the dust the moon.

V

THE IMPERIAL LAW

The right way is the weakening of the people, and the way of weakening is the law.

FRAGMENTS FROM THE SCROLL
OF LADY SHANG ...

... REGARDING ANTIQUITY

In the ancient time, the land was divided into squares, as many squares as there were families to work them. Now that all the world is at war, even the hedgerows are cultivated, and the paths and the furrows as well.

In the ancient time, the Son of Heaven contained the law and his princes dispensed it, as many princes as there was law. Now that all the world is at war, the law of one prince is the law of today and the law of tomorrow is another's. Thus it was that the land came to be bought and sold, and the law became political.

In the ancient time, a soldier served his prince as a horse its rider, as a limb its body, and "law" was the name of the way of serving. Now that all the world is at war, a state is the name of yesterday's battle and no soldier knows the monogram on his back.

In the ancient time, justice was written on the heart and the Son of Heaven read it, a different justice on every heart. Now that all the world is at war, merit is counted in heads and treason in backsides. Thus it was that the law lost its name, and justice became rewards and punishments.

In the ancient time, when an eldest son was born he was cut into pieces by his family and eaten. The younger brothers, it was said, thereby were benefitted, when anyone can see that, in those circumstances, there could be no younger brothers. Thus antiquity is not to be trusted.

... REGARDING SOLDIERS

Rewards are a civil measure and punishments are a military. Civil and military measures are the sum of the law, the latter twice the former now that all the world is at war. Before an army can be used to inflict punishments, it itself must be punished. To make an army no rewards are necessary, only punishments.

If a soldier is not in every way amenable, by no means train him. If an enemy is not in every way inferior, by no means attack him. Prudence is the law of an army, calculation its weapon.

When trained soldiers are commanded to stop, it is as if their feet were cut off. When they march, they are like flowing water. For disloyalty a soldier is permitted to take his life. For bad marching he is beheaded with a dull axe.

Before soldiers can be used, the law should be fixed. Being fixed, the law should become custom. The law being custom, weapons can be provided and soldiers can be used.

In the entire army there is no soldier like the sapper. Without him walled towns would not fall. So long as a single walled town stands within it, no state can be said to have fallen. It is the sapper who burrows beneath the ramparts. It is he who scoops away the footings and replaces them with timber uprights. It is he who gathers branches and ignites them. It is he who calculates how much longer before the beams burn through, and the tunnel collapses along with the wall above it, and the signal to attack can be given.

Though the sapper does not storm the breach, without him there would be no breach. Though all his skill be undermining, without it none would overrun. Though he himself takes no heads, for every head taken let the sapper receive one degree of freedom from the law. Though the sapper has no reason to run, for every soldier who runs let ten blameless sappers be torn to pieces by the chariots.

... REGARDING FARMERS

The land and the army are lawful occupations. If a man's wealth is in next year's crop, he will not run with it on his back. If neighbouring states are kept always in peril of invasion, no man will run there. The land and the army are one occupation.

Farmers endure and their hope is seasonal. With little alteration they can be used for war. Bravery might appear to be their only impediment, yet it should not appear so because farmers have none. Soil that opposes them with infertility, weather that oppresses them with drought and flood, their cattle that perish, their vermin that do not ... farmers have no choice but to despise the course of nature and to face it with rancour. Rancour is not bravery. There is no bravery in it. The rancour of farmers may appear to be bravery, yet it is rancour pure and simple, and it translates into killing under instruction.

The rancour of farmers is perfectly corrosive, no vessel can contain it. If the rancour of farmers is not injected abroad, it remains to envenom the homeland. Presently, for every crop that fails farmers will withhold the like in taxes. Presently, farmers will cease to turn their sour earth and will seek a sweeter terrain in private cause. Presently, like farmers, all men will have angry eyes and will clench their fists and will dismember the state. That, indeed, may be bravery, and against it no law can stand.

Thus it is said, "Anyone may be trained to kill who has the heart of a farmer." Bravery, however, should never be pardoned.

... REGARDING SHOPKEEPERS AND SCHOLARS

When a thief succeeds, he sells what he has taken. When a shopkeeper succeeds, he buys more merchandise. When a spy finds out, he sells what he learns. When a scholar finds out, he asks new questions. Thieves and spies can be paid off, shopkeepers and scholars never.

Shopkeepers and scholars ... their clothing does not warm them, their food does not fill them, they travail their thought and fatigue their limbs and suffer in their internal organs, yet they increase their activity. Of shopkeepers and scholars it may be said, "There is wine enough for any bottle, but a tube of less than a finger-length cannot be filled."

A shopkeeper strives not to live but to live better. A scholar strives not to know but to know more. The one seeks profit, the other fame. Those who seek merely profit, forget the rules of polite behaviour. Those who seek fame, lose the eternal principles of human nature.

A prince makes sure to hold the handle of profit and fame. Using the handle of profit and fame, a prince may turn even a shopkeeper and a scholar, and the name of that handle is "law."

... REGARDING REWARDS AND PUNISHMENTS

To control a soldier, give him merit for every head he takes. Let the form of that merit be one degree of freedom from constraint by the law. Thereby three benefits are accomplished. Soldiers are encouraged to take heads. Lawless dispositions are encouraged that are the best at the taking of heads. A prince pays out a currency he mints. Thus it is said, "If one understands rewards, there is no expense."

To control an official, blame him for every failure of the law. Let the form of that blame be one degree of withdrawal from protection by the law. Thereby three benefits are accomplished. Deprived of what sustains them, failed officials vanish. The law that fails does not fail, for it succeeds in afflicting officials. Freed of failed officials, the law of a prince will not fail. Thus it is said, "If one understands punishments, there is no pain."

To control the poor, promise exemption from taxes. To control the rich, offer to resign. Thereby three benefits are accomplished. A prince relinquishes what he does not have in order to gain what he might have. A prince is generous with what he does have in order to gain what he does not have. The promise and the offer usually suffice. Thus it is said, "If one understands rewards and punishments, there are no rewards and punishments."

... REGARDING THE WAY OF THE LAW

If the people are poor, where is their contentment? Law is the way. The poor are the punishment of the rich, and shame is the path between them. Thus it is said, "To weaken the strong by means of the weak brings strength to the law."

Were the poor to remove the rich, how would they themselves avoid affluence? Law is the way. To punish the rich, the poor need no other reward, nor do they receive any. Thus it is said, "To weaken one without strengthening another is the way of the law."

In everything there is an essential, that which makes it live, its power. Law is the way. A prince is what he is, not because he gets to the bottom of things but because he sees the power in each thing and makes law to remove it. Thus it is said, "A weak people means a strong law."

If the people are weak, who is there to lead them? Law is the way. It is the humiliated who prize rank, the licentious who seek office. Thus it is said, "The law recruits from the dregs of the people, then it reaches below."

If officials are vile, who is there to control them? Law is the way. Where rank and office are measures without portion, a prince bestows portions without measure. Thus it is said, "The way of the law is a ladder in a circle. Everyone climbs, no one rises."

In everything there is a quality, that which makes it different from every other thing, its measure. Law is the way. A prince is what he is, not because he understands anything at all, but because he keeps proper figures and alters the law to fit them. Thus it is said, "The law stands backwards on its head, though the people think they are looking at its face."

... REGARDING THE GLORY OF THE LAW

The law must be more than the man of the law, otherwise the law must die with him and have the trouble to be reborn in another. The law that dies is not law but custom. The law is not born, but uncovered. The grain of naked law when the husk of custom is shed, of that a prince is nourished.

One does not await a prince for the gift of the law. If a prince arises, it is because of the law. Should he not arise, yet there will be the law.

Intelligence is not needed to read the law. It is the law that reads the intelligent. In what sense can the law be said to read? In the sense of reading, which is to uncover the sense beneath the word. The law is simple because it is one thing only. The intelligent who are more than one thing only cannot read the law. The ignorant must help them to do it.

Government is not needed to impose the law. The law imposes itself, and upon those who govern. That is what government is, the receiving of the law.

Praise and slander are alike impossible under the law. Where there is law, there is no benefit in praising, no satisfaction in slandering. All benefits, all satisfactions, are awarded by the law, which is the highest degree of order.

All this is what is called "the glory of the law."

LADY SHANG, THE LEGALIST

In the times before the Emperor there was Lady Shang, the legalist. Whither she originated and when, whom she served and how, why she died, at whose hand ... of a certainty what remains of the great Lady Shang is the bone-carved figure on my desk.

This is a woman so old, so stooped, in all the years I have watched she has not proceeded beyond her base. She leans upon a staff taller than she that bends companionably. Across her middle nestled along a forearm she cradles some object. Her cowl descends upon it, her robe depends from it, her back and her staff curve around it, she protects it with everything. Of this object one end laps between her fingers, so perhaps it is merely her sash? On the other end at her elbow there is a tassel or a seal, so perhaps, after all, this is the very scroll containing Lady Shang's famous advice? Perhaps she is on her way to present it to her prince? Perhaps, since her eyes are averted and her mouth droops open in astonishment and grief, she is on her way back?

At least it is certain what that scroll contains. The legalism of Lady Shang is known to us all.

> "The army is to be divided into squads of five, the other four to be beheaded if one of their squad is killed. The people are to be divided into families, the remainder of a family to be beheaded if one of a family commits a crime that none in his family denounces. Virtue is brought about by punishment, righteousness by betrayal."

> "If, in the application of punishment, serious offences are regarded as serious and light offences as light, light offences will not cease. If light offences are regarded as serious, all offences will cease."

> "If punishment is applied at the intent to transgress, greater depravity cannot be bred."

> "Punishment of intent must be so severe that a wallet dropped in a roadway will not be picked up."

> "Punishment produces force, force produces strength, strength produces awe, awe produces humility, humility produces kindness. Punishment should be unrestricted because kindness itself has its origin in punishment."

And so on and on, the litany is familiar to every schoolboy. What is less clear is the nature of the woman who could advocate such law.

Judging by my little statue, Lady Shang was ugly. Doubtless the bone-carver was influenced in his figuration by the ugliness of those times. Lady Shang flourished in the Epoch of the Warring States. Ugly times bring forth ugly people. Indeed, in the Epoch of the Warring States beauty of person and beauty of polity were alike impossible. Within her Doctrine of the Ugly Official, Lady Shang says as much. "If a beautiful official be employed, the people will obey the official. If an ugly official be employed, the people will obey the law. By employing ugly officials, a prince ensures that the people serve only him." Such a doctrine supposes a plenitude of hideous candidates. No other period in the history of the mandarinate would justify such a premise. In the Epoch of the Warring States, apparently, it was no more than an observation of nature.

Of course it was not until the Epoch of the Terminologists that every word in the scroll of Lady Shang came to be understood. On occasion, however, unable to await posthumous clarification, Lady Shang herself impatiently provided the definition.

"Beauty," Lady Shang wrote, "is whatever works."

By ugliness, on the other hand, Lady Shang appears to have been referring to several defects. Eloquence was one. "He who loves force, attacks with what is difficult but sure. He who loves words, attacks with what is easy but useless." Learning was another. "Wandering scholars in unreasonable discussion ... cannon choke on such fodder." Wit was a third. "The endless repetition of crude and simple strokes ... that is how a battle-hammer crushes or an argument convinces." As for artistic temperament, "Not a skirmish has been gained by the thin of skin, nor a crusade lost by the thick." Elsewhere Lady Shang wrote, "Care for the elderly, filial piety, fraternal duty, social humanity, historic responsibility ... living for others does not work." And again elsewhere, "Ugliness is whatever does not work."

Which is why, at a time when all the world is at war, princes employ ministers as ugly as they. It is also why my beautiful statue of the ugly Lady Shang cannot be a contemporary likeness.

FRAGMENTS FROM THE BOOK
OF FEI-TZU ...

... REGARDING VIRTUE

When the strong are broken and the sharp are blunted, education has taken place. When the police are more terrible than any enemy, patriotism is possible. Virtues do not interest a prince, for the cause of a virtue is never virtuous.

... REGARDING NEED

It is more important to design a perfect house than to find a perfect tenant. A perfect house will perfect any tenant. Thus, architects are preferred to builders, builders to tenants, tenants to no one. Needs do not interest a prince. To rectify the needy, he employs the needless.

... REGARDING NAMES

So long as a hare runs wild, even a sage will chase it. As soon as it is on sale in the market, even a thief will hesitate before it. What is the difference between a hare in the field and a hare on the stall? Legal title is the difference.

Names interest a prince. All things must have their names, no two things the same name, no two names the same thing. It is only when everything is named with the name that is its name that the way of a prince is free. That is the purpose of naming, to free the way of a prince.

The method of rectifying names is to locate the one quality in a thing that makes it work, and to name it with that name. When names are rectified, correct actions follow. Thus, the name of charity is "privilege," the name of hope is "reward," the name of faith is "single-mindedness." When a prince acts with faith, hope, and charity, the single-minded are rewarded with privilege.

... REGARDING MEASURES AND CONDITIONS

If an arrow hits a mark at ten paces, it is an achievement. If a blind release splits a hair at fifty, it is clumsiness. What is the difference between the two shots? Measures and conditions.

Exceptions do not interest a prince. A prince is not himself exceptional. Were a state to await a prodigy to direct it, the state would fall before the prodigy arrived. Measures and conditions are more useful than prodigies. With correct measurement and controlled conditions, even the mediocre achieve results. The aim is statistical government by an unexceptional prince over a people inclined to be average.

... REGARDING LIKES AND DISLIKES

The people may be freed to vote when it is certain they will abstain, to gamble when they are afraid to risk, to trade when they wish only to possess, to compete when they themselves are interchangeable. Likes and dislikes interest a prince, and do not interest him. To govern his people a prince should observe their likes and dislikes, and by no means share them.

... REGARDING RESULTS

Measuring an abyss, a prince learns that it is a thousand snakes deep by dropping a farmer tied to a measured rope. Wishing to test the strength of his walled city, he defends it with exhausted soldiers. Results interest a prince. Observing results, a prince may discover anything.

... REGARDING STATISTICS

The statistical method of governing is to gather one number only, the smaller number that is needed to know the larger, and then to make law against the smaller number, less law and easier to enforce. Thus, knowing those who make their livelihood by talking, a prince can order the affairs of the useful. Knowing those who cultivate odes and history, rites and music, statues and brushwork, he can select his farmers. Knowing the brave, he can recruit his army. Knowing the beautiful, he can appoint his officials. Outlawing the lesser, he prefers the greater. Thus, a prince rids himself of orators and artists and heroes and moralists. In their stead he employs the accountable. Relying on statistics, a prince may govern forever.

... REGARDING MEMORY

The only impediment to the statistical method of governing is the memory of the people. In the dominion of a prudent prince, the people are recorded at birth and erased at death, and are permitted no memory.

FEI-TZU, THE TERMINOLOGIST

Preceding the Era of the Emperor with its blessings too numerous to record and its infelicities too inconsequent to mention, and following hard upon the Epoch of the Warring States with its defeats so devastating and its victories so costly it is profitless to distinguish between them, it was then that the Season of the Terminologists enjoyed a cultural climate of exhaustion. It was a period of political inertness, of mercantile prudence, of hermetic domesticity, and a general air of tetchiness. Fei-tzu personified the era, and his work, The Book of Fei-Tzu, exemplified it.

Fei-tzu's precise method was so subtle and complex that, to any but a seasoned Terminologist, it appeared simple to the point of idiocy. Operating on the premise that all notable ideas about the nature of the law were contained within the scroll of Lady Shang, Fei-tzu devoted his academic research to the elucidation of every word in Lady Shang's scroll, along with footnotes on punctuation variables, syllabic modulations, and consonant clusters, and appendices on the more flamboyant vowel aspirants. To ensure the purity of his results, Fei-tzu obeyed two control restrictions. Since its historical author was putative, never to add an unauthorized word to the historical scroll. Since transmission of the historical scroll from one aeon to the next had depended upon folk songs and street chants, always to include in the current version any new word that seemed to fit.

In short, Fei-tzu rewrote Lady Shang, rendering her complex ideology into memorable slogans fit for inscription upon ceremonial robes and street attire, a lively sideline that produced a steady income from his licensing of the manufacture and his sharing in the sales.

Fei-tzu's reason for employing his method is clear. The reason he gave for doing it is as follows.

"In the Epoch of the Warring States the word of men had for each a different meaning. For one man it had one meaning, for two

men it had two meanings, for three men ...† a thousand and one
meanings. Thus, each man regarded his own meaning as correct
and the meaning of others as wrong, though in the circumstances
how anyone could expect to understand the meaning of another
when it was his word only that had meaning for him is beyond
the understanding of any man of any meaning. No matter. In
the ancient Epoch of the Warring States how could there be certainty? There could not be. Now, however, is the Season of the
Terminologists. Now is the time of certainty, now and now only.
A moment sooner would have been too soon, a moment later too
late. Now is the time the words of Lady Shang will be understood
with one meaning only. For a thousand and one men they will
have one meaning, for a thousand men they will have one meaning, for nine hundred and ninety-nine men —" ‡

Of Fei-tzu's life-work, that single encyclopaedic tome upon which
he expended his entire career and to the cause of which he sacrificed innumerable colleagues, little remains, a few fragments
considerably charred. Of Fei-tzu himself, so entirely has every
trace been removed that he might have been a woman.

THE ADVICE OF LI SSU
REGARDING THE LAW

Sire, Fei-tzu made a mistake. He imagined that the law did not
exist before him, and without him there would be none. For the
sake of his study, Fei-tzu pretended to invent the law. The empire
could not tolerate such vanity, and that is why I have been permitted to end it. As always, sire, you have enabled the enforcer of your
will to select himself accurately. From our earliest days, Fei-tzu
and I were fellow students of the law, comrades, life-companions,

---

† Here there is a welcome gap in the text.

‡ Here, where the text of Fei-tzu breaks off abruptly, is commonly believed
  to mark the point at which Li Ssu killed him.

yet I killed him. How was this possible? Why, because we were students of the law!

Does the deletion of Fei-tzu suggest that the law itself has died? The law, once known, does not die. Would that it were not so, but it is. The law, however, was not always known. In the ancient time when the law was not separate from the nature of those bound by the law, no one knew the law, the law was contained within. When the law became political and every state contained a warring prince, still the law was not known, only the prince knew the law, for how else could the prince be free? Now that all the world is one empire, yours, and the warring princes are melted into statuary, every official knows the law, though no one knows the sum of officials.

Fei-tzu made known the law and then made a business of it. There were those of us who tried to stop him. Unfortunately only his fellows had noticed his work, and it was precisely they whom his work consumed. Before they could warn Fei-tzu of his peril, it laid waste to them. I alone escaped, sire, fleeing the study of the law into your service. Here at last I was empowered to curtail Fei-tzu. I did so comprehensively, but too late by many slogans to staunch the spread of the law.

How in time and time the tidings of the law seeped into the mandarinate, how eventually the statutes of the law permeated the enfeoffed commanderies through every prefecture into the remotest wards, how this very morning the velvet palanquin of your own least official sets him down at the gate of his ministry of petty claims, where he gathers his robes above his knees and runs giggling into the audience chamber to dispense his especial fragment of the law ... these are tales too told for telling.

Nowadays, wherever one travels in the empire, there are officials. Wherever there are officials, there is the infinite scaffold of mandarin and clerk. Who dares dismantle that apparatus? What emperor would wish it done? Why, perhaps such a deconstruction might discover that, within, there is no edifice of the law! No, sire, you and I must be content with the encyclopaedic excision of Fei-tzu and, when irritation warrants and opportunity avails, with the genital abridgement of the occasional thrusting official.

Now that the law is known, this much may be said. Once the law is known no one is free of the law, not he who is bound by the law nor he who binds all with the law. Though the law was fixed by whim, once the law is known no whims remain. When everyone knows the law, not even the law is free.

Here, then, is my advice. Obey the law! Perhaps there is law to obey?

As token of my imperial pardon in the matter of the death of Fei-tzu, I accept with humility your gracious gift of the little statue of the great Lady Shang. Ugly, wasn't she?

THE PERSON OF THE
FIRST EMPEROR

Thus the way of the Emperor was made smooth for him by others.

HIS ARRIVAL

The birth of the Emperor, regardless of its date, always has been celebrated on the first day of the first month of the first year of each decade so that he could be honoured centuries before his nativity yet come to reign no later than his middle age. The effigies burned upon these occasions represent, some say, the mystery of the Emperor's pre-incarnation. Others say they represent the Emperor himself, and dismiss the lack of resemblance on the grounds that our ancestors could hardly have copied what they had not yet seen.

Still, one might ask, why commemorate the birth of one's emperor by combusting man-shaped sacks of glutinous inflammables? One may as well wonder why invisible sects welcomed the seasons in the Emperor's name long before he had chosen one, and why, aeons before there was an empire, many a remote potentate mourned the date upon which his kingdom had been absorbed into it. The answer is that these traditions always have been so, and the Emperor has permitted their practice by ignoring it.

When the Emperor arrived among us, it was as if we had been expecting him. His palaces already were built. Most had fallen into disrepair, and the remainder were derelict. Several, among them the most imposing and notorious, were represented by no more than mounds and conflicting archaeological theories. The same was true of his ceremonials and his liturgy, and his regalia had awaited him so long and had been used by so many that it was in no fit state for his coronation.

By the time he arrived, we had been observing his twenty-seven feast days and his hundred-and-one days of fast for generations. The clergy habitually harangued us upon our laxity in commemoration, which did not indicate that our piety had declined but merely that our priests themselves no longer could recall even the anecdotal origins of these rites, and were unable to inspire us to continue to observe them.

The best we could manage upon his arrival was a kind of fond enthusiasm, a generalized gladness of the sort one feels watching one's mother bless the house with a gesture she considers silent prayer though it is only a manuflection her mother had employed to shield her eyes from the flare of the holy candles. He was our first emperor yet his arrival generated nostalgia.

HIS DIMENSIONS

Any consideration of the Emperor is hampered by the perfect embargo on coeval portraiture. There was, of course, the famous exception of the hard-wax casting perpetrated by the Imperial Cosmetician when she was supposed to be performing a whole-body depilation. At her death-bed confession, the effigy was revealed to have been a self-modelled hoax, though not before said cosmetician had enjoyed a lifetime of lucrative commerce based upon the reputation of her alleged achievement. From which episode can probably be deduced one relevant observation: the Emperor was hairy.

As well, the Emperor's long reign provided ample opportunity for imaginative representations of him in charcoal, tin, and wool, a few of which reputedly were instigated by the Emperor himself in envy of forms and physiques he would have enjoyed possessing. They are, therefore, inaccurate. Any authentic record of the Emperor's famous features was confined to the image daily impressed upon his shaving mirror, if indeed he was beardless.

It should not be concluded as many have that, following an unhappy episode in his personal life, an amatory rejection, perhaps, or a criminal prosecution, the Emperor suffered a paroxysm of demurral that prompted his decision to conceal a visage become loathsome in the eyes of a disdainful beloved or desirable to a hostile constabulary, or was otherwise unbearable or imprudent to reveal. No, it is simply that the Emperor preferred not to be viewed while alive nor graphically memorialized later on, a predilection so intense that official audiences with him took place through gauze, and his testament specifies that his corpse be thrice cremated. The solemnity of the latter instruction is undermined by the mischievous codicil that his sifted ashes be scattered over the breakfast of his enemies so that, with luck, they would contract whatever ailment had killed him.

There are verbal delineations of the Emperor in the diaries and the personal correspondence of contemporary folk who were fortunate enough to have caught a glimpse in a moment of unguarded visibility. The accuracy of these intimate individual word-portraits is attested to by the zealous eradication of all of them by the imperial constabulary. Which accumulated act of censorship must have been entirely successful given the activity of forgers to manufacture so many, several of which have found their way into the texts of sensational historians.

The enemies of the Emperor were numerous and varied, and their eyewitness testimony is distorted by ideological antipathy and political expedience and vogue. It is doubtful, for instance, that the Emperor's facial features contained what is caricatured, or that his organs exuded what is alleged. Even if it were so, it would be of little non-scandalous historical significance. Indeed, it is in the demeanour of the enemies of the Emperor that we can deduce the clearest manifestation of his corporeal appearance, once we neutralize their vituperation with an injection of anti-propaganda and accustom ourselves to rely upon the evidence of their behaviour rather than the object of their abhorrence. The residual portrait is banal. Once we subtract the lies perpetrated by his enemies, the face of the Emperor is surprisingly like our own.

The behaviour of the Emperor is another matter. Here the evidence is copious, the allegations are plausible, and the results are worth recording.

HIS BEHAVIOUR

In prophetic reaction to political styles of the future, the Emperor made an effort to appear non-charismatic. By all accounts he succeeded. Indeed, it is said that his most effective protection against assassination was neither the devious apparatus of disguise nor the distracting mechanism of unpredictable behaviour, but the blatant ordinariness of his daily routines and the utterly pedestrian manner of their accomplishment. Palace registers indicate that the Emperor ate moderately, drank appropriately, clothed himself in whichever fashion predominated, and performed his bodily necessities without ostentation.

The covert memoranda of well-placed and discretely perceptive underlings often do manage to record anecdotal insights based upon diurnal and nocturnal task-related incidents and corridor glimpses obscured by lowered brows. For example, from marginalia in volumes forty-three to eight hundred and eighty-seven of the commonplace book of a specific anonymous courtier, we learn that the Emperor ...

... "eschewed intimacy with anyone who sought his, granting favour and privilege in advance so as to offset importuning." A self-evident self-protective attitude, not in itself reprehensible.

... "caroused selectively and espoused consecutively." His consorts — how many, which gender, whether concurrent, sequential, or collective — remain a topic of learned speculation. Likewise the matter of his accumulated offspring, their lineaments, their complexions, their distinguishing deformities. There is no report of his ever having opposed a paternity suit. Indeed, there are several enledgered instances of his having "pacified aspirants and their mothers" with "honoraria," without bothering to read their claims.

... "accomplished his most useful tasks in the hours before dawn when the palace slept, everyone except the night guards who were instructed to perform their office in silence and, where possible, invisibly." That the Emperor never slept is an exaggeration or an admonitory motto. What is more probable is that he did not sleep in the conventional manner. It is known, for instance, that he possessed the rare gift of napping with his eyes open and his visage alive with apparent awareness, a talent witnessed by appellants who withdrew from the imperial presence believing themselves to have had a successful hearing only to hear no more of it and, of course, be denied a second interview on the grounds that none is heard in the same suit twice.

... "dreamt." It is known that the Emperor suffered violent recurring dreams. His screams before waking sometimes were uttered in awkward circumstances, during a judicial proceeding, for instance, or at a tedious social engagement. The contents of these phantasmagoria were confided to a few, a bed partner mauled in the process of the Emperor's awakening, a guest spattered at a banquet table, a foreign diplomat collapsed upon.

Many horrors could be construed from his lamentations in the moments before he attained entire day-consciousness. From those unconstrained wails it could be deduced that, as an embryo, the Emperor was intimidated by a cusped upright instrument that threatened to thrust through the amniotic sac and to engulf its tenant in venomous ejaculate; that, as an infant, he was imperilled by a flesh-mound with a salient promontory that penetrated his dietary orifice and inundated it; that, as a child, he was molested and abused and disgusted by unavoidable intimates: an uncle demented by war and obsessed with a recitation of its details, an aunt of intimidating cosmetics who clad herself in pelts, a cousin of the same age who killed himself at the earliest opportunity by an excess of confection and effervescent beverage. By interpretation of these findings, it is possible to conclude that the Emperor's adult phobias regarding machinery, suffocation, and nutritional poisoning mostly derived from early traumas.

... "was talkative." His garrulousness was never observed at governmental rallies, military exercises, displays of decorative female
calisthenics, and other events requiring keynote addresses. There,
the Emperor's locution bordered on the apt, with occasional
excursions into eloquence.

In personal interviews or small-scale colloquia, however, the
Emperor was ill at ease, which condition, in the aside-words of
a retired admiral of the imperial fleet then serving as Underbutler
of the Bedchamber, "fuelled his babble and stoked his jabber."
Though stenographic notation at personal audiences was forbidden, the whispered reports of bemused participants indicate
that private conversation with the Emperor did tend to dwindle
into monologue, monologue into pronouncement, pronouncement into harangue, harangue into soliloquy, at which point the
Emperor's self-absorption would enable the auditor to escape.
Survivors of such encounters agreed that the Emperor's episodes
of uncontrolled prolixity were the result of his awkwardness during silences, not symptoms of demagoguery but of shyness.

... "was an exhibitionist and a gifted performer." With respect to the
former allegation, the reverse was the case. The latter remains
a matter of taste.

It is safe to assume that the Emperor had no appetite for
mass movements, popular assemblies, folk dancing, and choral-
singing, though the governmental calendar did necessitate his
attendance at many such events and his enthusiastic participation
in most of them. Similar indices were his avoidance of protest
marches, congregational entertainments, and bacchanalian dithy-
rambs unless he was at the head of the parade or at the lip of
the stage or on the top of the pile under the festive table. All
of which could have been mistaken for extroversion, narcissism,
or, at the least, dissipation. They were, in fact, the Emperor's
various ways of avoiding crowds.

It must be admitted that pandemic entertainments did
proliferate during the Emperor's reign and, given his rank and

position, his entrepreneurial initiative with respect to them was
inevitable. At the legendary forty-night Festival to Alleviate
Famine Abroad, for instance, it was the Emperor who presided
behind the scene, monitoring the performance of the contributing artistes, and ensuring that the stripping of their assets was
entire. To distract the audience from the sight of those painful,
enforced contributions, it was he who came forward from time to
time to announce the accumulating total. Whether the Emperor
secretly enjoyed devising and orchestrating and dominating such
occasions was beside the point. Apparently he was good at it, and
performed vigorously if against his nature. Speculation beyond
that is futile and borders on treason.

... "was cowardly." This rumour is based upon the notorious episode
of exploding sewage gas at the imperial palace. It is an unavoidable fact that the Emperor was seen to be the first to flee — it
was assumed that his sudden headfirst emergence from an upper
window was the result of flight — and to take refuge in the moat
from which eventually he was extracted, the tail of his night-
shirt severely singed. At the time an epigram attributed to the
Emperor was much quoted, though it was almost certain to have
been coined by the aforementioned formerly nautical Underbutler of the Bedchamber: "Unless there are superior officers aboard,
captains should be the first to leave sinking ships. How else can
floating ships acquire captains?" The witticism was popular but
failed to quell controversy.

    Inevitably the scandal of the sewage gas explosion reminded
gossipmongers of the Emperor's craven escape from assassination
by relinquishing the sleeve of his ceremonial robe and hiding
behind a bronze pillar, though the two incidents bore no simi-
larity beyond the obvious. In the mysterious dynamic of public
awareness and extrapolation (of which more below), that particular folk-memory stimulated other recollections: the unmanly
irresolution of the Emperor's adolescence, his naive susceptibility to flirts of either sex, his championship of social misfits, his

failure to participate in the Tea Tray Orifice Scandal other than as an enthusiastic onlooker. And so on.

Given these indications of the Emperor's endemic timidity, his disinclination to instigate proactive warfare usually was mentioned in this regard, as well as his failure to arrive early enough to prevent the unhappy epochs before his birth. Rather, that such a diffident man had the courage to embrace imperial pre-eminence should have been interpreted as a wonder that entitled him to it.

HIS REPUTATION

To obtain a grasp of the Emperor's reputation little is required beyond an inquiring eye, an acute ear, an adhesive memory, and a strong stomach. With this equipment the diligent researcher into popular sentiment may collect, corroborate, journalize, and preserve for posterity gossip regarding the Emperor's ...

... "penis." As memorialized in equine statuary and civic obelisks, allowance should be made for architectural overachievement. His reputed priapism is probably an instance of rigid sculptural material becoming anatomic legend.

... "corpulence." Deduced from silhouettes in mural graffiti and doodle marginalia, the occasionally swollen appearance of the Emperor may be attributable to military dress and honorific regalia. A similar though opposite imputation is promulgated from another angle by enthusiasts in the anorexic, apepsic, and bulimic communities.

... "intelligence." One does not wish to succumb too easily to anti-imperial propaganda and attribute to the Emperor conspicuous intelligence. If they possess intelligence, public functionaries tend to conceal it, usually affecting its obverse out of respect for those on whose behalf they function. And so, it may be assumed, did the Emperor.

... "wife-beating." This inexcusable aspect of the Emperor's reputation, of course, is exclusively associated with the princess. As the consort of his youth, it would have been she who suffered the most reprehensible of his actions, or alleged that she had. In this case whether activity or allegation was the operative mode mattered very little with respect to the Emperor's reputation. As is common in such matters, even if no damage was done, the damage was done. It could not be undone without inflicting further damage.

The charge was based upon a single offence attested to by the princess at the divorce tribunal. She was convinced the Emperor had struck her. So intense was her belief that she developed a welt upon her body where there had been none before, though in an area even a well-aimed fist was unlikely to have penetrated. The more accessible target, her face, remained unimpaired except for a layer of sombre cosmetic deemed necessary for her tribunal appearance.

The Emperor failed to deny the wife-beating on the plausible grounds of his hospitalization at the time he was alleged to have inflicted it. Perhaps he did not bother with denial, believing that to call attention to the fact that he himself was the victim of the alleged assault would be seen as proof positive of his constitutional disinclination to engage in personal combat even in self-defence (see "was cowardly" in the previous section).

The tribunal was considerably moved by the princess's enthusiastic display of her intimate blemish, and a positive judgment on her behalf was secured. For reasons best known to her, however, the benefits of the settlement and the fame of her achievement in winning it against an eventual emperor did nothing to temper her vengeful pursuit of him. In spontaneous public rallies choreographed on her behalf by acolytes employed on a commission basis, it was made to seem that, during the marriage, the princess's actual bodily harming of the Emperor with whatever lay to hand had been a pre-emptive retaliation for his abuse of her, and that, following their divorce, his refusal to defend himself retrospectively was an instance of his aggression, albeit passive.

Because of the Emperor's strenuous avoidance of her after the divorce, the princess was forced to resort to contrivances to achieve an encounter where she could deliver her accusations in person, lying in wait to waylay him on a sentimental visit to the site of the giant willow, their ancient trysting tree (a hope sadly unrewarded), engineering accidental intersections along his regular routes to the grocery market and the garden privy (successful, but only once along each path), and countless other tactics and subterfuges recorded in the daybook of the local constabulary and in the memory of neighbours who reported the princess's consequent screams of frustration.

When the Emperor left home and moved to a foreign land to accept his destiny, the princess's allegations of mistreatment multiplied in inverse proportion to his proximity, and the stratagems for their transmission became more subtle. Courier delivery of a feculent bundle enclosed in a box of his favourite confectionary, pigeons carrying pathogenic toxins, fleas trained in collective infestation, journalists pretending neutrality ... the malevolent devices were numberless. Some, indeed many, perhaps all, may have been grotesque conceits of the Emperor's imagination or vaporous horrors generated by emollient powders and potions. If so, they were a measure of the extent to which daggers of malice launched by the princess continued to invade his consciousness, and the depth to which they penetrated.

An objective observer of the process might have been tempted to conclude that, with a resolve akin to and the reverse of a dedicated physician's, the princess sought to impede the closure of a wound that, kept open, would infect, fester, suppurate, and ultimately annihilate, decompose, dissolve, and scatter the person and the legacy of the victim. As it happened, it was she who predeceased the Emperor, which godsend did nothing to curtail her mission to discredit him and, for one long moment, seemed actually to accelerate it.

When the princess died in inappropriate circumstances, the outpouring of public grief was compendious, the tirade of blame deafening, and that among a people whose only concern for the person of the princess had been a vicarious interest in the more lurid aspects of her marriage! Those who had not mourned their parents, their siblings, their cats, mourned her. They who never had an unorthodox thought were certain it was the Emperor who had done her in.

At the funeral of the princess the progress of the cortege was slowed by flowers, toys, and sealed vials of heart's-blood hurled in its path. Mourners who achieved admission to the boneyard itself knelt upon a dedicated archipelago of diamondiferous topsoil, and witnessed the encasement of her black-gold coffin in a white-gold sepulchre visible on a sunny day from a distance of six cantons. There, at the lip of her grave, they petitioned the Emperor to extend her annual commemorative memorial-day by several months. The suggestion was delivered with menaces.

Even considering the tourist trade, the interment of the princess obviously represented an imbalance between expenditure and revenue. Nevertheless, the Emperor appeared at the funeral suitably attired in bespoke sackcloth, refused to scoff at the public hysteria, and acceded to all petitions regardless of their ridiculousness. At the filling-in of the grave, he was seen to conceal a grin. His mien was universally accepted as a rueful apology for his unspecified part in her irredeemable demise. It enabled the Emperor to be forgiven and the princess to be forgotten.

... "sophistication." The accusation was seldom made. Cosmopolitan taste, aesthetic delight, transcultural intercourse, and intellectual adventuring, though occasionally alleged, were never proven. They remained smudges on the Emperor's escutcheon rather than defilements.

REFLECTIONS ON REPUTATION

Reputation has no substance beyond report. Report is the whole of it, its origin, its occasion, its objective, its accomplishment, its residuum, not only its basis but its entirety. The reputation of any one of us depends upon who is reporting it, how he came by his opinion, his entitlement to it, his nature and his quality and his condition at the moment he permits it to be released, his (at the risk of wit-play) reputation.

Consider the Emperor's bitterness. Who alleges it? Why, he who considers himself wronged and attributes his misfortune, not to personal fault or natural happenstance, but to the dynamic of an embittered age when any admirable initiative and legitimate enterprise such as his is doomed, and failure is favoured, and incompetence is rewarded, such is the temper of the time! And so it goes, impugning only the reputation of the alleger.

The same may be said of the Emperor's fabled cynicism, apathy, despair, and abuse of cats. He may have embodied every deadly sin, the Shangian, the Fei-tzuian, or more or some or none. Reputation will not tell us. The reputation of the Emperor recedes from the person of the Emperor and approaches the identity of its reporters. In striving to delineate him, they indelibly imprint themselves.

The impulse to gather together the fragments of observation, the shards of gossip, the detritus of scandal, and to construct of them a reputation for another being is irresistible. Congenital liars speak of the joy of biographic dissembling and fictive assembling as the rest of us do of the ecstasy of the act of gestation. Apparently, to construct a chimera of the imagined from the fragments of the real is to emulate the divine procedure of amassing order from chaos, of generating body from particle, of particulating man from mankind. The excitement of doing it is irresistible. The attraction of it when done is unique. Who, after all, does not enjoy literature?

In our natural state the least of us is an original of untamed will and contradictory impulse who, once arrested and examined, alters. He must be apprehended and scrutinized again and again.

Our world with us in it moves on, and is incomprehensible. But characters wholly invented hold still. They are out of time or are in a time of their own. Their objects, when dropped, may rise; we are only entitled to protest when suddenly they begin to fall, for then the physics of pretence have been offended. Such a world is within our grasp. Its creatures are coherent. We understand them and are charmed.

To resist the delights of pretence is to prefer record to report. Where recording ends, reporting begins. With the one there is no pretence, with the other there is little else. Record shows us the world as it was, perhaps as it is, possibly as it will become. Report shows us a world of no substance beyond its articulation, a world of words, a reputed world, a world of repute. It should not be mistaken for the world. But frequently it is and, of that error, emperors are born.

There remains the possibility that, being aware of the self-reflective quality of reputation, the Emperor encouraged disrespectful speculation upon him and scandalous characterization of him as a means of enabling us to portray ourselves. Perhaps our envisioning and revisioning the Emperor — even after his death, perhaps especially then — is actually a method to embody the empire, to mortalize it, and by association to immortalize ourselves?

VII

THE LIMITS OF THE EMPIRE

There is another possibility. Perhaps the First Emperor has realized that the limits of the empire cannot be measured by conventional means? Perhaps he has decided that, for that great task, nothing will suffice but the apparatus of the imagination?

IMPERIAL QUESTIONS

When the Emperor left the provinces to enter the empire, did he move at all? Since there was no empire before his arrival, it can be argued that, if he did move, he carried the empire with him. What, then, did he enter? How was it different from the place he had left? And, if it was no different, why had he bothered to come?

The answers to such questions did not become clearer after he arrived. An important new question arose. What, in fact, constituted the empire? To argue that the empire was measured by the presence of the Emperor was to reduce its dimensions to those of a city, a room, a chariot, a tent, or, if one were to commit jocularity, a suit of clothes.

Nor was it helpful to define the region of the empire by the presence there of the imperial army or of the imperial law. At no moment in his reign can even the Emperor have been aware of the scope of either of those. Conscription, after all, is as little a product and as much a process as jurisprudence. The techniques of both are as flexible as wind, their results as variable as water. Besides, if the body of the empire were to be determined by the presence in it of soldiers and of litigators, were it not better to let it die?

Which raises another question. Is it true the empire is diminishing? That would be easier to calculate if one ever had known its extent.

What, then, of money? Surely all who pay tribute to the Emperor are within the empire? At last, it seems one has an answer! The empire is precisely the size of —

Of what? Of the size of the men who pay tribute? Of the size of the tribute they pay? Of the size of the place they pay it, or of the home they sold in order to raise it, or of the remote uncharted invisible location they skulk off to in the hope that they will never be summoned again?

Perhaps one needs to ask other questions? Should all men within the empire pay no more tribute, would the empire cease? Yes, or so we who pay it are told. So long as we pay tribute, does the empire exist? No, such as we always have paid tribute and yet there has not always been an empire. It is common rumour that even men who are not blessed to live within the empire also pay tribute, though not, of course, into a purse half so worthy as —

There, finally, is the glimmer of an answer! The empire has an extent, for there are men who do not live within it! What a pity that, living within the empire, we cannot know who they are!

THE EMPIRE AND THE WORLD

The empire did not contain the world. The Emperor knew this. So did the Emperor's principal ministers. Ministers of a lower rank realized it intermittently but succeeded in putting it out of their minds. Mandarins knew only that the Emperor ruled their world and did not consider themselves qualified to conjecture beyond.

And the people, what did they know? In times of war it did not matter; the presence of an enemy obscured the need to ask whence he originated and whither he withdrew. In times of peace all enemies were within; even those who were not, were recognized by their effect within. If, for example, the activities of a nation in the outer world damaged the empire, the Emperor was able to create the impression that what was required was a change of ministers of lower rank or a rearrangement of the mandarinate or a greater enterprise on the part of the people.

Even when the Emperor was obliged to travel abroad to warn a foreign nation about its policies, even then the thoughts of the people remained within the empire. After all, the Emperor only undertook foreign journeys when the situation was desperate. At such times one thinks of one's next meal and not of the travels of one's emperor.

"Hard times," said the Emperor, "do not cause people to question the integrity of the empire. Indeed, shared deprivations hold the empire together. Thus, although the people may know that the empire does not contain the world, such knowledge is not permitted to interfere with their ignorance of the world."

Of course he said it in the early days of his reign. Later he had no need to appear sardonic. His advisors did it for him.

THE ISLAND PROVINCE

The Emperor dispatched an expedition across his empire to the remotest of his provinces, a mysterious island where holy men were said to eat of the abundant fish and thus become immortal. The expedition returned with word that they should be sent out again but with a larger party that included attractive maidens. This was done, and nothing further was heard of any of them.

Since nothing definite was known about the Emperor's island province, courtiers told tales about it. Usually these took the form of pleasantries wherein ignorant primitives from the island were outsmarted and disgraced by courtiers. Although the Emperor himself composed none of these jokes, he seemed to be amused by them.

When Li Ssu asked the Emperor why he took pleasure in such cruel tales, the Emperor replied, "I find stupidity laughable."

"But," said Li Ssu, "such tales merely demonstrate the stupidity of their authors."

"Very good," smiled the Emperor. "Now tell us one we have not heard."

When an ambassador from the remote island province eventually deigned to visit the capital city, the Emperor was eager to interview him. When the ambassador appeared in the reception hall, the Emperor was shocked. The man was small, garrulous, intelligent, and clearly neither holy nor immortal. With all possible politeness the Emperor ventured to express his disappointment.

The ambassador smiled. "Sire, the tales you have heard about your island province are the product of the imagination of witty courtiers. My people are neither more nor less than myself. That is why I am their ambassador."

The ambassador then approached the Emperor, knelt, lifted the hem of the Emperor's robe, and kissed it. In doing so, he revealed to all the court that the Emperor had crooked legs. "Excuse me for observing," said the ambassador, "that you are no surprise to me."

When the Emperor visited the remote island province, he beheld the poverty of the inhabitants and was much troubled by it. When Li Ssu observed his master's grief, he approached the Emperor and said, "Do not be troubled overmuch by the wretchedness you behold. Who would expect the benefits of your reign to penetrate to the very ends of your empire?"

To which the Emperor replied, "Whether my empire ends here or begins is a matter of the direction in which one is travelling."

THE DWARVES OF TAO-CHOU

In the land of Tao-chou the people are dwarves. The tallest never grow to more than three-and-a-half hand-span. Displayed for sale in our markets, they are described as "offerings of natural products from the land of Tao-chou." How else to describe them? As artifacts?

The dwarves of Tao-chou confess of themselves a limitless contempt. Indeed, they boast of it. Which attitude would make them perfect slaves were it not that they also display a hunger for possessions, in particular, ours. What pleasure they have in property, what profit they derive from the ownership of it, even from its resale, is unknown, their reputation for stupid dealing being legend among us. In second-hand trading there seems no price too slight for a dwarf to accept, usually accompanied by his confession of profound relief at having got rid of so valueless an asset. Whereupon the tiny obsessive instantly rushes out to acquire whichever other of our treasures we can be persuaded to part with and, eventually, at a much reduced price, to repurchase from him. Hence the famous aphorism universally quoted upon the completion of any successful bargain or undetected theft: "like dealing with a dwarf."

There is no way one can hurt a dwarf of Tao-chou. They have anticipated every blow. Nor do they seek to avoid it, but accept it full in the face. Then they smile, or seem to smile, no, not a smile, more a stare of seamless candour, of fulfilled expectation, of satisfaction at a burden successfully borne, of a job somehow well done.

The dwarves of Tao-chou disprize everything about themselves, even their children. They do not abandon their children — indeed, they cling to them with a fierce possession — yet it is clear even to the infants that they too are loathed, in particular those destined to fail to achieve normalcy, which is to say the height of us. Frequently their children achieve our height, which is not surprising as most are the issue of our loins.

I am afraid we find the dwarves of Tao-chou irresistible. More than a little, their seductiveness is due to the aggression of their attachment to us, at least in the beginning. Once they have obtained our reciprocal devotion, of course, they disown it and do everything in their power to rid themselves of those among us weak enough to have become enraptured by such contemptible objects as they.

Where does it go this initial devotion of a dwarf of Tao-chou, where does it go when it is withdrawn? Is it transferred to another? Who can say? Disheartened by the experience of having loved a poisonous dwarf, one is little inclined to overturn rocks to uncover one's successor.

There is nothing so implacable as rejection by a dwarf of Tao-chou. You begin by offering love. You end convinced that it is you who have an ugly body, a contemptible personality, a treacherous character, and you are obliged for the lesson in self-hatred that is not one you will easily forget. Perhaps they select among us those least able to bear loss?

I myself have known a victim of such unequal love for a dwarf of Tao-chou that he took to following her in the streets, though she chose routes to avoid him and wore a variety of clothing of surpassing ordinariness that made it difficult to discern her tiny form fleeing amid the passersby. When from time to time he did manage to achieve an encounter, he would seize the occasion ostentatiously to turn his back on her. It was precisely after one such mishap that he happened to notice a market stall displaying the compelling specimen to which he presently is wed.

How do the dwarves of Tao-chou come to appear on market stalls? Most believe it to be the result of a thriving industry of entrapment and export, which lends a frisson to the purchase of what probably are illegal goods. Yet a visit to Tao-chou itself does not bear out the supposition. In all the land there is not the shop-sign of a single slave-agent or trader, let alone that vast machinery of selection, packaging, and transport that must accompany commerce in such an established commodity. The conclusion is inescapable. The dwarves of Tao-chou merchandise themselves! Such is the measure of their need to escape the despicable land of their birth!

THE FELLOWSHIP OF FFUT

In the court of the Emperor there remained those who recalled the empire at the moment of its greatest extent, and regretted the passing. Such a one was the venerable Ffut.

Every public or private statement, every waking thought of the venerable Ffut was related to his regret at the manifest decline of the empire. This state of mind was not expressed with the passive sorrow or the bewildered despair that befits the elderly. Instead, Ffut performed tantrums amplified by indecorous occasions. "Ah!" the old man would howl, scattering nuns around the Pool of Sepulchral Tranquility in the Garden of Seigneurial Repose. "Life in those days!" he would yelp, twisting the cheek of whichever grandchild. "Never again!" was his invariable conclusion, whereupon he would pout or caterwaul depending upon the proximity of his companions and the relative depth of their slumber.

Ffut was not unique. Every ennobled family contained an elder with congruent recollections. It was impossible to attend the remotest palace on the least political of missions without encountering them. Each old man required another to whom to address his complaint. All, by inclination, were deaf. In a corridor, behind a drape, within an anteroom reserved for those requiring privacy to prepare their petitions or to recover from the rejection of them, one was certain to find oneself surrounded by any number of these old fellows bellowing their elegies. Even the latrine was not free of them. In fact, it appeared to be their favourite resort, perhaps because the only other matter that united their fellowship was the issue of their bowels. Never, it seemed, had they suffered less obstruction than in the fluid days of imperial grandeur!

Did the fellowship of Ffut actually recollect anything beyond the reverberations of their own laments? Had the empire ever been as extensive as they claimed to recall? Had its dimensions been any greater than today's and, since nobody could judge these, was regret sensible?

Clues to the actual extent of the ancient empire were provided, not by the lamentations of Ffut and his fellows, but by the assumptions that underlay them. From their inescapable clamour one could deduce, for example, that at the time of its greatest amplitude the empire had contained grandchildren of acquiescent demeanour and plump cheeks. Apparently, imperial females in that far-off time had been hermetic until marriage and wanton upon demand within it, whereas in widowhood they had been undesirable, inconsolable, and short-lived.

Why, in that blessed era the Emperor himself had sought the advice of this particular elder now lamenting! Had that advice been taken, the empire would have avoided political degeneration, social denigration, and innumerable decrepitudes the most malign of which is constipation due to an absence in the diet of a specific sugared condiment to which one had become habituated in one's youth but that now no longer is imported because of the entirely avoidable loss of a specific far-flung imperial province.

Moreover, back then there had been no aliens. Nowadays there are aliens. Everywhere one looks there are aliens. They are most especially plentiful wherever one does not look. Why, during the time of the ancient empire one never beheld an alien except across the ridge of one's second knuckle at the instant before one's arrowhead entered his throat! Whereas now, of course, ah, now ...!

That particular conviction explained the clamour of Ffut and his fellows every time they encountered an alien. They thought they had seen a ghost. Their terrified clamour on those occasions inevitably reached the ear of the Emperor and caused him to cause Li Ssu to address the problem.

THE ADVICE OF LI SSU REGARDING ALIENS

Sire, truly it may be said, "The empire is the home of aliens." Even in the capital city, even before the gates of the principal palace, the street is full of aliens. How does one recognize them? By their dress, by their accents, by their occupations. Yet one must use discretion, for it is the custom of the empire-born to ape the manner of aliens.

The fashion is particularly popular among the young. Which imperial family does not contain one son or daughter of exotic demeanour and incomprehensible inflexion whose aspirations eschew improvement and who prefers the diminished expectations habitual to those of foreign extraction? Who among those who are empire-born has not himself in his earlier years indulged in similar fantasies of debasement?

The situation is further complicated by the fact that every alien seeks to appear empire-born. Indeed, it has been observed that the most effective way of distinguishing between the alien and the empire-born is to observe not the manner of their performance but the nature of their intent.

Consider, sire, that beggar. Where in all the vastness of the empire has one encountered the like? His entire body is at war, fingers attacking thighs, legs jerking contradictorily askew, cheeks alive with spasms wrenching from his unthinkable lips the grotesque dialect of what must be the least melodious of foreign lands. Here, then, is an alien!

Yet, sire, observe him again. Is there not in all his twitching a pattern, a symmetry, a discipline, even a ritual? And, if one is prepared to stand before him long enough and resist the impulse to kick, can one not also perceive an intent? That remaining arm, for all its apparent flailing, does it not in fact repeatedly traverse the length of that repulsive body, directing our attention to the emaciation, demonstrating the uncoordinated helplessness? Does it not always end its odyssey palm outstretched and empty? Even that interminable chant, is it anything more than exhalation? Are all its words not moans?

And what is the result of this incessant obsessive beseeching? Why, paralysis! Does any of it disturb the languor of that neck, the flaccidity of that gaze, the quintessential lassitude of that arse?

In all the time you, sire, have been watching, has that beggar stirred a hairsbreadth from his place on the pavement? Has he ever moved? Is this not the identical beggar one's very father, when only a boy rushing from encounter to encounter, paused before to steal a coin? Of course it is he! If not, is it not precisely such a one, perhaps the son or the son of the son of that original beggar who may himself have writhed on the curbstone of his father and of all the beggars who fathered that one in the aeons before there was an emperor much less an imperial street to recline upon and an imperial palace to beg before?

Surely sire, for all his exoticism, this beggar is no alien but, shame betide us, empire-born!

Why, then, does he seek to appear other than he is? Because that beggar knows, as all beggars know, that the streets of the capital city are full of aliens, and it is to one of their own that men are most likely to cast coins. And what is true of beggars applies as well to certain ministers of state who —

To return to the matter of aliens. If on every thoroughfare every acrid overcoat and incomprehensible shriek is likely to signal an empire-born imitator of aliens, how are we to recognize a genuine alien, should there be one and should we happen to stumble across him? In this, as in all matters of perplexity, one turns to one's emperor.

Here, sire, is my advice regarding aliens.

In all the empire there must be none. There must remain only the reputation of such for, without it, how should the empire-born know themselves to be unique? It is for that reason that you will devise the universal status of Internal Alien. Thus the aboriginal becomes an immigrant and the emigrant remains a native. Who, then, can doubt the universal pervasiveness of the empire? Who need come to it or leave?

GENERAL MENG

When Meng entered the empire, he was suspect. First, because he was an alien and an alien had tried to assassinate the Emperor, though an alien, too, had saved him, so on that score no decision could be secured. The second reason for suspecting Meng was that he was an architect and a general. An architect built, a general tore down. How could anyone perform a single project that incorporated the arts of both?

Furthermore, Meng suspected us! Why else would he have disguised himself? A man of such accomplishment must needs have passed many a debilitating night over wick and taper, would not have escaped the humiliations of apprenticeship, might have survived recurrent bankruptcies but could never have evaded unscrupulous competition and that especial treachery of colleagues that precipitates emigration. Yet, so profound was his distrust of us that Meng concealed his corrosive bitterness and

his understandable cynicism behind an unwearied countenance
and an open smile!

The Emperor might have required such an impostor to take
his own life forthwith, if only as a defensive contingency. With
Meng he chose a subtler device. The Emperor employed him. How
demeaning for the redoubtable Meng to be caused to perform the
tasks of a common property surveyor! But perform them he did,
and not without a feigned enthusiasm.

Woodworm, dry rot, hide suckers, galloping mould … such
repugnances were his daily office. Yet his records reverberate like
anthems of rectitude rather than litanies of decay! Who but Meng
would have filed the following? "From the internal eaves speci-
mens of putridity, from the nether recesses of the sub-cellarage
crawlspace samples of ineluctable gunge: such repugnances con-
firm our earlier observation that the natural agents of decrepitude,
when compacted for generations, serve to reinforce an antique
domicile otherwise susceptible to bombardment." Or this? "Road-
way, market square, temple, abutting one upon the other down
the unscalable perpendicular of the cliff: the disturbance of any
portion of the ulterior tier, indeed the undermining of a single
particular boulder (see insert cross-sectional projection 'Q' high-
lighted black), and the entire village will precipitate itself into the
gorge." Or this? "Were that region not already a part of the empire,
I should recommend its immediate invasion."

There is no indication that the Emperor read these reports.
There is every indication that the Emperor did not read them, for
Meng was accorded preference, esteem, and extensive promotion.
Doubtless some flunky employed to scan tiresome documents had
responded to one of Meng's more inappropriate observations with
some such comment as "Why, the man's an imbecile!" Which
ejaculation in the unexalted confines of that invisible bureau could
have appeared to be an unprecedented spark of vivacity. By the
time such a response filtered upward through echelons to the
ear of one whose voice might be heard in ministries beyond, is it

not conceivable that it had become transmuted into an acknow-
ledgement of initiative or, what is even rarer in such dreary
precincts, praise?

After that, who knows what collision of happenstance?
A remark over tea amplified along corridors? An abstract testi-
monial transmitted by nonentities hopeful to associate themselves
with distinction? The name of Meng progressing from memorandum to memorandum, perhaps as the result of the misspelling of
the name of quite another, some deserving minion, some actual
benefactor of the public weal, some unassertive hero such as you
or me who thus was condemned by epistemological dysfunction
to a lifetime of invisible service to emperor and empire in a grubby
pavilion miles and miles from the imperial throne?

Unless, of course, one concludes that Meng's various promo-
tions were an indication of his inability to perfect a single labour?
What, after all, was the good of any of it? The sort of data Meng
collected, the conclusions he deduced, the advice he proffered
might have been of some use had they applied to a malevolent
nation that the Emperor intended to subdue. But Meng's survey-
ing projects carried him to all sectors of the known world within
the empire. What was there to fear from those?

Within knowledgeable court circles it was authoritative gossip that all the works of Meng were but diversionary devices to
distract attention from the Emperor's true motive in soliciting
them: to measure the parameters of the empire. Such a project
must needs have been kept secret. Should it have been noised
about that the Emperor did not already know the extent of his
own empire, panic would have prevailed, perhaps despair. Meng
must have remained ignorant of this ulterior purpose for his
employment, judging by the fact that he cheerfully continued
to perform it.

Even had he been aware that most of his work was irrelevant
and that, once their incidental calibrations had been noted, all
his reports were disregarded, perhaps he still might not have been
troubled. The frivolity of Meng also is well known. One example

will suffice. In response to the award of his military commission, Meng appallingly addressed the Emperor thus: "In my native land I was a general. For my symmetrical arrangement of the limitless graves of my soldiers I was rewarded with the title of 'architect.' In the empire as an architect I have surveyed the limits of the internal world. For my reward, sire, you have named me 'general.' Alas, I have no luck with princes!"

Be that as it may and regardless of sensible deductions, Meng's career in the empire accelerated at a rate unprecedented among those of us who cared to watch. Meng, the surveyor of bleak hinterlands, became Meng, the designer of grand imperial projects. What a decline! Though all the world, of course, saw it as a rise.

It happened thus.

In every province Meng surveyed, what came to be called the "Great Demolitions" followed. Sometimes these took the form of eyesore clearances with the implication of prettier structures to follow. Sometimes the luxuriance of a natural topography or the excellence of an indigenous housing stock or the depth of a resident community dictated more subtle measures. In such regions the incitement to tribal conflict was effective, and rarely was it necessary to foment outright civil war. More often than not the empire-wide tradition of territorial disparity had the duel effect of physical degeneration and social abandonment resulting in emigration due to sadness. Vast areas could be cleared of human residence by these methods, and rather slowly which fortified the impression that nature itself was at work.

Whichever the machinery of a particular demolition, plenty of residual rubble remained. Indeed, some historical observers conclude that the aggregate purpose of the Great Demolitions was to provide a bountiful resource of wasteland.

Whether Meng knowingly brought about the Great Demolitions or even was aware that they followed in his path as blight in the footsteps of a dragon, it surely is to them and to their consequences that he owed his apotheosis. Every time a city was despoiled or a province became destitute or a region suffered decay, out of the inevitable ruins and refugees, like a maggot from an apple, a grand imperial project was born! And each was designed by Meng!

Not that he meant to do that either. As Imperial Architect, Meng was commissioned to produce his grand designs piece-meal, and he was forbidden to conceptualize their entirety or cumulatively to recall their parts. Thus it was that he came to design the Interprovincial Subalpine Tunnel that subsequently became the Imperial Reservoir, all the while believing that what he was doing was levelling a valley with backfill. Thus transpired the Imperial Archive which vast repository Meng claims he was told was intended for use as the Great Granary at Ao, hence its unique facility for the alphabetic storage of, if not every kernel, at least every silo-full.

Had he lived longer, the gullibility and the loyalty of Meng doubtless would have explained all manner of bizarre imperial projects, horizontal monstrosities like the Great Trench and ver-tical ones like the Imperial Tomb, not to mention the Burning of the Books and the Interment of the Scholars. Suffice it to say that, in his time, the distorted integrity of Meng eventually was exhausted, and with his famous sigh he was impelled to accept or compelled to solicit his next advancement without realizing the scope of his mandate or knowing the reason for his labour.

Contingent to his duties as Imperial Architect, Meng was licensed to conscript. Not that he exercised that power. For a man as ambitious as Meng must have been in order to have risen so consistently and so high, visibly to have enlisted the aid of others would have been to confess the absence of his own entire suffi-ciency, and to retard his ascent, and perhaps to invite his downfall. No indeed, Meng was too wily to fall into the trap the Emperor had set by empowering him to conscript! Instead he recruited by utilizing charm.

What charms did Meng possess? Neither above nor below the common height of a man, Meng did nothing to compensate for this humiliating lack of stature. In fact, he repeatedly drew attention to his littleness by failing to cultivate the companion-ship of tiny women. Of Meng's several putative wives only one was reported to be of less than medium height, and she may have been his mother.

What body Meng did inhabit probably was deformed beyond description. Such a conclusion is inevitable because he deliber-ately eschewed the prevailing fashion of sandals, vest, and truss, choosing instead to dress warmly. In consequence, every knob and hump, every hairless stump, every pustular private and carbun-cular extremity was enforced upon the imagination of everyone who beheld him fully clothed.

Of course, all these concealed horrors were disguised by that face, the frank and cheerful expression of which belied his nature. Meng, it appears, was a self-loather. "When I am dead," he is said to have said to one of his wives or a daughter, "memorialize me thus: 'Here lies one who despised himself'." Some in his presence believed the repulsion they felt to be their own. It was not so. The loathing of him was his.

Apparently Meng's auto-contempt was related to his occupa-tions. "I have never seen," Meng is known to have said, "the result of a single of my labours. Thus I have the courage to go on."

When asked why, since he despised both his professions, he did not pursue another, Meng replied, "So long as men need other worlds to live in, architects will find employment. The same is true of soldiers. One way or another I shall not be out of work."

When it was demonstrated to him that, despite his personal debilities and professional disinclinations, men flocked unbidden to his service, Meng shrugged, "I have observed that all men fol-low any man as unlike them as themselves. Likewise the reverse." Which remark demonstrates the most irritating of Meng's pro-pensities: his impenetrable whimsy.

By all reports, then, the demeanour of Meng, like his enter-prise, was negative in character and self-mocking in practice. Who would not feel himself superior in every respect to such a man? Doubtless that is why, given the humiliations of life at court, so many of us were comfortable in his presence. If that is charm, so be it!

When ultimately he was honoured for the completion of all his labours by being made First Commander of the Imperial Armies, it was widely reported that Meng accepted the title with a laugh. He more than others must have realized that the empire, whatever its extent, contained no armies at all. Meng himself said as much, or that is what Meng actually said generally is taken to mean. "In history or in prophecy," Meng actually said, "the army of the empire is the largest and the least. The largest for its incalculability. The least for the same reason."

Why, then, laugh?

General Meng was a silly man. We at court did well not to take him seriously.

THE LAST WORDS OF GENERAL MENG

The Emperor has surveyed the empire. Which is to say, the Emperor has named himself, made uniform the width of wagon axles, and founded a random mathematical religion. Which is to say, the Emperor has ended the previous administration. In some of these enterprises I imagine I was privileged to assist him.

Now the Emperor has made it known that he requires me to find a reason to terminate my life. Perhaps this instruction does not emanate from the Emperor, but from those at court who have envied me my career despite my lifelong attempt to give it to them? No matter. I have long possessed the sufficient reason required.

From the earliest days of my service I was granted the power to enlist workers. In doing so for many years in every sector of the empire, I unintentionally amassed the greatest standing body of permanent conscripts the world has known. So that he himself need not hesitate to employ my inadvertent army, let it be reported to the Emperor that I have opened my belly. Thus.

THE GREAT TRENCH

That was when the Emperor caused the Great Trench to be dug. There is much speculation as to why he did it. To protect us, it is said, against invasion from the barbarians to the south. Why, then, dig trenches to the north as well, to say nothing of those elsewhere in every part of the empire beheld by men? Moreover, do the dimensions of the empire themselves not protect us in every direction from foreign invasion? Were the barbarians to straddle their ponies and to urge them at us until they dropped in dust and foam, were they to mount others and to gallop at us again, were they to stop their wild ride, were they to lay camps and to clear new pastures and to breed new ponies and to mount those and to ride and to stop and to mount again and to ride again, surely they would never reach us? Should one of them find a way through the inconceivable wastes of our infinite borderlands, should a single son of the barbarians penetrate into our very midst, after generations of incursion would he not have become one of us? Would we notice him?

It has been thought that what the Emperor actually is doing is building a wall. That speculation vanishes when it is remembered that every sector of the project is said to contain not one wall but two, though the second — compiled of the excavated detritus of the first — by definition is invisible to us. What, everyone asks, is the use of two walls, equidistant, parallel? And, since those probably delineate our border, who is to say which wall is ours? It is difficult enough to interpret matters pertaining to the empire. Why bother to concern oneself with at least one structure of two that may not be a part of the empire at all?

By means of this reasoning it becomes apparent that the important phenomenon is not the walls, assuming that there are two, but what lies between them, the eyeless tract where workers stand casting spadesful in both directions, the corridor that deepens as the mounds rise on both sides. And that, of course, is the Great Trench.

This illumination does not, by itself, solve every mystery. If in fact the Trench is a vacancy, who is to say where it begins and where it ends and, in a sense, whether it begins and ends? And if such matters remain uncertain, is it not possible that anything we perceive and everything anyone perceives may be an aspect of the Great Trench, perhaps the very Trench itself?

Such speculation borders on the poetic. Is it not better to avoid speculation and to forget trenches that instigate it? Yet, however much the mind demurs, irresistibly one is drawn back to the Great Trench, for it alone contains the empire, it alone excludes the world.

Or does the Trench contain the world, and exclude from it the empire? That, of course, would depend upon the shape of the Trench, would it not? And of the world? Though one would be able to deduce the shape of the world, would one not, from an accurate perception of the Trench? And there, indeed, is the problem! Who has seen the entirety of the Trench? Who, since the Trench obviously is unfinished because work upon it apparently does not cease, ever will see it?

Rumour has it that the great plan of the Great Trench is round. How that is deduced is unfathomable because every single sector of the project is of no particular shape at all, not even straight. Indeed, in his only directive concerning the construction of the Great Trench the Emperor is said to have said, "Need it be straight? No! Should it become straight, modify so that it is no longer straight. Nor does my instruction imply a series of straight trenches contradictory to one another. No! All straightness is prohibited to the very matter of the taking of a shovelful. From the moment the spade leaves the shoulder, an indirect motion is prescribed. Should ground and spade-head come into contact at an angle, however obstinate the will of the digger it is unlikely that his incision will be straight. And if no incision is straight, how is it possible that the shape of the Great Trench will be other than that intended?"

What, then, is the shape intended? Who, other than the Emperor, can say? It has never been alleged that he did. Doubtless he does not consider it necessary to say. Does the Trench itself not proclaim its shape? Beyond that assertion what is left to be said, even by an emperor?

Perhaps the Emperor does not know its shape? Can he any more than we describe what he cannot perceive, for of the Great Trench this much can be said with certainty: from any point of view it is invisible? Periodically the Emperor himself mounts the utmost tower of his ultimate palace and, if he can perceive the veriest shadow of excavation, that sector of the Trench and the next on either side are filled again and dug again, and filled and dug again and again until, to the exacting perspective of he who authors the whole of it, not a vestige of the Trench remains.

So successful is the Emperor's surveillance, so scrupulously is it enforced by those who supervise the digging, so devoutly is it implemented by those who dig that, the farther we withdraw from the vicinity of the Trench, the more it becomes enfolded in the crenulations of the land. Indeed, should we hang upon the horn of the moon and gaze outward into the ellipse of the world, the Trench would be the only great work of man of which we would be unable to perceive a trace. That much can be said with certainty.

The view of common wayfarers is blocked by the inner wall. The inner wall is a portion of the outpouring of the contents of the Trench, and it rises as far above the ground upon which we stand as it does above the higher ground we move off to in order to discover ground high enough to peer over the inner wall that must forever rise above us. The same, we guess, may be said of the outer wall, though it will have to be a barbarian who says it.

In moist parts of the empire, temporary roofing has been laid across the hiatus of the Trench as a protection against flooding during the rainy seasons. From the point of view of those workers thereby enclosed, the improvement is referred to as "sealing." Retrospectively it has been noted that sealing also provides a greater stability to the outpourings on either side of the Trench, as well as an imperial highway atop it enabling the emperor's chariot to avoid the delays of crowded roads while affording terrestrial pedestrians a refreshing glimpse of him in transit. Indeed, the device has proved so popular that much of the temporary roofing has become permanent, and there appears to be some movement toward sealing even those segments of the Trench that are dug in deserts. Should the trend continue, it is not impossible to imagine a future day when the Great Trench is entirely enclosed, thereby giving the false impression of a single great wall.

If there is one thing anyone can perceive from any vantage it is that the inner wall above the Trench is uniform in height above the level of the ground. Which suggests, of course, that the Trench is uniform in depth below it. Any of us can perceive that. And, presumably, from his side so can any barbarian. It is interesting to be able to deduce one half the depth of the Trench, and we are grateful to the Emperor for permitting us that certainty. It almost allays our desire to behold the Trench itself.

Of that desire we never shall be free. How else to explain the devotion of those whose entire life is passed beside the inner wall?

Wherever one travels in the outskirts of the empire, one sees these people. All else but the inner wall is of no concern to them. Theirs is a perfect devotion and we, of course, respect it, never inquiring their motive, never offering to aid their enterprise, never impugning their success.

At no point known to anyone does the inner wall dip below the line of sight, nor has there ever been found to be an aperture in it. And, naturally, it is forbidden to construct man-bearing kites. So, if it be their objective to catch a glimpse of the Trench behind the inner wall, these devotees have no more luck than we.

Yet failure does not disperse them. They are there and there they reside, ragged, tentless, never speaking to one another much less acknowledging our address, seldom seen to eat, sleeping only when the ground-fog is impenetrable. They have been there as long as the inner wall. The Emperor never has forbidden them their fixation perhaps because, as long as they reside, there is no need to post soldiers to guard the Great Trench.

Who are these people? There are among them, it is said, those who themselves have laboured at the Trench. Why should those who dug it need to be near the Trench again? Perhaps because there is a pleasure in the digging none but those who performed it can recall? Perhaps because they wish somehow to possess the result of their digging? Perhaps because they are not sure even now that the digging has been curtailed? Could that be why they have been seen to throw foodstuffs and blankets over the wall? Why else would they ignite fires below the wall and scream prayers into it except to encourage their fellows beyond it, and to assure them that they and their work and its purpose and its success are not forgotten?

Regarding the purpose of the Great Trench, we are fortunate to possess the Emperor's very words. Unfortunately, they are in the form of a conundrum. "The digging of the Trench is the meaning of the Trench," the Emperor said. "After it is dug, the Trench will lose its meaning, though it is only then that the common measure of men will confer upon it any meaning at all."

THE IMPERIAL CENSUS

The length of the empire, its width, its height, its depth, its duration, are proportional to its intensity as a concept, the velocity of its influence, and the trajectory of its style, every one of which can be calibrated though not, of course, directionally, refraction of dismay as well as momentum of decline and impact of demise being precisely calculable only in retrospect.

The population of the empire, the rates of birth, death, immigration, emigration, the age, sex, pigmentation, superstition, marital status, and economic location of all its citizens, their domestic and public, individual and collective, interior and exterior loyalty, inclination, behaviour, and reactive reconsideration thereof, whether authentic, obedient, assumed, habitual, theatrical, instinctual, obsessive, ceremonial, or arranged are precisely equivalent to the statistical conclusions required.

VIII

THE GOVERNING OF THE EMPIRE

When we named the date for our revolution, the First Emperor declared it a national holiday so that our massing in the streets appeared to be in his honour. When we looted the shops, the First Emperor declared all property common so that we would not be guilty of theft. When we decided to disband our revolution and go home, the First Emperor declared that the revolutionary army was required for the defence of the empire, and we remain conscripted.

THE PARABLE OF THE GOVERNING

When the Emperor travels, it is within a closed carriage. When he emerges, it is at night. In his wayfaring, he follows the course of the sun along the byroads of the empire, never sleeping twice under the same astral configuration. Within his principal palace, he continues from chamber to chamber under zodiacal ceilings, and the underground passages he moves along are no wider than his person.

The course of the Emperor, though determined, is random. His presence is the space he has just passed through. What of him remains? Tales, the same tales told and retold according to different, indeed contradictory, impulses, an enormous coil of related tales unwinding behind the receding cloak of the one whom we take to be him.

It is no wonderment, then, that the governing of the empire is invisible. How, therefore, can it be known? How does one discern the course of a whirlwind? By observing the track of its devastation. Which is to say, by collecting tales.

PEH YI

How Peh Yi arrived in the empire, why he had come and whither, no man could tell. Rumours that he had been a companion of the Emperor's youth and formerly was known as the "Jovial Peng" remained unconfirmed. When the Emperor was asked his opinion on the matter, he publicly was heard to laugh. Perhaps Peh Yi himself had forgotten his origins. When asked, he made it clear that he was blessed with a poor memory, which faculty was an important part of his artistic temperament. When that statement of Peh Yi's was reported to the Emperor, he is said to have laughed again, though witnesses to the event cannot be located.

Once among us, Peh Yi quickly developed a repertoire of classical imperial ballads. He sang them in an inappropriate accent with unexpected rhythms, which increased our desire to hear him. Those songs were too well known to be heard again except when sung by one who made them seem as if we were hearing them for the first time. When asked about his failure to perfect his pronunciation despite more or less mastering our language, Peh Ti reputedly replied, "Is that not the definition of an artist?" though it is possible that, because of his diction, he was imperfectly understood.

Peh Yi never alluded to his native land. Indeed, he deflected our inquiries on the subject into testimonials of his enthusiasm for life in the empire. Peh Yi took pains to persuade us that the empire was the domain of his desires and the haven of his art. Nevertheless, every aspect of his performance reminded us of his origins which remained unknown. Thus did he secure our affection. We, after all, were empire-born. Whatever the intensity of our loyalty to the Emperor and the extent of our enterprise on his behalf, we were but exercising the imperatives of our birth. Peh Yi, however, had chosen the empire. In effect, Peh Yi had chosen us. Could we do less than devote ourselves to the admiration of him? Indeed, we were charmed by every indelicacy of his phrasing, every superfice of his thought, every error in his technique. We prized Peh Yi above empire-born musicians despite the excellence of their art. Peh Yi had more than art. Peh Yi had love. Ours.

It is not difficult to say what it was Peh Yi did musically that so charmed us. He made a love song sound like a military march and a military march sound like a love song. Whatever he sang became an anthem and left us enamoured of the empire and, by extension, of Peh Yi. How he accomplished this seductive transformation is knowable only among musicians. For mere listeners, it had something to do not with the songs themselves but with the intervals between them.

In fact Peh Yi made little music. At concerts we usually interrupted his performance with so frequent applause and of such duration that rarely was he able to complete a song, and seldom did he have time for many. Even when we permitted him to conclude a single resurrected imperial ditty, our zealous rhythmic participation in it plus our residual acclamation for the preceding one and anticipatory appreciation of the next invariably drowned him out.

In the midst of our hysteria, idly plucking at his instrument, Peh Yi would amble toward the lip of the stage, endearingly stumbling against his accompanists and precipitating them into the wings. Once the platform was cleared and he was as close to us as his prestige permitted, Peh Yi would speak. We understood little of what he said. We expected that. A singer, after all, is incoherent without his song. Why else would he bother to sing?

Some of us claim to have heard Peh Yi mention his failed crusade to collect together a body of patriotic musicians who would represent imperial music, thereby relieving Peh Yi of his burden of solitary adulation. Others recall his tearful commitment to remaining in the mainstream of imperial song despite his failure to discover another musician who also was in it.

I myself distinctly remember Peh Yi's announcing something about his needing me to defend him against music critics and other traitors to the empire. Whatever else he seemed to say on the occasion of that particular concert, by the time he had begun the next song in his program — a lilting lament of vanished virginity fetchingly syncopated — I and thousands like me already had emerged into the street and were marching in pursuit of anyone in the vicinity manipulating a critic's writing brush. Once out of range of the concert hall, of course, we stopped, looked at each other, blushed, and went home.

It was inevitable that Peh Yi would attract the envy of empire-born musicians. Their especial grievance seemed to be that, at the height of Peh Yi's fame, the only concerts in the empire were performed by him, and the only jobs available to musicians were as temporary replacements for those accompanists whom Peh Yi accidentally had elbowed off the stage. But Peh Yi refused to be drawn into aesthetic controversy. With his imprecise sensitivity to our language how could he have been expected to respond? And so we responded for him, though in the immediate aftermath of a concert it was difficult to remember in which direction.

On one occasion, the Emperor himself was required to respond on Peh Yi's behalf. At least, it is to Peh Yi that these words of the Emperor usually are taken to refer.

"In the empire there are men of especial privilege. Such men prefer to work by word of mouth. Words of mouth make no mark except in the memory of the person to whom they are spoken, and such traces can be deleted or altered by other words of mouth. Any agreements thus obtained can be accommodated to the changing needs of the men of especial privilege.

"For the enterprise of men of especial privilege it is essential that they render themselves lovable. By perfecting clumsiness in matters of the body, they succeed in appearing vulnerable, and thereby secure the protection of those less ill coordinated. By engineering crises, they attain a position of prominence in affairs. By offering themselves as victims, they obtain charity of those who do not wish it to be implied that anyone victimizes. By seeming guileless throughout, they encourage the exercise of guile on their behalf.

"Those of their colleagues who do not share their disposition, soon succumb to irritation and are vanquished by frustration and resign the liaison, choosing instead to work alone or with others of less devious persuasion or, in despair, no longer to work at all. Therefore, one need not concern oneself with the problem of controlling the associates of men of especial privilege.

"But the men of especial privilege, how does one control them? One deals precisely as one deals with thieves. They are permitted to exercise their craft so long as nothing major is stolen."

It was immediately after that putative defence of him by the Emperor that Peh Yi gave up public performance. His farewell concert consisted of no songs at all, merely his announcement of his imperial appointment as Internal Ambassador of Indigenous Chants. After which he disappeared, smiling, into the Ministry of Culture forever.

We, of course, continue to attend concerts, especially now that the empire once again somehow is full of musicians. But it is not the same. We shall not forget our Peh Yi. We shall never know if he loved us in return and would have killed on our behalf. Many years later, after we had the opportunity to study the Emperor's defence of Peh Yi and had come to understand it to have been an attack, almost a dismissal, perhaps a banishment, we sent a petition to the Emperor asking why, if he disapproved of such a man, he had taken Peh Yi into the government.

"To protect you from him," came the reply, thereby proving that, when given the chance, an emperor can be as obscure as any musician.

THE CHILDREN OF THE KING
(IMPROBABLY IMPUTED TO PEH YI)

The king of the Westland's daughter, the son of the Eastland queen,
Loved each one the other because of the wall between.
    Loved each one the other because of the wall between.

The wall was the highest, the darkest, raised by the hands of men.
Coral, sharp carbon to hold soldiers out, flint to hold soft lovers in.
    Coral, sharp carbon to hold soldiers out, flint to hold soft lovers in.

The king of the Westland's daughter longed for her Eastland soul.
Roses and promises, sweetmeats and sighs, wafted she over the wall.
    Roses and promises, sweetmeats and sighs, wafted she over the wall.

The prince of the east bade his mother the queen open the wall to his love.
Every petition was met with a stone laid upon dark stones above.
    Every petition was met with a stone laid upon dark stones above.

The king of the Westland's daughter, the son of the Eastland queen,
Their love grew all the taller as the wall grew in between.
  Their love grew all the taller as the wall grew in between.

The folk of the Eastland and Westland watched as the love grew tall,
Watched as the lovers tore their fists beating against the wall.
  Watched as the lovers tore their fists beating against the wall.

The folk of the Westland, weeping to see the wall grow between,
Bade their king dispatch his gold to the court of the Eastland queen.
  Bade their king dispatch his gold to the court of the Eastland queen.

The queen of the Eastland, weeping when the joyful news was told,
Bade her folk make a hole in the wall to gather the Westland gold.
  Bade her folk make a hole in the wall to gather the Westland gold.

The king of the Westland's daughter, the son of the Eastland queen,
Bade their love be patient now the hole grew in between.
  Bade their love be patient now the hole grew in between.

Here knelt the Westland princess, here her Eastland love,
One upon gold, the other on stone, reckless of danger above.
  One upon gold, the other on stone, reckless of danger above.

Finger to finger they fumbled, palm against palm they touched,
Arm around arm, breast upon breast, lips upon lips, and such.
  Arm around arm, breast upon breast, lips upon lips, and such.

The king of the Westland, smiling, beheld what wealth had wrought.
"Lover on lover, east into west, cheap at the price," he thought.
  "Lover on lover, east into west, cheap at the price," he thought.

The folk of the Eastland, laughing, by promise of wealth made bold,
Widened the hole and widened the hole to gather the Westland gold.
  Widened the hole and widened the hole to gather the Westland gold.

The king of the Westland's daughter, the son of the Eastland queen,
Loved each one the other because of the wall between.
  Loved each one the other because of the wall between.

The wall was the highest, the darkest, raised by the hands of men.
Coral, sharp carbon to hold soldiers out, flint to hold soft lovers in.
  Coral, sharp carbon to hold soldiers out, flint to hold soft lovers in.

There between Westland and Eastland, ruin that once was wall.
There lie the prince and the princess: rubble beneath the fall.
  There lie the prince and the princess: rubble beneath the fall.

THE EMPEROR'S VACATION

When the Emperor was obliged to vacation, he convened his ministers and announced his intention.

> "Were I to leave during a time of crisis, it would be thought I had fled. Were I to leave during a time of tranquility, it would be thought I had retired. Therefore, I have selected a time when the affairs of state are agitated, but not disastrously so. Barring, of course, an unexpected situation.
>
> "One by one in private I have confided to all of you my destination. To each I have mentioned a different place, and in one case only perhaps I have spoken the truth. Thus, while you are progressing in your attempts to find me, the unexpected situation will develop to the point where truly I am needed or truly needed no longer.
>
> "The date of my return, of course, remains a mystery. In my absence, how else can it be ensured that you will continue to work?"

THE EMPEROR'S RETURN

When the Emperor returned from his foreign visit and revealed its location, difficulties began.

"Why," asked his Minister of State, "did you bother to go? Everyone knows that a shared polity such as theirs can contribute nothing to ours."

"And," said his Minister of Justice, "their barbaric reciprocity can scarcely be of interest to us."

"And," said his Minister of Culture, "their dances are nothing but vulgar displays of athletic prowess, and their literature is slogans. What can we obtain from such a people?"

The Emperor considered these comments in silence. Then he withdrew and made preparations.

When the time came, the Emperor convened his ministers and addressed them. "It has been said that I should not have gone abroad, that I have nothing of value to receive from a land that has the misfortune to lie outside the empire. I would like to correct this misapprehension."

The Emperor caused three foreign dignitaries to be wheeled forward in the iron cages they now inhabited. "May I present," said the Emperor, "the empire's new ministers of State, Justice, and Culture."

THE EMPEROR'S PRISON

When the Emperor visited his imperial prison, he caused a platform to be built in the centre of the courtyard and the prisoners to be assembled around it. Then the Emperor mounted the platform, and he spoke. "In the days of our fathers, prisoners taken in combat were ransomed or executed. I will not ransom you because that would reinforce foreign armies. I have no wish to execute you because that is an act abhorrent to nature. Nor do I intend to keep you in my prison. Not only is my treasury afflicted by maintaining you there, the empire is impoverished by the lack of your labour. Henceforth, each among you will pursue the occupation he desires and the manner of life to which the fruits of his labour entitle him. Henceforth, you will all be free."

Then the Emperor directed his Minister of Labour to pass among the prisoners and to record the occupation desired by each.

In the darkest corner of the courtyard one prisoner stood alone. When the Minister of Labour reached this prisoner, he listened for a moment, stopped dead in his tracks, and stared at the man. Then he hurried back to the platform. "That man," he said to the Emperor, "that man must be executed."

"I have observed," said the Emperor, smiling at the assembled prisoners, "that government officials often solve a problem in such a way as to create a new one. Does the man refuse to work?"

"No, sire," replied the minister.

"What occupation does he desire?" asked the Emperor.

"None that is available," replied the minister.

"I have observed," said the Emperor to the assembled prisoners who smiled back, "that government officials are not always the most inventive of my subjects. What was the man's occupation in his native land?"

"In his native land," trembled the minister, "he was emperor."

For many moments the Emperor stared at the prisoner who stared at him.

Then the Emperor sighed and said, "Execute him." And it was done.

A NOBLEWOMAN

A noblewoman approached the Emperor and presented this problem: "My husband will not permit our intolerable son to enter our house again, not even to attend the banquet in honour of our wedding anniversary."

To which the Emperor replied, "You must have two banquets, and make certain that these arrangements are announced at both. All will believe your son was invited to the other. None will know your disgrace."

A COMMON GIRL

"My mother," said a common girl, "is sick from spirits. As long as I can remember, there have been times when she is sick from spirits. Then I assume the duties of the home as well as the care of my father who becomes more than useless when ashamed. Now, however, I am concerned with my own life, and I find it difficult to fulfill my filial responsibility."

To which the Emperor replied, "Your mother must leave home. Already she has stayed too long. You must release her, however unwilling you are to do so."

A FARM WOMAN

A farm woman said, "Five of my girls have borne children to their brothers of whom there are eleven, including the eldest whose seed I carry now. My husband no longer sires, not even upon his granddaughters. Since losing interest, he has become concerned, especially after the priest of our village spoke against such practices and named them vile."

"In your house there are how many beds?" asked the Emperor.

"Two," replied the woman. "When there is snow in the room, only one is used."

"The problem," said the Emperor, "is insulation."

"Thank you for the riddle," said the woman, and in view of her condition the Emperor forgave her.

A BEGGAR'S CHILD

On the curbstone of her deathbed a beggar woman advised her daughter. "There was a time of queens, a simpler time there is no doubt of it. If one was starving, one knew who to ask for bread. If no bread was forthcoming, one knew who to blame. Always one turned to the queen.

"Kings are a different matter. One can hardly ask a king for bread. Kings do not understand bread as queens do. Even when they do not give it, even when they have none to give, queens respect the lack of bread and grieve for those who do not have it. Kings believe the lack of bread to be the fault of those who lack it.

"Kings have never known the pleasure of sinking fingers into the flour, into the paste, into the dough rising like flesh. Kings have never breathed the sweetness of the oven. Perhaps queens have never made bread either, but they at least can imagine the making. Unless one knows the making of bread, one can never read the eyes of those who have none."

When her mother was dead, the beggar's child presented bread to the Emperor. "Because," said the child, "you are hungrier than I."

THE PARABLE OF THE MARKET

The Emperor was so full of compassion for the poor that he went into his tower that overlooked the marketplace, and he sat in the tower and watched the poor who sold fish and salt and vegetables, scarcely enough to live upon. If he saw that the poor did not sell their wares because of storms or because the wares were not good, then the Emperor would weep and bid his courtiers go down among the poor and buy their wares and dispose of them in the river. When all the wares were gone, only then could the Emperor enjoy his meal there in his tower high above the marketplace.

After a time the Emperor noticed that commerce in the marketplace was failing. Even when there was no storm, even when the fish were fresh and the salt was pure and the vegetables were plump and fine, even then the buyers did not come. And every day, surely it was every day, the courtiers had to be sent down among the stalls so that the wares might disappear so that the Emperor might cease his weeping and take his meal. Soon there were no buyers at all, none but the courtiers.

One day the Emperor did not go into his tower. He sent his courtiers off among the stalls, but he went to the side of the river and he concealed himself among the rushes. There he waited.

After a time people began to gather on the bank of the river, women and children mainly, although there were a few old folk as well among them. After a time it seemed the whole district was there and indeed it was, all those except the poor who sold in the marketplace and the courtiers who purchased.

After a time, laden with the produce they had bought at the market, the courtiers began to arrive at the side of the river. Instead of casting their goods into the river as they had been instructed, the courtiers sat upon the bank and waited. The people waited too. So, in the rushes, did the Emperor.

After a time others began to arrive. These were, the Emperor noted, all those who kept stalls in the marketplace, all the poor whose plight so burdened the Emperor and made him weep. And, wonder to behold, there on the bank of the river a market began! Quickly, without much haggling, the poor bought back their merchandise and paid the courtiers — the Emperor could hardly believe his eyes — and paid the courtiers the very gold the Emperor had provided to the courtiers that morning! Then with great good spirits and much laughter all the wares were distributed among all who were there, folk and courtiers alike! Then the courtiers took the gold they had received, all the Emperor's good gold, and they disposed of it in the river!

After the market by the river had dissolved, after the people with their goods had gone home and the courtiers with their goods had gone toward the palace, the Emperor sat alone among the rushes. He sat a long while alone among the rushes and his countenance changed colour many times. Then the Emperor sighed a great sigh, so great a sigh that all the rushes quivered. Then the Emperor stood, brushed the grasses from his cloak, and returned to his palace.

LU WEI

Lu Wei was gifted with an immense penis, which engine he operated by voluntary muscular control. In his youth as a sea-pirate he employed no other weapon, his booty being mostly the result of ransomed maidenheads and self-rental to the crew. Having thus laid the foundations of his fortune, Lu Wei returned to his family estate, boiled his parents alive, and toasted his inheritance with a cup of the soup. Similar uncorroborated rumours that he was the Emperor's secret father as well as the lover of the Emperor's former wife or of the Emperor himself or was the Emperor's bastard son or hers probably also are without foundation, though so pervasive as not to be ignored.

What is beyond dispute is that Lu Wei was a prodigious merchant. He bought cheap and sold dear. By this rare stratagem he accumulated thousands. With these he bought additional commodities that, however much he paid for them, he sold again for more. To his thousands he added thousands. With these he bought houses and land. Chattel, cattle, tenants he disposed of at auction. Subdividing everything else, he sold twice what he had bought once. To his thousands he added millions. With these he bought castles and villages and, eventually, an entire alien kingdom. This he presented to the empire shortly before his unsolicited appointment as Imperial Minister of Finance.

Being the Emperor's principal advisor, Li Ssu did not oppose the appointment of Lu Wei. At the ceremony of inauguration he merely observed, "I have heard it said, when a sea-pirate becomes a land-pirate, he neglects to wash his sword. I have also heard it said, when pirates become policemen, prisons fill with victims. Perhaps such things are to be expected as an empire dies?"

Reportedly, the dimensions of Lu Wei's penis kept pace with his ascending status and, by the time he obtained his ministerial post, Lu Wei behind a desk required the secretarial support of his wife, a veiled virago of uncertain vintage who lingered at the side of his swivel throne and manipulated a portion of his presence into that upright posture essential for command. Otherwise, the couple spent many happy hours at the window of Lu Wei's ministry, observing the decorative obelisk in the courtyard and its ceremonial ejaculation of coins.

Between times Lu Wei presided over an economic polity based upon the dextrous practice of tactical distraction. It was implemented thus.

When imprecise ethnographic reverberations were felt in certain unimportant backward provinces of the empire upon the collapse of a few picturesque cottage industries such as schooling, housing, and medical treatment, that distant rumble of events was obscured by the commencement of a program of public works to widen the Ministry of Finance with the addition of several dozen vaults.

When the news arrived of empire-wide crop failures due to the consumption by starving crofters of seed potatoes and unripe grain, the Ministry of Finance issued a proclamation to the effect that bailiffs, pawnbrokers, funeral directors, prison guards, fashion designers, and representatives of other essential services thenceforth would be personally invited to watch the Minister of Finance take his lunch.

When a subterranean palpitating flutter became a terrestrial communal throb, an empire-wide skyward undulation, a universal seismic reeling stagger and a roar into the midst of which before the gates of the imperial palace a horde of the impoverished linked hands and precipitated themselves onto a protest pyre fuelled by defaced pension vouchers and warrants of arrest for debt, Lu Wei convened an emergency session of the Imperial Cabinet of Ministers to debate his scheme to enhance profitability by curtailing the arts.

Being human, Li Ssu did not oppose the proposal. Instead, he calmed himself and said, "In matters of small craft Lu Wei is a mighty seaman. However much he pays to obtain the office of a particular official, he always gives it away for more. Then, when his treasury of political indebtedness is sufficiently swollen, he expends a little to purchase damaging secrets. Recalcitrant fellow ministers he disposes of by scandal. Others he persuades to support him, as today, by their silence in debate. What is not clear is why he does it. If the empire truly is dying, what will be the usefulness to Lu Wei of such an eminence? Would it not be better for him to gather foodstuffs and blankets, and build a raft?"

By way of answer, the wife of Lu Wei, still clutching a portion of the ministerial presence, burst out from behind her husband's desk and expired at his feet in a paroxysm of demonstrable loyalty.

The Cabinet of Ministers offered to adjourn.

The Emperor refused, poured everyone a cup of tea, and waited.

Seated by an open window and moved beyond prudence by the invasive odour of public cremations, Li Ssu took a shallow breath and spoke. "Sire, Lu Wei has been employing that monetary practice known to all the world but you as 'fluctuating the empire.' At that level of defilement, buying cheap and selling dear are too subtle to mention. Now you and I observe that, beginning with his late wife, Lu Wei is in the process of decreasing the number of his associates by means of acolytic over-excitement. Presently the Ministry of Finance will contain none but he. Is it your intention, sire, that Lu Wei eventually rid us of himself through loneliness? If so, I have heard it said, once the destination is perceived, there is always a shorter way."

The Emperor sipped his tea and signalled Lu Wei to resume delivering his ministerial advice which the fatal performance of Madam Lu had interrupted.

Extricating himself from the stiffening hand of his late consort and votary, Lu Wei coughed, rearranged his notes, and continued. "The common people," the minister said, "do not care about beauty. The common people care only about usefulness. As long as they have soup for their mouths, they do not care whether an artist designed their soup bowls. Your majesty does wrong to maintain artists in your empire. They waste your treasury in idle ventures. They impose beauty upon those who will never see more than the soup before them. Expel the artists, sire, or execute them!"

When Lu Wei had finished speaking, the Emperor beckoned him closer. When Lu Wei was near enough, the Emperor spoke.

"In my left hand I hold a bow. It is made of laminated rose-wood. An artist laboured a year at little pay to shape it and it is most beautiful. In my right hand I hold an arrow. Its head is beaten gold, its shaft is ivory, its tufts are peacock feathers rare and exquisite. Truly it is a beautiful arrow. When I lay the arrow to the bow, I may draw the bowstring smoothly and with power for it is spun of the sinews of the unicorn."

So saying, the Emperor released the arrow.

"Thus we may see," said the Emperor turning the corpse of his Minister of Finance with his toe, "how beauty may also be useful."

VOICES FROM A VILLAGE

What is most peculiar is that we never have been told the Emperor's name. Are we meant to call him by the name of his era? Or of his policy? Or of his fate? Even those names will be known only in retrospect, and collecting fragments of the past to obtain a hindsight of one who plummeted through it is hardly our concern. It is difficult enough to dig out last year's frozen dung for this year's fuel. Besides, what are we to call him now? His titles are so copious as to require a wax seal longer than any single edict it is fixed upon. Where in all that is his name? The absence of the Emperor's name seems to us entirely inexplicable. Were anyone to try to remove our names or even to overlook them, we would resist to the death and beyond. What else in this nameless village have we to protect?

◆

In our village there is one who fights for prize. We attend his every combat, no matter how little he pays us to come. Should he be beaten into insolvency, we would still wish to watch him fight and even, perhaps, pay him to do it. Thus far, that has not been necessary. He remains unthrottled, and each fight he wins earns him enough to pay us to cheer him on to attempt the next. Fighting for prize, after all, is a matter of pride.

◆

In our village the saying is: stand still or how will fortune find you? Other villages have other sayings but the meaning is the same. Like all sayings, this one is necessary because what it implies never happens. Everyone stands still. Fortune finds no one. Which probably suggests that misfortune is due to our failure to observe some other saying. He who truly is at rest has no need to put up his feet, for instance. Perhaps we are not truly at rest? Perhaps our stillness is lethargy, our serenity indifference? Perhaps we are like the bird in the saying? Which saying? Any saying with a bird in it. Thus, saying leads on to saying and that, one might say, is the way of it.

For another thing, we are forever enumerating. The Three Cardinal Vices, the Seventeen Mandatory Suppressions, the Twenty-Seven Feasts, the Hundred-and-One Fasts, the Infinite Chain of the Future, the One Link of the Emperor ... it seems that priests and lawgivers must first know how to count. Which is, of course, another saying.

I, myself, am free of the servitude to sayings and enumeration. My primary principle is: never mind. It is precisely that profound sense of resistance to tuition and mistrust of discipline and indifference to advancement and contempt for achievement with which I seek to inculcate my students. In my classroom, progress is punished as a lapse in tranquility. As a result, my students regard me as no schoolmaster at all, but as one of their own number, and by no means the least. In a word, ever thence ever thither.

◆

Long hair alters the appearance. Not of the face. Beards do that, but in such a way that it is clear to any beholder that the possessor of a beard deliberately has sought to disguise his face and is not to be trusted. Beards, therefore, are not dangerous.

Long hair is another matter. The possessor of long hair does not sit or stand or walk as he used to, nor in the same manner from moment to moment. His deportment follows the rhythm of his hair. Shadow, light, the dampness of the air, the wind that blows from one direction only but is deflected into every direction ... these are the masters of long hair, and they are forever changing.

When growth is as high as the fence posts, a farmer can only say that all the fields are grain and his is somewhere among them. Therefore, long hair disguises utterly and is most dangerous. In our village it is not permitted.

❦

Each dynasty begins with a ruler of superlative wisdom and ends with one of unspeakable stupidity. Why? Because the store of virtue contained in the sage ancestor is depleted by his heirs. How, then, is the Emperor to free us from the wheel of degenerating rule? By forbidding dynasties beginning with his own? By governing inanely so as to give us hope? By monitoring the intelligence of his governance so as to enable the moment before its moment of maximum enlightenment to bring about his death? It is for the Emperor to decide. At this distance from the capital city, we have no way of measuring destiny. Therefore, brethren, let us pray that he is the first and the last of his line.

❦

When papers were discovered that revealed the secret dealings of former rulers, the rumoured intervention of the Emperor attracted attention to them until at last the lowliest peasant in the remotest of villages knew what they contained. "Such evils," he said, "are almost beyond belief!"

"But," said his wife, shifting one child to her breast and stirring the gruel that would feed the other eleven, "do you really believe any of it?"

"Were it not true," said her husband, "why would the Emperor have tried to suppress it?"

"But," said his wife, replacing the wad of straw that was allowing rain to seep through the ceiling onto the fire, "how could such things have been?"

"Life in those days," said her husband, "was hard."

"But," said his wife, adding rainwater to the gruel so that there might be enough to feed her husband as well, "how have things changed?"

"Thank the gods," said her husband, "our emperor is not guilty of the evils practised by the ancient regimes."

"But," said his wife, breaking cow dung to feed the fire, "I still find life a little hard."

"Now we know for certain," said her husband, "that the Emperor is not responsible for the evils of our times."

"But," said his wife, removing her shawl and hanging it over the empty doorway so that the wind would not topple the cradle, "how do we know he is not as evil as they?"

"Woman," said her husband, "you know nothing of politics."

"No," said his wife, and she went out to gather fresh cow dung.

Sipping his gruel, the husband walked over to the cradle and gazed at the face of his sleeping infant. "Thank the gods," he said, "that the Emperor has permitted us to discuss the evils of the past. What else in this blessed age should we do for entertainment?"

◆

When he first appeared among us, we did not suspect him. His shabbiness, his evident ill health, his entire disguise was perfect. The most surprising thing about him was that we did not suspect him. He sat among us at meals and seemed as little satisfied. Like us, he watched his plate until it was removed. Like us, he sighed, and rose without complaint, and stood among us staring into the empty village street. Like us, he shuffled out to meet the night. It was only when he did not appear again that we took note. As always, it was difficult to sustain interest.

The entertainment, then, came as a complete surprise. At first it seemed nothing more than luck, the accuracy with which our gestures had been recorded. Our very turn of phrase, our intonation, our grimace, our stare ... it was particularly uncanny how he reproduced our stare.

Then we became aware of a certain distortion in his rendering. We, for example, never watched our plates until they were removed or, if we did, never with such anguish. That was exaggerated, burlesqued. But, then, perhaps that was his intention? The empty village street contained no answers. Perhaps our concentration upon it was absurd, even comic? So it could seem to others.

It must have seemed so to others, for the applause he received in neighbouring villages was boisterous, and his compassion for our village was much praised. Of course we too applauded his entertainment. At least we did not protest. In any case, we did not discuss it. At meals we never spoke. After meals there was only the empty street. When could we have discussed it? In any case, we probably had forgotten.

THE EMPEROR RIDES TO WAR

"A man proceeds from being alone to thinking he is not alone, but he is always alone. A man begins alone and, whatever he thinks, he remains alone though sometimes he is alone with others. To be alone is to be a man and can be mastered. To think one is not alone, that is dangerous."

So saying, the Emperor spurred his horse and rode on.

Those he left behind watched his figure recede, the iridescence of his cloak, black in the night, red in the day, rendering him invisible at little distance.

"Who was that?" said one.

"Where?" said another.

"When?" said another, called to her child, and went in to dinner.

At the door the child turned and whispered into the twilight, "Good night, father."

Miles down the road the Emperor whispered, "Child."

◆

Confused in a wood, the Emperor approached an encampment of militia and said, "I seek the war."

"Have you lost it?" said a soldier.

"That," grinned another, "is our job."

An officer glanced up, leapt to his feet, and shouted at his men to rise, but the Emperor already had dismounted and settled himself beside the fire. To these rancid veterans the Emperor told this tale.

"She dwelt beyond the Trench. We met, she loved, we parted. I weary with the weight of this and wish it to be gone. She was blooded on a beach by one who stroked her later so that she spoke no word about it until she told me of the girl she had been. She feared I would speak of it. I promised I would not. She straddled me and revolved entirely upon me until we could not breathe. She fed me brandied cherries with no stone. We spoke no tongue together but a polyglot of several, conned at school for other purpose, never used. Has it come to your attention how little can be said? My empire broke her land. There had been, she thought, a war. Perhaps I had forgotten it? Perhaps I had not been informed? She took me to the village of her childhood. At the foot of a wood in an undergrowth of bindweed, I stumbled on stone fragments. When we knelt, they were gravestones. 'Broken by us in the war,' she told me. 'They could not have our dead.' She thought I would return. I gave her cause to think it. Her eyes burned on my back like resin. A futile anecdote."

"Why, then," said a soldier, "tell it?"

"To those whose job it is to die for me," said the Emperor. "I have nothing else it pains me to give."

After a night of silence the Emperor rode on.

◆

In a clearing the Emperor came upon a billet of volunteers, certain farm lads seeking peril. One of them had walked a hundred leagues to find a recruiting officer who would ignore his narrow chest. Another had collected pebbles along the way to show his father that all lands were the same. Another boasted of the farms he would burn in combat, another of the narrow-chested alien farm lads he would detonate. They recognized no emperor. They knew the war was not a farm.

To these laughing boys the Emperor told the tale of the night the princess betrayed him with another, and then returned to his bed to betray the other with him. "So that," the Emperor said, "my shame might equal yours."

Then the Emperor rode on.

◆

As they marched toward the battle, conscripts told each other of the enemy they would meet. Moving among them unrecognized, the Emperor overheard their tales.

"They are children," one said, "deaf to shouts, resistant to discipline, beyond humiliation. They have no faces, only mouths. Their weapons are razor teeth and venomous projectile vomit. Pursued, they sink into the soil. Ignored, they rise and taunt you. They breed by fragmentation. Cut down one, a dozen surround you. Explode a squadron, you are engulfed, devoured."

"They are old folk," another conscript said. "Chief among them are the dead. Every night, all night, even when there is no war, they fight. The graves yawn and the bones creep out and link together with a clank, the skull of a scholar on the neck of a princess on the spine of a soldier on the hip of a tart on a priest's crooked leg with a milkmaid's knee and a beggar's club foot. The dead fight the dead with the will of the dead and the swords of the dead for the cause of the dead, and the bones tumble down double-dead in the mud. Rib cages shiver, fingers snap, jaws crush to powder, teeth rattle out. 'Emperor! Empire!' chatters a skull, and the dust rolls down the bones like blood."

"They are women," another conscript said, "two-edged swords where their sex should be. He who is taken prisoner is required to kiss their queen. Through the long night of her crisis, she grasps him with metallic arms and presses him to her. Spikes sink into his face and body and, gradually, through them. Towards morning her arms relax, and he drops between

her legs into a deep well where he is received upon horizontal
blades and is flushed away."

"They are barbarians," another conscript said, "shaggy, nameless. What renders them invincible is that they have no desire for
good things. Bring them velvet costumes, they tear them to shreds
among the thickets and declare them not as useful as hides. Give
them delicacies, they allow them to rot, then find them inferior
to fermented mare's milk. If only they would acquire our taste for
good things, they quickly would become our slaves and give up
the war. But they refuse to learn, and I fear the worst."

The Emperor rode on trembling. He had not encountered the
enemy before.

◆

An innkeeper stood by the roadside and spoke to the horsemen
riding past.

"We have all grown old in the service of the Emperor, none older
than myself. Yet it is a sweet service. None sweeter than my own,
for it commands me to stand by this roadside and beckon such
as you into an accommodation made humble by the whim of
fortune and noble by the spirit of the pilgrims it has sheltered.
We are all pilgrims, are we not, upon the one road to our several
graves? Of which mine is the nearest, though who is to say his lies
not beneath his next footfall? No, no, enter! Within is none to
do you ill nor one of any intent at all save I, your host, who bids
you sup, and sleep, and rise again, and resume your quest with
all the godspeed and good health the forbearance of our imperial master empowers me to afford you. So, so, and your bearers
may forage my garden for nuts. Tell me, sire, by your array I judge
you the first among them, is there to be a war? I construe your
silence! Excuse me, sire, I must tell my wife! And our hostel upon
the highway to it! Sire, you are welcome! Only our partner the
Emperor would be more welcome than you!"

Seeing that he had been recognized, the Emperor rode on.

◆

In the entourage of the Emperor there rode enthusiasts. They embraced causes. They also embraced each other. Such a one was Madam Fu. Hers was the cause of peace and it embraced every other cause, even that of war. Madam Fu reasoned thus. "When war is waged for the cause of peace, war is better than peace for, without it, how should peace be won?" Such reasoning was intended to please the Emperor, for it enabled him to wage peace or war without losing the support of Madam Fu.

In recognition of her service, the Emperor accorded her privileges. Always these took the form of forays abroad. When Madam Fu forayed, her enterprise in the cause of peace was tireless. Wherever she went, Madam Fu created the impression that, whether or not the empire was at war, the Emperor's desire for peace was proved by the fact that she had been dispatched.

Here is the record of a speech by Madam Fu on the occasion of one of her departures: "The armies of peace are on the march! I am in the vanguard! Into the bowels of the partisans of rancour the dagger of peace shall twist! From the mouths of the enemies of peace shall fester forth —"

It was at this point that the enthusiasm of Madam Fu was interrupted by her assassination.

And the Emperor rode on.

◆

A general said, "It is correct to speak of a war to end all wars. It is correct to speak of a war to end all civilization. It is correct to speak of a war to end all life. While one is speaking of such wars, one can wage others."

Another general said, "When a captain of soldiers refuses to commit an atrocity, execute him. That man thinks war is a matter of numbers, and too many numbers is an atrocity. Such a man is an accountant, not a captain of soldiers."

Another general said, "When a general speaks of a war as his war, replace him. It is only a matter of time before he wages war against one's other generals."

Another general said, "In times of peace, disloyalty is difficult to locate. For the sake of maintaining loyalty, one should never confess to being at peace."

Another general said, "All wars are fought for the public good. This is easy to demonstrate when one has obtained a victory. It is more difficult but not impossible to demonstrate when one has suffered a defeat. The only war one cannot prove to have been for the public good is a war that will not end. In such a case one must use ingenuity. By replacing one's army with soldiers from the state invaded, one can demonstrate that, although one continues to own the war, there is in fact no war under way."

Another general said, "On campaigns one must bring along women. What enemy, when it beholds bright hairdos among a phalanx of hobnailed shields, can fail to understand that one intends not only to conquer but to civilize?"

Another general said, "Defeat rigidifies the will. Likewise pain and grievance, punishment and deprivation, capitulation, humiliation, servitude, and shame. How, then, is it possible to lose a war?"

To which the Emperor replied, "And what need is there to have one?" And rode on.

◆

Of the advisors who rode with the Emperor, only Li Ssu remembered the Tale of the Great Defeat. All the rest had succeeded in banishing it even from their most idle banter. Now that the Emperor ignored every indication of the new disaster that awaited him and still rode on to meet the war, Li Ssu dared to remind him of it.

"I have advised you, sire, the whole of my thinking life, yet never have you permitted me to rid you of my presence. It must be that you require my contemptible chatter, if only for the pleasure it affords you to ignore it. It cannot be that you have wondered why, as a young man, I came so far unbidden and have stayed so long unheard. Yet now that I am grown useless with years, it occurs to me to tell you the reason I sought your service in the beginning. Of all the information you possess surely this will be the most trivial.

"I had heard, sire, the Tale of the Great Defeat. I was no witness. You already were Emperor, and therefore had suffered it. But the hearing of it was sufficient. My absence during the Great Defeat was my fault, and the shame haunts my sons. I came to the empire and entered your service in order to help to write the Tale of the Great Victory. Then, I thought, then I shall die most grateful, and my sons will praise my bones!

"Now, sire, I perceive I fail again. You are about to suffer the Eternal Defeat, and I shall have watched you ride out to meet it. My sons, sire! Who among them ever will forgive me? Ignore these tears. Consider them oratory.

"The matter is this. The war you approach is one you might not lose. One unlost war leads to another. The empire, sire, is in danger of failing to die! You, sire, are in peril of becoming a god! At the very least, a dynast! In comparison to that, what is the great defeat of having become an emperor?"

Nevertheless the Emperor rode on.

◆

Looking down on battle from a great height, a chaplain folded his hands, sighed, and sermonized thus. "In a war fought between tribes of giants who are deaf and mute, it is not important that they are giants. Were they pygmies, it is their deafness and muteness that would be remarkable. Not to them, of course. Isolated by terrain and tradition, inbreeding soon would have cancelled out individuals with hearing and speech and, after a few generations, even the memory of those faculties. Nor would anyone recall when the enmity between the tribes had arisen, nor why. It would be assumed that enmity always had existed and, without speech being possible, the means of expressing this instinct would be by war which, likewise, must always have existed. And so there would be war, gigantic, silent."

"Thank you for the curse," said the Emperor, and rode on.

"Above the pennants, through the smoke, just there do you see, not there, that is bone, beyond the drums, across that gap of blasted stumps, that carcass there, and there the mud, well, just between those shreds of mules, above the pennants, above the flames, I could have sworn, just there, right there, yet there again, look now, look there, that flash of more than gold, is that not he?"

The Emperor peered in the direction indicated, but he could not see the emperor the soldier saw.

When the soldier had finished dying, the Emperor shot his own horse and walked home.

When asked why he had not stopped the war, the Emperor replied, "I helped one soldier to die. So you see, I arrived too late."

MOURNING THE REVOLUTION

When our revolution was dead, the Emperor permitted us to mourn. Indeed, he encouraged us to do it. "Mourning," the Emperor said, "is important to a people, for it renders them less inclined to reprisals against those who are the cause of their grief."

And so we mourn. Especially we mourn the death of our revolutionary leader. Had he not, after all, led us in the path of our desires, if only for a short while and, as it now appears, only by permission of the Emperor who had encouraged our revolution by delaying his suppression of it? Had our leader not shown himself to be uncompromising? When the Emperor permitted him to kill himself, did he not accept the opportunity instead of requiring extermination?

And so we mourn. We mourn the loss of our dreams and, of course, the loss of our dreamers to whom the Emperor accorded martyrdom. We mourn the defeat of our reforms, though the Emperor has said he will pass on this information to his succeeding generations who will, no doubt, in time respond. We mourn the end of our new society that, as it now appears, was merely a transition to the Emperor's second reign.

And so we mourn. Of course, we do not mourn alone. We are joined in our mourning by all the enlightened citizens of the world outside the empire who, as long as they could admire our revolution, had no need to indulge in one of their own and, now that they have seen our revolution fail, can turn their attention to important matters.

And so we mourn. The Emperor will inform us when we have mourned enough.

THE TRIUMPH

There came a time when the last of the enemies of the empire was vanquished. "Now," the Emperor said, "there can be peace!" No one apart from Li Ssu appreciated the joke.

THE FESTIVAL OF THE FALL

The Emperor, it must be said, was magnanimous in victory. The fact that the laurels were withered beyond wearing, the fruits inedible, the roots already propagating malevolent tubers too remote to be culled, too abundant to be extirpated, seemed not to concern him, or concerned him only as any other matter of futile husbandry. The empire was his to cultivate. For the time, he decided, it would be become a garden of repose or, at the least, of respite.

To a people brought up on warfare and the subtle venting of Lady Shang's legalism and the commercial proliferation of Fei-tzu's terminology, the Emperor had little to recommend beyond "rest and recreation," something no one as yet had been required to enjoy.

The instruction bewildered everyone. Failure to satisfy their Emperor or to understand his command caused a miasma of despair to settle over the empire. The mood accorded with the season that was bleak with stubble and smelt of leaf mould.

"It is time," Li Ssu advised, "to institute a festival of thanks-giving. At the very least it will remind the people of how to laugh."

Rural festivals featuring legends of birth and evergreen religiosity, Li Ssu had noticed, flourished at a time of the year when winter weather made welcome any thought of incarnation. Spring, on the other hand, already contained sentimental folklore associated with anthropomorphic animals performing lurid rites of disguised sexuality. Summer required no festival, being naturally preoccupied with the languorous cultivation of the implantations of spring.

The portion of the agronomic calendar that was the most difficult to reconcile with a compatible mythology, Li Ssu reasoned, was the semi-season currently under way. Situated between mid-summer and mid-winter, diametrically opposed to spring and lacking its lubricity, it was as yet unnamed, and without a body of legend and unifying ritual.

Li Ssu concluded thus: "A season such as this favours the culling of the elderly, the pruning of the infirm, the uprooting of the fruitless, the incineration of the remnants, and the pickling of the dead. Thus the crops are gathered, the fields are laid fallow, and their produce is preserved. The mood of the day suggests the tenor of its tales, the burden of its balladry, the curve of its choreography, the menu of its banquet. Perhaps, sire, in observation of the annual custom of trees, this season might be named 'the fall'?"

Thus was inaugurated the holy day commemorating the commencement of the Emperor's second reign. It was named the Festival of the Fall. Planning for it began immediately.

Every hamlet in every district of every province of every canton of every region of the interminableness of the empire would be instructed to cleanse itself and its vicinity of every trace of recent warfare. Damaged property would be restored or razed, plundered fields ploughed up or ploughed under. Cattle infected with battle-madness would be culled. Domestic pets grown accustomed to foraging would be exterminated.

Every household would be persuaded to resign its dead. The corpses and their parts would be amassed and entombed, the grave mounds decorated with aromatic shrubbery and designated as public parks. The fallen foliage and that about to fall would be made to bear a distracting tint.

The focal event would be an empire-wide harvest feast of thanksgiving. Wildlife having been slaughtered, eviscerated, and hung according to the delights of the chase and the protocols of butchery, the meat would be prepared in accord with timeless recipes, to be consumed with theatrical gusto. Fermented fruit would be bled of its liquor which, fortified with hallucinogenic fungi and addictive pharmaceuticals, would be served in non-corrosive drinking vessels. The patron saint and the presiding genius would be the jovial Peng, the wastrel friend who had died somewhere of overeating yet inhabited the Emperor's heart as few others did.

The performance of folk music, folk dance, and folk pageant, the execution of painting and the recitation of rhymes would aid digestion and complement post-prandial slumber. A good time would be had by all to be followed by a time of good for all.

Events did not transpire as planned.

Immediately following any war, the restitution of a land, of its infrastructure and its chattel, is premised upon the will of the people to carry it out, something that itself requires the sort of psychic energy possessed by those whose recollection of war is merely historic. Such was not the case in the empire where everyone was pretty well convinced that any reconstruction merely would be the construction of a new target. This condition of the public temperament was not a matter of embitterment, but of practical observation and accurate short-term memory. The credulity needed for renewal would take several generations of innocence to acquire.

On a material level, the stuff required for a harvest festival was not available. Wild game brought down by surplus military armament was shredded beyond consumption, or it still contained unexploded devices the accidental ingestion of which delivered consequences that could not be mistaken for wind. The meat of domestic fowl that had free-ranged the battlefields and of cattle that had grazed the aflatoxic pasturage was provocatively pre-spiced, but lethal. Vegetables could not be imported from far enough away to exclude the stench of blood-soaked soil, and fruit ripened in gaseous air had altered its shape and lost its colour. Commercial sweets prepared in refitted crematoria tended to be insolubly caramelized. Intoxicating beverages were plentiful, though in the circumstances it was inadvisable to supply them to congregations of more than two.

The only aspect of the proposed feast that was universally agreed upon was the Emperor's suggestion that the symbolic presence of the jovial Peng, his effigy sculpted in jelly, should form the newly traditional centrepiece of each banquet table. Everyone hated the idea. Still available to living memory, it seemed inappropriate to recall Peng at a time of universal penury and alimental privation. The very thought of the capacious spectre of that amiable leech drove many otherwise reasonable individuals to commit acts of self-wounding and pre-emptive emigration. For the Emperor who had intended the cult of Peng to be an iconography of the meta-seasonal virtues of friendship, this popular repulsion marred the patriotism of the occasion.

The Festival of the Fall was remembered but not again attempted.

IX

THE IMPERIAL PHYSICIAN

Scholars who do not study medical books are unfilial. Even scholars have ageing parents.

THE PARABLE OF DESPAIR

There was a time the Emperor was afflicted with despair. He did not know it was despair that afflicted him. He thought it was digestion. Yet how else to account for the fact that, although he no longer had the slightest desire for delightful foods, matters entirely unconnected with eating sickened him?

It was Li Ssu who suggested that the Emperor subscribe to the practice traditional among common folk in despair, and sit beside a river.

"It is not despair," said the Emperor. "The manna is off."

"In that case," said Li Ssu, "let us turn our attention to matters of state."

And the Emperor threw up.

PAINTING ON SCROLLS

It was the Emperor's fascination with the progress of rivers that caused him to invent the practice of painting on scrolls. Previous to his enthusiasm, scrolls had served only the functions inherent to them: the storage of rice paper, the provision of many-layered fly swats, the compression of flowers, the preservation of spools. Subsequent to the Emperor's undisguised delight, painting on scrolls became an obsession throughout the empire. As themes, rivers figured largely, likewise mountains intersected by paths interrupted by ravines populated by an occasional hanging bridge, a recluse hut, an inaccessible temple, a pilgrim, a wayfarer, a hermit, a sage. In scrolls even mountains flowed like rivers.

Never rolled without unrolling, never viewed without reviewing, never present without presenting, foreground rise and remoter crests, receding perspective and broken lines, over-lapping composition and multiple vanishings ... it is, after all, the action of a river that most resembles the use of a scroll. Observ-ing at the range of the distance between his hands, proceeding at the tempo of his wrist's rotation, the viewer of a scroll beholds his own dimensions. Like rivers, scrolls are self-portraits. He who has not the joy of a scroll can always watch a river.

The Emperor first encountered the Imperial Physician while watching a river. Amid the myriads assembled at vantage points along either bank, the Emperor noted, only one carried a scroll. Of inordinate antiquity behind the eyes, with the hard features of a dispenser of small benefice among too many beggars, this sinusoidal person bore a scroll collapsed in the manner of a para-sol, concealing its true employment from all but the Emperor.

Certain he had found his physician and at last could stop attending rivers, the Emperor instructed Li Ssu. The candidate was drawn into a tea house and was entered upon the Three Cri-teria. It was then they noticed that she was blind.

THE FIRST CRITERION
(QUESTIONS AND ANSWERS ABOUT LIVING MATTER)

LI SSU: What is the art of the physician?

PHYSICIAN: The physician treats the body as the dredger-man the river. Perceiving a channel, she clears debris to ease the current.

EMPEROR: If the current be deathward?

PHYSICIAN: The veriest rill of the least tributary does not doubt the sea.

LI SSU: Explanation?

EMPEROR: (*rising to return to the riverbank*) She means life is like a river.

LI SSU: Do you mean life is like a river?

PHYSICIAN: Death is like a river. Life is like a scroll.

EMPEROR: (*who has stopped rising*) The scroll of a river?

PHYSICIAN: A scroll like a river, like a scroll.

EMPEROR: (*sitting*) Next question.

LI SSU: What is the craft of a physician?

PHYSICIAN: The analogizing of the parts.

LI SSU: Explanation?

PHYSICIAN: The bodily parts are analogous to the imperial rivers, the pulmonic tract to the Yangtze, the crasso-intestinal to the Yellow, the fellic to the Wei, and so on. Acupoints are named according to the imperial reservoirs, pulses to the canals, viscera to the marshes, orifices to the paddies —

LI SSU: Yes, yes, and what is the purpose of the analogizing?

PHYSICIAN: Contemplation.

LI SSU: Of what?

PHYSICIAN: Pebbles.

EMPEROR: The physician contemplates pebbles?

PHYSICIAN: It does no good to contemplate mountains. The lowliest pebble contains as mysterious striations, as profound declivities, as evocative concavities, as surprising dissymmetries, as unknowable impactments as the most sacred of mountains. Yet the pebble permits what the mountain cannot: access to its nature. Contemplate the mountain in a pebble, and you begin to understand the living bone of which a man is made.

LI SSU: Contemplation to what end?

PHYSICIAN: Tonification.

LI SSU: Explanation?

PHYSICIAN: When the five viscera are assessed, the seven orifices revealed, the nine pulses measured, the eleven tracts charted, the ninety-three acupoints encircled, needles are implanted and moxa is burned, sedation is instilled and tonification is achieved.

LI SSU: And disease is cured?

PHYSICIAN: Disease is enabled.

EMPEROR: The physician enables disease?

PHYSICIAN: The physician is the origin of disease. Without
    her there is none, with her there is nothing other. The
    nature of the physician is the enabling of disease.
LI SSU: And her practice?
PHYSICIAN: The ministration of venomous medicaments.
LI SSU: The physician, then, causes diseases and
    prescribes poisons?
PHYSICIAN: To the patient, not to the body.
LI SSU: Explanation?
PHYSICIAN: A body is the patient in a moment. A patient
    is the body in a lifetime. Minister to the body, yet the
    patient dies.
EMPEROR: For a physician, you seem uncommonly occupied
    with death.
PHYSICIAN: Uncommon for anyone but a physician. Yet it
    is not death that occupies me, but that especial measureless
    current of which birth is the source and death is the
    narrowing that speeds the flow.
LI SSU: What especial current?
PHYSICIAN: Why, decay! You are not a physician?
EMPEROR: Were he, would I require another?
PHYSICIAN: You do not require the one.
LI SSU: You decline the job?
EMPEROR: She has begun it.

THE SECOND CRITERION
(THE VITAL AXIS)

"The life-breath of a man expires in expelling as vapour from
cooked rice, as mouth-clouds on a frosty morning. The exhalation
of the earth, rising skyward, falling, replenishes the reservoirs,
makes navigable the canals.

"In the mountains at the snow line, sparse in foliage, of boulders plentiful, there amid the scrub-bush, ancient rockfall, elder
moss, there is born the river, born in tumult among ice-crags amid

snowfields combed with blowholes, dropping sheerly down the rock face to the cauldron pool beneath.

"Spindrift columns boil from the gorge. Mist-breath clings to the forest wall. Trackless the forest, measureless, dumb, compact of thicket, curtained with night. Elsewhere the river, the mother of rivers, hurtles through labyrinths, fathomless, bleak, pulsates in caverns enroofed with tree roots, infiltrates earth-pores, seeps to a salt marsh, rises like a river, lies like a lake.

"Here an island temple hollow with crows, a broken bridge no more than a board, a barge half-sunk where a jetty stood. No men yet, only relics of their passing. Water-reeds, bending, paint the wind. Here antique pavilions too remote for tenants, vacant the horizon, seamless the sky. Indolent the river, loitering nearly shoreless, water by its ripples, pleats in unstained silk. Here a boat and boatman pole a boatman's boat. There the fisherfolk wade legless to the shin. Brush and ink in ink-play animate, reflect, water without surface, river without depth.

"'Not one by one alone nor one into one only, but one as a part of another, the other as a part of the one' ... such are the words of my scroll. 'Perfect Waterway, Yellow Ancestor, Uncarved Block, Primal Unity, Vital Axis, Spiral Core' ... that is the name of its river."

THE THIRD CRITERION
(THE GREAT INNOCENCE)

When the physician finished thus recounting her scroll, the Emperor who had been expecting pictures ventured to express his disappointment.

"Pictures?" asked the physician.

"Painted pictures," said the Emperor. "I would have thought the idea self-evident."

"A scroll containing pictures?"

"Sorry I mentioned it," said the Emperor.

"You have, sire, seen such a scroll?"

"Never."

"Then why would you suppose I carried one?"

"Hoped, not supposed."

"Ah," said the physician, unfolding her parasol that was only a parasol, and taking her tea. "The Great Innocence!"

"Beg pardon?" said Li Ssu.

"I would have thought it," she said, "self-evident."

Restraining the sword-arm of Li Ssu, the Emperor said, "Explanation?"

"The Great Innocence," said the physician, "is the name of my garden." And she told them of it.

"In my early life I was an impractical romantic, giving up schooling before my qualifications were complete, selecting companions for the discomfort they caused my elders and the perils they brought to me, abandoning one occupation after another, and, when I could find no way to resign, behaving so as to enable my superiors to dismiss me.

"Although I gloried in my failures, they were not enough to sustain me, and I managed to squander everyone who meant anything at all. My husband, whom I had betrayed beyond others, estranged my children from me and vanished with them. My parents were lost to me by bigoted misunderstanding and died before we could be reconciled. My sister stole my inheritance and erased my name. After too much importuning, even my companions withdrew their charity and no longer recognized me in the street.

"At last I had tasted all the windfall fruits of impractical romance, and I resolved instead to cultivate the flat pastures of utilitarian pragmatism. It was then I composed my scroll and built my garden."

"Was that before or after you went blind?" asked Li Ssu.

"Blind? Ah, you mean the use of my eyes! No, they have always been turned inward. But I was telling you of my garden."

"Proceed," said the Emperor.

"The first chamber has nothing of garden in it. A white alcove, roofless, a blank wall at the far end, the sky containing only sky, the flagstone floor without a pattern, one door in, the same door out. Why visit such a chamber? Why, to lose the world! To prepare your eyes for my garden!

"The second chamber cannot be entered, only glimpsed through lattice windows along a corridor. A rock and a tree bedded in gravel backed by a grey wall, solid in a certain light, invisible in another, the rock venerable, the tree holy, the wall unblemished. Why look at such an in-scape? Every time a window permits, the pattern in the lattice frame has altered, the angle of the viewing has become another, the duration of the beholding is not the same. A rock, a tree, a perfect wall … your passing makes them garden.

"The third chamber —"

"What has all this to do with the matter at hand?" said Li Ssu.

"All what?" said the physician.

"Trees and rocks, walls and alcoves, what have they to do with —"

"Despair?"

"You," said the Emperor, "noticed?"

"Yours," said the physician, "is the only disease that warrants the use of a garden."

"Ah!" said the Emperor.

"Self," said the physician, "evident."

"And," said Li Ssu, "we have had enough of your flippant, disrespectful —"

"Proceed," said the Emperor.

"To enter the third chamber of my garden you must pass through a moon-gate, across and under the curved rim, precisely through the breadth of the centre, stooping without, unfolding within, receiving respectful posture, accepting preternatural grace.

"Despite the manifold beauties of the courtyard you now inhabit, it is a remote pagoda that beckons. Seeking it, you pass into a courtyard as beautiful as the other but farther from the pagoda, and so into another nearer and another farther off … a series of interlocking courtyards wrapped around each other like fretwork pieces in a puzzle. A screen of seasonal grasses altering previous visits, a corridor of foliage various as the wind, a quick-silver brook in dragon convolutions, a balustrade bridge so intricate it fails to depart its shore ... the way to the pagoda is never straight.

"Here are secret alcoves with hidden rewards, light-shy flowering lichen, primordial mural moss. Here are borrowed landscapes with stolen vistas, a window framing the horizon in sunset, a gallery overhanging the garden of another. Dead ends and diversions, perplexities and false perspectives, symmetries broken, rhythms contradicted, repetitions belied, expectations misguided ... wherever you delve, my garden lies deeper! However you rush past, my garden stays ahead! And just before the great pagoda, an astonishing boulder of quartz! And just beyond —"

"Very well," said the Emperor.

"Not so, sire!" said the physician. "I have not yet recited my calligraphy. On every principal stone there is a text, across every vacant lintel a slogan. The pathway to the pagoda itself spells out the immemorial word —"

"I meant," said the Emperor, "I agree."

"To what, sire?" said Li Ssu.

"To seeing her wretched garden."

"No need, sire," said the physician. "I myself see it daily."

Li Ssu offered the Emperor tea. The Emperor accepted, but left his cup untouched. In the distance a songbird began to be heard.

"Wherever I happen to be," added the physician.

Li Ssu poured himself tea, and watched it cool. In the distance, the songbird was answered by another.

The Emperor began to speak, then stopped. So did the songbird. So did the song.

"A scroll that cannot be held," said Li Ssu, "a garden that cannot be inhabited, they exist only behind your eyes?"

"How else," said the physician, "are they mine?"

"Your scroll and your garden," said the Emperor, "they are yours only?"

"How else am I a physician?"

CALLIGRAPHY IN THE
PHYSICIAN'S GARDEN ...

... ABOVE THE ENTRANCE GATE

"A physician who has not been ill cannot accept a patient.
A patient cannot be treated without becoming a physician."

... ALONG A CORRIDOR

"To stunt a tree by constricting its roots, to condense an essence
by boiling its stock, to copulate with a twisting of limbs, is to
prolong vitality by containment."

... UPON A DRAGON BRIDGE

"To transpose the vegetable kingdom into architectural forms,
the animal kingdom into theatrical enactments, the cosmic
infinitude into little gods, to transform heaven and earth, truth
and knowledge, the circle and the square into a mandala, to
reflect the moon in a pond, the seasons in a garden, your beloved
in a mirror, is to know the unknowable by artifice."

... UPON A PRINCIPAL ROCK

"Property is a state of mind, a lie one conspires to tell oneself.
Who in this life has owned a thing except his life? And that, he
reliably may be informed, is on loan. Commodity is real. It is
the possession of it that is not. Currency is real. The ownership
of it is not. My house, my garden, my cat are real. That they are
mine is an illusion."

... UPON A DANGEROUS CURBSTONE

"The gift of second sight at the cost of the first is the power to
review the past without being distracted by the present. It is the
usual defect of the seer."

... **ACROSS THE LINTEL OF THE PAGODA**

"Archaeological excavation uncovers not civilization but its layers. Nothing is discarded, although the earliest fragments, the bottommost, are prized. These are recognized by what lies beneath them. At the point of virgin soil, archaeological excavation ends and geological excavation begins retrospectively. In science little is prized though all is admired. The objects of art are the detritus of science."

... **ABOVE THE EXIT GATE**

"If you cannot imagine a garden, memorize a scroll. Failing both, sit by a river. As a last resort follow politics. Patient, heal thyself."

THE DEPARTURE OF THE IMPERIAL PHYSICIAN

She was released again to the bank of the river to minister to those blind with despair, and to await the day everyone keeps a garden or holds a painted scroll and rivers are unattended and physicians pursue useful trades.

THE PARABLE OF THE PAVILION

The Emperor had a pavilion where he could be quite alone. It was built well away from the principal palace. Nobody was permitted to enter but he himself. Not even his courtiers could set foot in it. Only a songbird shared the single chamber with him, and the Emperor fed it with sugar that he carried in the pocket of his dressing gown.

Because he always appeared refreshed after a day spent in his little pavilion, there was much curiosity in the court regarding the Emperor's occupation during his periodic retreats. Certainly the little pavilion was less comfortable than the palace. It contained no decoration of any kind, and the furniture was nothing other than one hard chair. Nor was the view from the window particularly stimulating, screened as it was by trees and vines.

By a process of elimination, then, interest centred upon the songbird. Despite its pedestrian appearance surely it possessed a miraculous quality? How else to explain the effect it had upon the mood of the Emperor? Plans were launched to examine it.

When the Emperor was touring a distant province, a courtier entered the little pavilion and carried the songbird into the palace. There it was inspected by wizards, historians, counsellors. All arrived at the same conclusion. There was nothing, absolutely nothing, to distinguish it. Indeed, it was an exceedingly mundane bird. There were others more colourful, more tuneful, in every chamber of the palace.

Perhaps, someone suggested, there was a mysterious virtue in the sugar the Emperor fed the bird? A pastry cook was summoned, and the songbird was fed some sugar. It ate readily enough but nothing remarkable transpired except for the fact that, while it was engaged in the act of eating the sugar, the songbird stopped singing. More sugar was provided, and still more, until the ignorant creature so stuffed itself that it suffered a convulsion and died. An autopsy was performed but again nothing remarkable was discovered.

When news reached the palace that the Emperor had completed his tour and was about to return, the court convened in emergency session. Since the absence of his songbird was bound to reveal to the Emperor that his sanctuary had been entered, and since every courtier had been responsible for the invasion, it was decided that the entire court would flee the palace.

When the Emperor returned and discovered the absence of courtiers, he laughed, and spent the remainder of his days moving from chamber to chamber in his magnificent palace feeding his songbirds. Since he never again required his little pavilion, he did not learn that it had been violated.

X

THE AGEING OF THE
FIRST EMPEROR

When a reputable soothsayer offered him eternal life or, at the least, longevity, the First Emperor declined. "How many others," he said, "am I expected to watch die?" Instead, he accepted a degree of ageing with a prophecy of termination.

THE CONGRESS OF THE AGEING

Meanwhile the days were so similar as to be interchangeable. To distinguish between them, the progress of their hours and the passage of their light required notation in memoranda and the maintenance of diaries.

The nights, however, were always individual, populated by visions so vibrant with event and intense with significance that they obliterated everything at the time of their dreaming and superseded each other in the recollection.

The Emperor knew that, with respect to the day and the night, when the one became the other and the other the one, he would have achieved the soothsayer's promise, and the moment he had always contained at last would contain him. So he waited patiently.

It was then there transpired an event that might have been either of the day or of the night, and was probably something of both. It came from nowhere and went to nothing, but it altered the course of his journey if not the destination.

To fill the time remaining the Emperor had undertaken the occupation of the ageing: a search for the roots and the branches of his ancestry. He told himself he was doing it for the benefit of his progeny, so that they might be bequeathed something worth possessing. But it was not so. As emperor, an abundance of his worldly amenities that exceeded the days remaining to expend them had left him with an abiding sense of poverty which there was little time to correct. So what might have seemed an unsolicited gift to the unborn or an idle self-indulgence was, in fact, a quest for adequacy.

Also he was intrigued at the prospect of telling a story in reverse, of beginning at the end to discover the beginning.

History, the Emperor concluded, was precisely that: his story told backwards with some data in it, but only enough to generate something more. The progress was accumulative, the application of it increasingly obscure like peering into the sky at night watching time recede and accuracy diminish until at last anything might be so, even an origin.

His parents, the Emperor found, were of little help. In their lives they had made no reference beyond the banal to their own progenitors. Once, to keep himself from weeping while administering punishment to his son for an offence too minor to recall, his father had grunted between strokes that his own father bore across his back a lifelong scar from the flat of the blade of a bronze jian, and it had made a man of him. Another time, the Emperor's mother, cheering herself during the reheating of the broth that she thinned daily, had muttered the fond reminiscence that her mother could time an egg without a timer and gauge the age of a fowl by the lay of its plumage. Beyond that, nothing. Neither of the Emperor's parents had worn imperial robes nor seen the interior of a palace so, to that extent, they could be trusted. They would have divulged more had they contained it. Of their heritage, however, they were sparsely informed.

Records, of course, did not exist, the Emperor's predecessors having attained insufficient fame to merit them. And so, based upon no documentation, the Emperor resorted to extrapolations of the scant evidence available. Thus, his father's selection of a juvenile victim to discipline and his admiration of a simple scar led the Emperor to imagine his paternal grandfather to have been a pugilist who stomped the unconscious. Thus, his mother's elevation to legend of domestic trivialities and her taste for inexpensive comestibles suggested a maternal descent from a line of fantasists and petty thieves. By this line of reasoning the Emperor's putative ancestors became a negative hierarchy declining to a pair of parentless creatures in a primordial garden, the original father an amiable innocent provoked by an emotion he did not understand into sacrificing a body-part, the original mother a winsome snake charmer with a propensity for stealing fruit.

Troubled by the results of a quest that had produced such unembraceable precursors, the Emperor convened a congress of geriatric contemporaries who were likely to have adopted the same genealogical hobby. He hoped to compare his notes and methods with theirs to see where he had gone wrong. The delegates were not informed that it was a congress to which they had been summoned. Their invitations were perfumed, so they thought it was a reunion.

These ancient worthies included Madam Ng and her litigious husband, the assassin Kao and his old peasant woman, the Lipless Wang, the Jovial Peng, Peh Yi, General Meng, the Imperial Physician, and others whose names or eponyms the Emperor had managed to forget but which were recorded along with their addresses in the diary section of the Imperial Archive. Some failed to appear citing infirmity as if that were not the universal condition, others because they were dead or claimed to be. Kao's invitation had been returned unopened with a notation from the courier that Cold Mountain could not be located, and in any case was unscalable. General Meng's was rejected as "deceased or moved," and the Imperial Physician's as "unread." The Jovial Peng's was re-addressed to Peh Yi, who ate it.

As well there were unofficial delegates not listed in the agenda. These included a former imperial latrine attendant soliciting a commission to smear the memory of the princess with semi-non-fictional scatology authenticated by palace gossip, a veteran of the Great Trench petitioning for the recovery of the bones of his parents and theirs and theirs from one of the walls so that he could get started on his own genealogy, and a survivor of Lu Wei's fluctuations who broke down before beginning and had to be carried from the hall foaming with vituperative reminiscence. Several others wishing to contribute were held back at the door by the imperial guard, among them a reputable soothsayer who recently had received an ethereal message addressed to the Emperor from a source unknown even to the recipient. The information it contained, the soothsayer blurted out before being comprehensively curtailed by the guards, was a matter of life and death or, rather, of prolonged living and interminable dying, which was to say —

The rest of medium's message, the officer in charge gathered, had something to do with the intensification of a previous prophecy made to the Emperor regarding the desirability of longevity. Precisely what that new information was neither the officer nor his lieutenant could make out, though it was they who were closest to the throat being throttled.

After a short period of settling in during which their dentures were unpacked, their appliances adjusted, their trusses secured, and their cosmetics applied and applied again, the delegates assembled in plenary session. As a venue the Emperor had chosen the broken terrace of the cobwebbed Pool of Sepulchral Tranquility in the unweeded Garden of Seigneurial Repose historically populated by the now departed but still derided fellowship of Ffut with its attendant bevy of carer-nuns. Disused for decades, its amenities were few but the setting was evocative. It was there that the congregation gathered.

Even fuelled by vegetative ferments and intoxicant powders dispensed or injected by skilled attendants, however, the delegates had nothing to say to one another, their only commonality being a shared enthusiasm for compiling self-histories which, according to their invitations, the Emperor shared. And so they sat in embarrassed silence around the empty pool waiting for the Emperor to read their submitted genealogies, and for the proceedings to begin.

Overall, the Emperor noted, their written testimonies presented a pattern of investigation and a trend of deduction that were invariable. Precisely like his own, all followed a downhill trail that led to a boggy conclusion. Had each testifier begun with a different initial premise — an other than admirable self, for instance, or a fallible one — the process of retrospective analysis might not have led to the same atavistic product. But they did not, and it did.

Moreover, many of the genealogies ended when the elderly compiler evidently had dissolved mid-sentence into slumber. Apparently the more of it that was conjectured and invented, the more the history might have been anyone's, and the teller lost interest and dozed off. While he perused their submissions, the Emperor was peripherally aware that the same process presently was being repeated among the delegates in their after-dinner hammocks. By the end of his reading only the Emperor remained awake. That, he concluded, is the way of stories that fail to become tales: they lose the reason to be told.

Following these reflections, the Emperor roused his fellow amateur genealogists, thanked them for their submissions and participation, rewarded each with a trinket and a pension, and disbanded the congress. He dismissed his attendants and stood down the imperial guard, intending to spend the rest of the night alone beneath the stars, contemplating his quest and wondering how to proceed. Withdrawing to a hammock by the dry pool, long-since emptied of the waters that had proved so therapeutic to the long-since dead, the Emperor wrapped himself in robes, tried to think, and fell asleep. Which was where and when the Congress of the Ageing began.

Around midnight the Emperor stirred. Something had set the hammock rocking, but there was nothing there, nothing but the rustle of leaves at the bottom of the pool and the afterglow of a thin moon to see them by, and the breath of a breeze that made them dance. The Emperor yawned. It must have been the breeze that had nudged the hammock. It had passed, and now the air was still and the twilight dim, and the shutters of his perception began once again to enclose the visions behind them.

Again the leaves rustled.

Peering at the basin of the dry pool as into an open grave, the Emperor saw a foot moving along the bottom. It did not appear to be attached to a body. There, on the other hand, scurried a footless leg. Then, as the moon passed out from behind the cloud that had filtered its beam, a curtain was raised before him and below.

From shallow end to profoundest depth the pool was replete with spectres. They were arranging themselves, it seemed, in formal echelons before a presiding authority whose rostrum was the rotting remains of a fallen diving board. In the chair — it was, in fact, the bladder of semi-deflated beach ball — sat an unclothed figure of skeletal demeanour and simian proportions. At its side, eternally chomping an apple core, reclined a recording secretary with calcite breasts and worms for pubic hair.

Ranged before the dais in sloping ranks of diminishing decrepitude, a horde of ghastly delegates had assembled. The foremost tiers were occupied by compendiums of body parts, among them the legless foot and footless leg whose late arrival and scuttling for position had disturbed the leaves and roused the Emperor. On either side were limbs and appendages that might have been pieces of any body, and were too replicative to belong to one. Some ankles, wrists, and knuckles, the Emperor noted, wore the remnants of jewellery. One hand twisted by malnutrition clutched a writing stylus.

Beyond these and below were gradations of greater entirety, many bearing the marks of the forces that had curtailed them ... an exploded thorax with a military decoration, a spine with elongated cervical vertebrae still sporting a noose, the upper segment of a lusty cadaver with its cranium embedded in a shapely pelvis. Adjacent to these, its face forward but its back to the front, hunched a fleshed torso of familiar design. At distance the Emperor could not be certain but thought that, along the spine, it might display a scar.

Far to the rear at the deepest level of the penultimate row, their winding sheets in tatters but their features intact, were the pair of spectres the Emperor sought. His mother waved shyly, and at her urging his father did too. The Emperor wished to respond but found that his arms would not move.

Secure in the knowledge that he could wake if necessary, the Emperor settled down to watch. This theatre of the dry pool, however, was not presenting its masque of the dead for his diversion. The phantoms were engaged in a private plenary just begun: a gruesome colloquium with a specific agenda. If they were aware they were being beheld by one of the living, they showed no sign of performing to please.

The primary order of business, indeed it seemed the sole order of business, was enlistment. It gradually became clear that one candidate only was being considered, and that the nomination already had taken place. What remained was a vetting of the candidature, leading to an expression of universal suffrage by those fragments with enough sentience remaining in them to deserve the privilege of the ballot.

From the ensuing discussion, the Emperor had the impression that the various methods of polling and accounting were perennially debated and remained unresolved, and that the delegates enjoyed revisiting this issue at every congress. Block voting, apparently, was difficult to arrange amid generational units of three that shared no historical century with other units. Given the proliferation of body parts, one-member-one-vote was a dead issue, though a wag in the front row suggested the sufficiency of a show of hands, thereby occasioning a general chortle. It occurred to the Emperor that, in the circumstances, proportional representation was an excellent notion and he tried to introduce it, only to realize by the lack of response that either he was not heard or he had not spoken.

Eventually it was decided that, on this occasion, whiteballing was to be the electoral procedure. The application being considered would be approved if a single member of the forum could be persuaded to agree to it.

Sponsors had no vote or voice in the debate but, even if they had, a positive outcome would not have been assured. There did not seem to be a single good word to be said on behalf of the applicant. One of the ears had never heard of him which, considering the intervening aeons of time and layers of soil, was hardly surprising. Yet, incongruously, it was the candidate himself who was held to blame for being out of touch. "He never once," tutted a tongue to universal chagrin, "wrote home."

Universal blackballing appeared inevitable until the chairman intervened. His recording secretary leaned over, removed the apple core from her tireless jaws, and whispered advice into his earhole. The presiding cadaver looked up, rattled its thorax, and addressed the multitude.

The peroration delivered from the rostrum was more in the interest of delaying a foregone conclusion than in directing an outcome. Delegates were reminded that their own candidatures at one time or another had been contested, the chairman and his charming colleague having sat through every case. As a measure to correct overhasty judgmentalism, the delegates were cautioned, those very archives could be displayed if necessary. Nevertheless, by popular demand for anecdotal entertainment, several were requested. The chairman turned out to be an excellent mimic and the recording secretary a supple mime. Together they enacted a few humiliating case histories to the delight and applause even of those spectres being burlesqued.

Diversion over, prejudices had been tempered, the rush to judgment cooled, and discussion was enabled to resume.

The rest of the debate was profound. For one thing, it was argued, no member of the candidate's family — each of whom, however primordial, was present — had been called upon to sacrifice an equivalent worldly grandeur in order to assume residence among them, and a certain degree of recalcitrance and delay in this exalted case perhaps was forgivable. Nevertheless, it was refuted, the famous candidate's natural allegiance to his assembled family was suspect. The applicant himself had not applied for membership. Because of his stubborn continuance in the world above, the petition for his admittance had been filed by proxy. Again the parents of the Emperor waved. Again he could not find it in him to reply. At that moment he realized that the nominee was he.

In the colloquium that followed, speaker after speaker lustily articulated tales of the candidate's bad behaviour in the mortal realm they had relinquished long ago. None of this gossip related to his suitability for inclusion in the realm below, but the denizens relished the retelling. They were encouraged to do it by the recording secretary, her stylus keeping pace with her chewing.

These hearsay anecdotes, the Emperor realized, could have been rumoured by anyone in the empire. What was made of them down here, however, was scandalous or ludicrous or both. The Emperor's first marriage, for instance, was portrayed as a lopsided affair between a lunatic and a saint. The Emperor's private thoughts at the time were reported as malign accomplishments, his covert wishes as vicious enactments. His oaths muttered in irritation were cited as his intention to murder an entire gender. During the spectral diatribe it occurred to the Emperor that the princess's predecease might have had something to do with the bias of the report.

Inspired by venomous allegation requiring no proof, similar calumnies were asserted as fact with respect to the Emperor's reputed abhorrence of popular music, his fear of the ocean, his antipathy to cats. Of his vertical employment of horizontal tea trays, the less said the better, though it was not. Under such distortive scrutiny the Emperor's life became unrecognizable to him, and his mind began to wander.

Watching the congress pursue its debate, the Emperor was reminded of something he had witnessed once and had spent the rest of his life trying to forget. In the first year of his reign a virulent cattle infection had begun to spread from farm to farm in a rural area of the empire. In an effort to arrest it, each farm in the district was required to construct and to employ a dedicated extermination facility: an immense sealed chamber into which a deadly gas was introduced and whole herds simultaneously were disinfected and dispatched. To promote the cruel but necessary program, the Emperor had visited such a facility and had peered in through the window.

The difference between those doomed animals and these bickering human relics was manifest. The dying of the infected bovines was finite, their agonies terminal. Once they had begun it, however, the demise of the phantoms was perpetual. With every new arrival to their ranks, they revived it. This pathetic congress of affiliated remnants was doomed never to finish its dying! Surely ignorant unregenerate extinction was preferable!

The Emperor stared into the chamber of the pool seething with an energy so much like life, so entirely of death. The prospect of his joining this company in the row behind his parents appalled him. It was, he concluded, to be delayed as long as possible, even at the risk of longevity. Somewhere in the remoter regions of the ether, a reputable soothsayer smiled.

During the Emperor's ruminations, the debate had been concluded, the vote taken, the ballots tallied, the result announced, the gavel sounded, and the minutes filed. It occurred to the Emperor to request a postponement of judgment or a suspension of sentence but, even had he found a voice, it was too late. Their decision ratified, the phantoms were not to be denied or deferred. As a body they broke their ordered ranks and ascended the floor of the pool, making their impaired ways toward their newest recruit. "Pull him in," they chanted in a variety of dialects and archaisms. "Welcome him home!"

Paralyzed where he lay, the Emperor could not evade them. Hands caught at his ankles. Fingers mounted his thighs. The touch was feathery, the grasp insubstantial, the pressure unyielding, the impetus firm. To his surprise he found himself tempted to give in and to permit himself to be claimed. His thighs and his buttocks, his back and his shoulders, his nape and his brow ached with the effort it took to resist. Were he to yield, the Emperor knew, it would be he who had flung himself into the pool. For a long moment he teetered at the edge like a man at the lip of a waterfall drawn to surrender himself to the sweet course of the current and the caress of the vapours and the promise of the rocks below. Then he broke away, and fell out of the hammock.

The pool was empty, the leaves astir, the clouds aloft, the moon abed, the dawn impending, the day assured. When he was certain he was awake, the Emperor packed up, returned to the palace, and burned his research.

XI

THE IMPERIAL HISTORIAN

The First Emperor was aware that a book such as this some-day would be compiled. He knew there was little he could do to control it. Even if he said nothing unconsidered, he could not be certain those words would be included, not as he had spoken them, nor that they would be understood in the sense he had intended. The First Emperor knew that words he had not said would be attributed to him, as would thoughts he had not had, actions he had not taken, along with the noxious paraphernalia of tales partly true or utterly invented. That is why the First Emperor eternally reformed the practice of literature so that editors would have better payment, more fame, and greater loyalty than authors.

THE FIRST LETTER OF THE
IMPERIAL HISTORIAN

In my family it is the left ball that hangs lowest. My father recalled
that his father's left ball hung half a diameter below his prick. My
father's prick and left ball were precisely level. In my case, the ver-
tical distance between prick and left ball was that between left ball
and right. Had I had sons, there is every chance their balls would
have been level, and their sons would have begun the sequence anew
with the initial advantage shifting to the right. The scrotum of my
great great grandfather must have resembled mine. That is, if the
generational rhythm of testicular pendulance never permits the left
ball to descend lower than one-half a diameter below prick-tip —
my grandfather — nor to ascend beyond a half-diameter above the
right ball — my grandsons, alas hypothetical. Since ball diameter
and prick length tend to preserve the same ratio of size as obtains
between prick length and width, this speculation is not based upon
a uniform prick. It does, however, postulate a stationary right ball.

   Such matters may not seem to deal with the question you
have addressed to me. But I wish you to understand the nature of
the one whom you have addressed and who now addresses you.
You will not be able to understand my reply if you do not understand my nature. It is not a nature easily cowed. Nor is it a nature
that refuses to see things as they are, and to speak of what is seen
and to name it with the name that it must bear. Things would
have been easier for me had I understood the practice of evasion.
I have never been able to understand it nor those who practise it,
for their nature is not mine nor mine theirs. You have asked what
you have asked and you were free to ask it and I was gratified by
your asking and you must bear my reply, however tedious. It is

not beside the point. Tedious, perhaps, but not beside the point. Nor tedious if you have a heart for suffering and an ear for valour. Which I do not claim. Suffering, yes, not valour.

Mine was no public war and my wound proclaims no valour. Suffering, yes, though not as you imagine, for the knife was sharp and the surgeon skilled, and the movement of his wrist was sudden and single. Even when they applied the iron, even when I saw it cherry-red except at the tip where a mantle of ash capped it and was struck off before it touched me, even when I saw the hiss of steam and the sweet smell of my flesh, even then the sensation was that of ice. When pain came, it was not in the groin but in the elbows that had dislocated and the writing hand where my nails had impaled my palm. It is for that reason that I employ this scribe and not to impress you with the dignity of my office.

You do wrong to assume my importance. It is not as if I had direct access. The nearest I have approached the person of the Emperor is through messages I have addressed to him. Once I even posted such a message, though whether it was delivered into his presence and read to him with incisions and corrections or few or none I did not learn nor expected to. It is sufficient that, after years of indirection, at one time I did address the Emperor and may have been heard. To my knowledge he has addressed me only once and that was upon the occasion of my offence, and then only by means of his monogram on the blade.

Dear friend, my father was not unknown to your father. On the contrary, they were friends, as indeed were their fathers and, perhaps, theirs before them, though such questions are dark and deservedly so, though well worth the asking, for who is not what they have been? You, then, will understand why I consented, not to the knife for there was no resisting it but, after the knife, to remaining alive. It is my book. I must complete my book. Do you think that, without my book, I would have consented to live one moment beyond the knife? You cannot think it! Did not your father choose death rather than dishonour in the matter of a tea tray? The son of such a father cannot think less of me. I could not choose to die. I must complete my book. It is of no consequence what happens to my book. Perhaps it will be installed in the Imperial Archive where it will repose forever, dustless, brittle, unread. My book is named The Book of the Emperor. It is his book. The use of it is his. I am named Historian to the Emperor. I am his. The use of me is his. My only use is to complete my book. All other use of me ended with the knife.

I must complete my book. It is not that I want to write. I want to have written. The writing, that is a matter of the severest pain. How could it be otherwise? Of course I do not understand the nature of my offence. It is enough that I have suffered for it. That I suffer still means that I continue to give offence. Since I am permitted to live, it must be that my offence likewise can be borne.

Undoubtedly it was the early chapters that offended since they alone were complete at the time of my punishment. How can such matters offend? Perhaps because they are not true? Yet you and I who write history know that they are true. They only are not fact. I do not pretend they are fact. There is no fact of earliest times, none that we can know. People lived, people died, insects sang. Of what use to us are they? Of what importance?

Perhaps my offence was in recalling earliest times? The Emperor has made it known that time began with him. That is not fact. It is truth. I accept it. My work asserts it. Even the earliest god, half-man, half-worm, cloud-born, sea-garbed, even such a tale attests the imminence of the Emperor aeons before his birth. Where is the offence? Perhaps in daring to have written? Yet now I am permitted. I have even been elevated to the office you address. My writing must be approved. It must be commanded.

I could have chosen to die. Indeed my father urged it. How could I have chosen to die? Had the Emperor wished me dead, he need only have ordered the blade raised or the iron of fire withheld. I did not choose to die. I chose to submit to life. My choice was permitted, and I was wounded, and I was healed, and now with dishonour I sow the long rows of my words and gather my harvest of pain. Such is the state of the man you petition.

I must complete my book. In other circumstances undoubtedly I would intervene on your behalf. Have I not dared? Was
it not I, a mere apprentice scribe, who committed satire, and
that to save a courtesan despite imperial edict? Was it not my
artistry in that cause that enabled me to obtain my first elevation? How much more would I dare for the life of one as dear
to me as you? But now? You cannot expect it of me now. Now
I must complete my book.

Dear friend, for the sake of our fathers forgive me. Dear
friend, for the sake of yourself heed my life. Dear friend, after
the knife choose to die.

THE SECOND LETTER OF THE
IMPERIAL HISTORIAN

The Whoring of an Empress! The Dismemberment of Pleats! The
Great Ramification! The Plenipotentiary Device! The Tea Tray
Orifice Scandal! The Revocation of Newts! The truth of them
must be told! And if you and I and such as we —

Among many starving dogs what is a small packet of meat?
The gift of a detester of dogs! You believe I exaggerate? A service
you do not admire, a reputation you already possess, a rank to
which you need not aspire in a position you never sought at a task
you cannot fulfill ... in a word, mine. Truly, colleague, do you not
understand? That is the benefaction of one who wishes us to eat
one another! Do not covet my office! Do not intrigue at my downfall! I am aware that you have not and do not, but in view of your
recent accomplishment — for which, I assure you, my heartiest
admiration — you might. Do not do it! I beseech you, do not!

Should you choose to pursue, I shall be required to retaliate
to your discredit as, indeed, will you to mine, and then what will
become of us? I have instigated inquiry. My position is secure.
I have nothing to fear of you. It is you, colleague, who is in peril.
Even should you refuse to aspire, beware! There are precedents.

One is offered a blessing, one bows one's head to receive it and extends one's hand, and the blessing is withdrawn and one is asked what it is one solicits! After such an experience would you ever again believe an advantage possible, a reward real? Would you not despair and make an end to your life or even to your work? And should you incinerate everything, who would be at fault? Not he who deigned to give audience to your "solicitations" and whom you will die cursing!

Colleague, the path to high office is paved with the calcifications of such as we! And who rides triumphant over our detritus? Precisely he whose immortal progress you and I and such as we should most seek to —

Do you not think I myself have had to withstand improvement? Consider my fifteen volumes of celebratory eulogy commemorating the imperial circumcision, albeit putative! Do you imagine such a feat went unacknowledged? Consider the matter of my anthem! Of all my anthems! But consider —

Very well, then, do not consider. Yet, this I require. Permit me to complete my book. I realize that you do not seek to impede it. Why would you? Is not my book as much your concern as mine? More, even, for when I have done with it, why then I shall have done, but you and all men such as you or worse will know the humiliation of acknowledging it to be complete and to be mine, and which of you then will dare to undertake —

Colleague, abstain. At least, delay? You will not regret forbearance. You will benefit from it. Will not my vacancy be the greater because, before I vanished, I completed my book? Then, of course, my chair is yours, likewise my brush, my pot, this chattering chattering chattering scribe. As for the remainder of the gorgeous retinue of my most puissant office — including that raucous fruitier who considers a citron a day a debt worth litigating — let them pursue me to my terminal abode and entomb their rancour there, for the coffin-mould that enshrouds and the mud-slugs that inhabit must recompense us all our corporeal —

Colleague, colleague, who else has a chance of understanding me? And now that ambition has entered between us, how can I hope that you, even you, most especially you —

Shall I even dispatch this? But I must complete my book. Who has profited less from it? Who has lost more? Yet, now the sacrifice is done, now the shame is habitual, now except on damp mornings the anguish is past, is there not a species of comfort in the thought? A curious kind of pride? Or is it merely a loyalty to the implacable imperial perpetrator? A grudging professional admiration? Perhaps, at moments a persistent fondness, even a sort of a positive —

Of course I do not condone it! How could I approve my own mutilation? I could not!

Very well, then, let this not be dispatched. Yet sometimes, kneeling at my book, staring at the desert of a page, not daring the indentation that might lead me trackless into voids beyond retreat, I think, I dream, I almost breathe aloud ... one clear act of savagery, how I wish it had been mine!

THE THIRD LETTER OF THE IMPERIAL HISTORIAN

The difficulty of the writing is this. There is nothing that is not the Emperor. Were he less, it would be known, for example, that tea trays are not he and the writing need not concern itself with those. Yet the father of one who was as dear to me as you met death in just such a matter, and even tea trays must be considered. How much more so wars, shaving bowls? One can hardly exempt oneself.

Merely because there is no evidence that the Emperor is concerned with anyone's destiny, which of us has the tranquility to conclude that his own destiny is not concerned with that of the Emperor? Indications are to the contrary. To add to every other difficulty, then, it is certain that one's very self must become a part of the writing that already is and, one suspects, not inconsiderably, a part of every other self. Can such a book be completed? When can it be said to have begun? Has there been a moment one has not been writing it?

The difficulty, of course, is not the writing, though that is almost impossible. The difficulty is the making of such writing a book. Here one feels not so much the pervasiveness of the Emperor as his entire absence. After all, The Book of the Emperor is not in itself the Emperor, nor his empire, nor his reign. It is, somehow, less and more. Less in duration and more in depth, less in depth and more in extension, less in extension and more in comprehension, less in comprehension and more in comprehensibility. In other words, are these my present ruminations not merely an evasion of the writing, however much they be expressed in words, however many of those eventually be included in my book?

If only the Emperor would decree an extent! If only he would make it known that "here" imperial matters end and "there" begin, and he himself is by his nature "thus" and "so," and "thus" and "so" and "here" and "there" must end, begin, consist the book that bears his name! Then, dear friend, I should fly to my scribe and hush her idle chatter, and watch her brush melt bats' wings on her scroll until all is done and done. Instead of which I squat upon an earth mat and address this letter to the dead.

One cannot, of course, overlook the possibility that the Emperor is aware of the difficulty, and that he permits the writing because he knows it cannot succeed. It is not every historian who would bear the expense of doing it. I do not refer to matters of the body. If it were required I would relinquish more, if I had more of that kind to lose. I mean, rather, that which I myself have severed that no man else can grow: the hope of ever writing any other thing. And if I, the sole author of the only book to bear the Emperor's name, am prepared to resign that hope in this or in any other world, what need has the Emperor to mutilate more than me? And, since he has accomplished that in every way save loping off my life, must he not require me to hope I may succeed?

THE FOURTH LETTER OF THE
IMPERIAL HISTORIAN

Forgive this mode. In times less devious I would not have had
recourse to direct correspondence. Now it is perhaps the only
evasion. Yet, should you accept this intact and deny yourself the
advantage of neglecting to read it, you will be rewarded with the
most extraordinary gossip.

It has emerged that there are restrictions beyond! Have you
understood what I have said? Without, there are restrictions!
I have learned this from no braggart, but from such a one it is
impossible to doubt even should the allegation have been made
in words and not, as was the case, in the apertures between them.
A famous practitioner, though none of course that you and I may
know, but in the world outside the empire most famous. Indeed,
I assure you, feared. Nor are restrictions confined to him. (I say
"him" so that you will not be imperilled by the knowledge of his
gender.) Several of his former colleagues have been the recipients
of proscription! Another actually has achieved banning! I realize one need not believe everything one infers, that deduction
is the offspring of desire. Yet, constraint, suppression, erasure ...
tantalizing, are they not?

Why, you will ask, should such a one remove himself from
such a place to this? There may well be an answer. I shall be fas-
cinated to receive yours. To assist your deliberations, he is dumb,
blind, and lacks limbs. I jest! No wounds appear. It is by other
manifestations that one must judge the seriousness with which
he was taken. Certainly his judgment remains impaired. In the
empire, for example, he intends to pursue "achievement." I think
he means currency. That may be why he came. Is it to be believed?
One can become bored even with having made something happen! And you and I thought we understood decadence.

Further, despite the fact that he has vacated a condition to
which most of us would not dare aspire, he seems astonished
at our contempt. He was expecting admiration! Well, well,

sufficiently indulged would even I maintain perspective? Could even you resist vanity?

It is thought that, in his native land, he fomented irreverence. Apparently he disobeyed commands. In any case, he must have received some. Surely he could not have dreamt them up himself, else he would recognize in us a greater compatibility. Perhaps he did not contradict. Perhaps he intended irrelevance, even whimsy. Perhaps he did not intend anything. Perhaps accidental effect is his style. Or is that suggestion merely another of our perverse, monolithic, cynical, distortive, empire-like manners of perceiving? I expect he would think so. He laughs a lot, though it may be a respiratory gasping brought on by travel.

When I visited, he was studying to learn the language. Unable to address him with subtlety, I could not advise. In any event, what would I have said? My personal restrictions are of no use to him. Who can proscribe for another? Now that he is among us, he must cultivate in his own way the servitude of the free.

Of what, then, did we speak? Why, of my book! He seemed interested. He could be seen to smile. "Here," he said, "one considers such matters?" Then he smiled. Like a slap. I should have replied. I react badly in situations. I thought of you. I rushed home to address you at a distance.

Aware of your desire to be the first among us to achieve the dream of all, I made discreet inquiry on your behalf. Direction, distance, climate, travel-clothes ... the sort of thing I should need to know, were it not you who was planning to —

I cannot be certain of the location of his homeland. Doubtless it lies far to the west, for he expressed incredulity with respect to the Great Trench. In that connection, he also implied that, without the evidence of a single measurable prohibition regarding my own book, I have no reason to assume the existence of the Emperor! I have not the space to recount his other regional jokes. Should you manage to achieve whence he originated, doubtless you will soon have gathered a collection of your own.

I shall investigate further, though not in such a manner as to alert. I am well placed to inquire. Who is to know I am not engaged upon the Emperor's very business? Should my babbling scribe suspect, I shall once again silence her by showing my wound. The wretch is superstitious. A single glimpse of the scar, and she does not think me other than the Emperor's own.

Well, well, so I am. I am a man upon whom the Emperor can depend. Believe it, were I not beyond suspicion of other than inaction I would not have risked a word aside in a fishmonger's queue much less a letter in an oilskin in a carp. Nevertheless, upon reflection, would every man have dared as I have dared? Even the surgeon was astonished, though I indemnified him from every consequence were his cauter to fail. Had I been confident I could complete the incision once begun, I probably would have administered entirely to myself. Pardon the boast. In the event, in fact, what else was there to do? I had guessed as well as anyone the reason I merited pain. Should I literally have awaited imperial decree? And if it had not come? No, friend, no, in this as in all things, I anticipated command and I obeyed without compulsion. What is our freedom else? Nor, believe me, even in that day and age were surgeons less expensive than —

My friend, forgive me! It is envy of you that causes me to justify myself. My office makes me visible, but who will know you to be gone? I must complete my book, but what have you left to relinquish? How I envy you your dotage, your lack of fashion! Were I your elder and your lesser, would I not fly? Oh, colleague! To be restricted! To be banned! To have been heard!

THE FIFTH LETTER OF THE
IMPERIAL HISTORIAN

The Emperor unified the weights and measures and regulated the coinage. He revised the system of calligraphy making it coherent in every part of the empire and he standardized the length of axles so that one network of roads served all wagons.

He fragmented the feudal domains and set up a non-hereditary bureaucracy based on competitive merit. He demobilized the armies of the old states and melted down their weaponry into metal statues of their former generals weighing sixty thons apiece, kneeling. He executed the old nobility and transported their descendants to the capital city where he could watch them. He subdued the barbarians and placed between them and him a wall or a ditch or a ditch between two walls with a roof. He built his tomb and his archive, and neglected to forbid the writing of my book.

There! How dare you say I am "out of touch"?

On the chance that this will reach you in a legible condition, I condescend to reply to your various other allegations which, despite their careless method of delivery, I believe are addressed to me? I trust you will not object to the unsanitary vehicle of my response? In times like this etcetera etcetera.

Of course the empire is dying! I do not require your youthful illusion of "futurity" to approve the practice of my profession nor the profession of my practice. It is when a man himself is in decline that he is most concerned with the explanation of his life and the ordering of his immortal reputation. It is when an empire itself is about to die that it is most necessary to record the songs and the legends of what soon will become the world's bright past. That the Emperor permits my book indicates that we are in the midst of extinction. You require further "proof of our collective mortality"? Linger amid the living and you will obtain it!

"Offering neither a discovery of new material nor a novel interpretation of the old, what can forgive yet another book on the subject? An abiding interest in the Emperor? The shelf life of previous volumes? The former is a historian's incentive, the latter an archivist's. Where, one longs to ask our current Imperial Historian, where in all his prolix endeavour is his consideration for the reader without which no other purpose obtains?"

Why, it is just there! In my book! How can you imply otherwise?

In my book the reader will discover a faithful record. There he will receive an objective in-gathering of verified historical material without bias, without selection, without formulation or preference or device. Myth sifted of the supernatural. Folklore purified of the improbable. Law embodied not in abstract code nor obscure precedent but in the actual behaviour of moral men. The dead consoled for their sorrows by the handing on of their stories. The unborn instructed in the ways of the living by the stories of the dead. Out of all the empty tales of the world I conjure truth!

My only "endeavour" has been to remove the least stain of invention, the veriest vestige of intervention, and then to withdraw the remainder of my inconsequent self into the refuge of a preface, well satisfied that (along with the occasional parenthetic note) the enterprise of a lifetime presents to the reflective judgment of the reader purely the matter itself. Is that not "incentive" enough? Enough to excuse my "prolixity?" Damn your eyes!

"And where in all these tedious evasions is our Emperor? Perhaps already dead? There are those labouring in pavilions less remote from the throne than that of our Imperial Historian who have been heard to reckon that nothing short of the death of the Emperor could make possible the continuing machinations of a Chao Kao and his league of malevolent eunuchs. Yet is the reverse not possibly the case? Unless the Emperor lives, what reason has Chao Kao to machinate? On the other hand — "

Who's in, who's out, who lives, who dies ... pah!

Permit me to instruct you in a topic upon which, though your years proclaim you an apprentice, yet your manner reveals you to be an accomplished barbarian. The ancient ideogram for "historian" represents a hand holding a vessel used to contain the tallies at an archery contest. I am charged with keeping track. Where in that is the "independent judgment" you demand? The earliest recorded duty of the first historian was to memorize and to recite the interpretation of the results of divination whether by tortoise shell or splintered bone or leaf division. "Commitment?"

"Nonconformity?" "Risk?" I am a historian! A receptive palm, an accounting eye, a throatless voice! No more! No less! Indeed, no less!

Nor am I concerned with "the complexion of today." I was once, and I gave offence. My punishment is difficult to contemplate though easy to recall. Now I offend no more. In short, I am not an itinerant strategist alert to changes of the times and quick to turn them to his own advantage, one who abandons inopportune loyalties, who relinquishes the losing side in order to join the winning, who bends his knee and extends his tongue and — But perhaps you already are familiar with the posture?

I do not know how you obtained an early version of my manuscript. If, as you report, you borrowed it with my "blessing" or even, as you imply, at my solicitation, I can only imagine that I mistook you for another: a colleague, perhaps, in need of a paragon, an enthusiast in pursuit of a reflected glory, a potential patron estimating my price for his inclusion in a footnote, a manifest historical villain negotiating my fee for his revisioning. And it was that error of my discernment that permitted the unwisdom of inviting a cannibal to dine.

What is more probable is that you bribed my garrulous disingenuous scribe, in anticipation of the proof of which she has been made mute and discharged. Fortunately, what few textual emendations yet remain to be made I am competent to undertake in my own maimed hand.

Yes, it is true I have suffered "the palace punishment," that I am "a mere remnant of the knife and the iron, a mutilated creature fit only to be a demi-official in the women's pavilion." How astute of you to point it out! And is that not the greater reason to contribute to my work rather than to seek to consume it? You are able and entire. Should you fail to achieve your fame, perhaps your sons will triumph, or theirs. What hope have I? Truly it is said, "He could not accomplish his aims, so he wrote a book." And, if compassion for me fails to satisfy you, pray consider my book! Mine is such a book —

Imagine a perfect body, entire and intact.

Or, rather, imagine a structure not separate from the body it supports, a part of that body, the part that supports it, implicit, integral, present in every limb, as a sapling in a seed discoverable there.

Or, rather, imagine a form that is the result of its structure, neither excessive of it nor deficient but developed in response to the development of that structure, developed simultaneously as in the morphology of the skeleton of the fetus that continues to grow after birth and modifies throughout childhood and ossifies but late into middle age.

Or, rather, imagine a meaning that is the visible manifestation of a structure, the vitalic embodiment of a form, the organic impetus of the architectonic integrity of, say, the stone arch, a boulder supporting the boulder above, bearing downward on boulders beneath, deflecting its weight to boulders beyond, keystone to bedrock, coping to base. And should but a pebble be removed? What then would remain? Mere fragments of fact and fable tumbled into natural chaos! Splinters of my basic annals compounded with my chronological tables! My sturdy thematic treatises pulverized between my hereditary houses! My memoirs of statesmen and heroes sifted with my own biographic dust! Heaps of encrusted relics over which the seasons pass, waiting perhaps to be gathered again by some unknown hand into a shape I neither intended nor —

Oh, horror! In an age unenvisaged among folkways undreamt of, a passerby stoops to examine a shard, finds another to fit, lays a third as a through-band, and by such rude mechanics manages to build —

Build what? A cairn in a landscape not yet evolved? A rough stone altar to gods unborn? A dyke to withstand who knows which beast from incursion upon what occult husbandry? No! No! A maimed book of my broken half-told tales bearing the name of another!

If you do not wish futurity to hold you responsible for the collapse of what else might have stood forever, each part

supporting every other part and supported by it, the perfect
model of perpetuity and insight, of entirety and grace, a book
that tells something in all places but all in no place and cannot
be skimmed, a book where, yes, you may discover the conspir-
acies of a Chao Kao and his league of infamous emasculates
though not by name nor attached to their deeds, a book where
you may uncover the secret corpse of our very Emperor concealed in a silo of fermenting grain though that unpermitted
tale must be told of another, a book where you may enjoy the
maddening to suicide of the legitimate imperial successors,
the sawing in half of the loyal imperial advisor, the eventual
implosion of every degenerating descendant and the retrospective illegitimatization of the entire spiral dynasty, in
short a book of bald truths in veiled words too intricate for
amendment, too subtle for offence, too evasive for —

Ah, damn!

If you would not throttle at parturition the only proper issue
of these poor mutilated loins, I beseech you, desist in your critique.
At least abate until installation is achieved? Then, of course, my
book is yours to abuse as I suppose you must if you too are ever to
attain the sanctified asylum of the eternal Archive.

THE FIRST PEER-REVIEW

In my province the Emperor is a little-known figure from a remote
sector of cosmopolitan activity and a not greatly considered one.
There are some in our region — cultural historians, a small lot not
noted for their research zeal or purchasing power — who might be
interested in learning more about his life and his work. But he never
lived among us, and it may have been a while since he lived at all.
In my view The Book of the Emperor does not contain enough of
him to encourage any archivist of my acquaintance to learn about
him. Nor does it reveal enough about him to make any common
reader wish for more. I cannot comment on his drawing power in
another province.

The situation might be different were this submission to reveal an overlooked paragon or a misprized genius or a misrepresented villain and popular bandit with an ambient alias, someone along the lines of Otto the Unruly whom the present peer-reviewer had the good fortune to uncover and the perspicacity to pursue in several scholarly odysseys that themselves have become the stuff of archival legend.†Judging by the submission under assessment, however, the Emperor is nonesuch. In this account he emerges as something between a melancholy has-been and a taciturn never-was, perhaps a natural choice of protagonist for the submitting historian?

With regard to the text, from the point of view of words it seems well enough written, though frequently lapsing into literature. For the reader who successfully resists the impulse to be drawn into the flow of its eloquence and is able to ignore the impulse of its invention and refuses to resign his critical faculty to the seduction of its perception and the music of its phonology and the wit of its tropes, it soon becomes clear that the narrative, to the extent that one exists, is fragmented beyond repair, and the textual fabric contains too many individual voices for a single informing attitude to emerge.

There do appear to be some prevailing thematics and a few unifying structurals — the inadvertency of power, the comicality of endeavour, the indices of mortality, the prevalence of tea trays, to instance a few — though only if one is prepared to search for them amid the counterpoint.

In short, by any normal standards A Book of the Emperor is impossible to read.

Nor, once read, does the reward justify the effort. Poetry, song, monologue, documentary, memoir, what can only be described as

---

† See Otto the Unruly: a Judicious Appraisal; Otto the Unruly: a Judicious Reappraisal; Otto the Unruly: Injudicious Bits And Bobs ... all inexplicably catalogued in the Imperial Archive under "Otto" rather than the author's name!

outright art ... the mixture of modes is dazzling and intolerable.

Separated out, the individual pieces are impressive if flamboyant. Taken together they present the plurality of life itself, hardly a comfortable scenographic for what, because of its obscure plot-argument-development continuum, its arcane topic-theme-sense dynamic, its remote tenor-purport-import exponential, and its negative prospect of provincial interest, inevitably must be an audience of cosmopolitan academicians. And how many are there of those?

Even such a readership is unlikely to be pleased by A Book of an Emperor. As displayed here, the overall disrespect for institutions of higher learning and greater intelligence and deserved privilege suggests that the author, be he an imperial historian or a lesser lackey, could just as well be a failed student or a disgraced professor or a might-have-been academician of indelible embitterment. For instance, in the natural course of academic studies we all have encountered a lascivious teacher. Few of us, however, would be tempted to generalize our particular experience into a wholesale condemnation of the institution that houses and feeds the offender, and offers him the protection and the security that enables him to carry on his important intellectual work even if it is practised within a merely provincial academy where —

The point, I think, is made.

And so, to move on to the matter of subjective opinion.

Once exposed to this material, even in the brief intimacy of a peer assessment, the tone and the style and the energy of the author adheres like something foul on the heel of one's shoe and is as difficult to shake off. Upon completion of the reading, one lays aside the manuscript in a daze of altered consciousness from which it takes a day or two of productive endeavour to recover. Correcting undergraduate term papers is a salutary antidote, as is a prolonged session of martial arts followed by a scorching sauna. Normality regained, what, one might ask oneself, has been learned from the experience? "Not," in the words of Otto the Unruly, "a lot."

The style of the text blends event and legend, record and probability, assertion and interpretation with whim, whimsy, and imaginative flight, producing an untrammelled accumulation of invention beyond the tolerance of modern historiography and the parameters of any respectable archive much less the Imperial one.

As a contribution to knowledge the submission is beneath computation, unless "none" be taken as an admissible grade. Its scholarship is similarly immeasurable by conventional standards and, one suspects, equivalently absent. It goes without saying that the author's interest in provincial matters is non-existent. Are there other articles or books on the topic or in similar areas? I think not. Who would bother?

That a remote colleague and much rewarded contemporary has chosen to expend decades of his endeavour, perhaps the whole of it, in the preparation of such a manuscript and chooses to submit it in candidature suggests a level of self-disparagement or a degree of suicidal negligence or, to give the so-called Imperial Historian the benefit of the doubt, a simple stupidity that one might be tempted to observe in other aspects of his career and his life.

Some Book of Some Emperor is not recommended for inclusion in the Imperial Archive.

THE SECOND PEER-REVIEW

Given my personal history, academic persuasion, and pedagogic temperament, I find the character of the Emperor as portrayed in The Book of the Emperor strangely compelling, particularly in his early years, and then more for the path he might have taken than for the one he took.

Surely the pre-Emperor was confused, but no more than the majority of my students. Nor, indeed, than I at their age, which compatibility enables my empathetic understanding of them, and coincides with my rather distinguished reputation for pastoral care.

Because he was talkative, the emperor-youth was attracted to those who said little and implied much, and that through alternate agencies. Thus his transfixion in the presence of the princess-youth whose inability to sustain thought required her to perfect a luminosity of gaze. Thus his fascination with Madam Ng who spoke rarely and smelt delicious. Thus his susceptibility to the incantations of a mellifluous balladeer.

Under appropriate guidance from a charismatic elder, these characteristic disabilities need not have hardened into defects of character. To mitigate his confusion and to channel his anger as well as to learn a trade, the stripling might have sought out a shaman. As indeed did I, and now as my students do in me, recognizing shamanism to be the practice of one's heart and the source of one's reluctant fame.† Under such benign guidance the post-pubescent Emperor could have avoided marriage, foregone adultery, and eschewed enthusiasm. How different then would the course of his life have been!

Yet, however fascinating, what has all of this to do with The Book of the Emperor and my peer judgment regarding its admittance into the Imperial Archive? Why, everything!

Inevitably, the role of a particular shaman in the life of an individual postulant tends to remain tantalizingly obscure. In The Book of the Emperor, for instance, that there is no recorded reference to an attendant shaman need not indicate that, in his formative years, the Emperor had none. Indeed, a determination not to mention the name of one's shaman generally is considered proof positive of the man, a paradox I have encountered amidst my own graduates and been required to correct.

Thus it remains impossible to determine whether the Emperor might have been a shaman's initiate or one of his competitors or

---

† See my humble contributions to the holdings of the Imperial Archive: Shamen I Have Known and Been; Shamanism in the Theatre, The Theatre in Shamanism, My Place in Both; and, of course, Me, Myself and I: A Mirror to Nature.

a member of his entourage or of his audience, a compelling field for conjectural research that the Imperial Historian never undertakes. Had he, one might have been tempted to accept his submission into the Imperial Archive. Since he failed to, one is compelled to reject it.

THE THIRD PEER-REVIEW

It had, of course, been the original intention of the employees and the appointees of the Imperial Archive to assess this collection at once in its entirety. Piecemeal assessment over many years perhaps requires some explanation. As chair of the present review committee and presiding curator of the Imperial Archive, it falls to me to provide it.

Traditionally, where the assessment procedure has been interrupted by illness or boredom, or the archival standards have altered, some projects have been returned to their submitters stamped "partial assessment only" without a further explanation, or with no such stamp but containing clear internal evidence of not having been read beyond a certain point or at all. Naturally such an incompletely adjudicated manuscript often is resubmitted, usually after years of revision by its author who, in the way of authors, despite our institutional confession that the fault was ours not his, somehow suspects the reverse to have been the case. Were his manuscript more compellingly written, more fully researched, more stylish, other styled, racier, less racy, repunctuated, unpunctuated, better scribed, he reasons, it might yet attain a full reading. Honestly, it makes you weep!

And so to the matter at hand, the current and, one hopes after several decades of regrettable delay, the final peer assessment of The Book of the Emperor.

As mandatory third reviewer, I also have reservations about the submission. Unlike my two colleagues, however, it is the inherent politics I find especially disturbing. That they are there is inappropriate. That they are required for interest or for popularity is unproven. Many of our best-read historical archives — the Otto the Unruly franchise, for example, and the fashionable series on shamans and gurus — contain no politics at all.

Would that the same were true of The Book of the Emperor! Politics are blatant on every page, even those seemingly distant from the theme: "The Assassination," "Painting on Scrolls," "The Parable of the Gerrhi," "Imperial Gossip," to name a few. In whole sections — "The Imperial Law," "The Limits of the Empire," "The Governing of the Empire" — the latent anti-imperialism borders on sedition, and probably is actionable.

During my reading of The Book of the Emperor, however, I hourly reminded myself of the fact that, while it would be difficult to isolate and to modify a political attitude that permeates the material and infects its very fabric, it is entirely possible, likely even, that the opacity of the text itself conceals any relevance to contemporary governments and to current governors. It could be argued that, though The Book of the Emperor does contain dangerous implications, its profuse and imaginative eloquence obscures them. I argue it, and my fears are calmed without being entirely removed.

Of course it should not be forgotten that any volume contained in a prestigious archive such as ours could become a recommended text and enter a school curriculum, and that physical sensibility or disrespect of intellect, while sometimes delightful in itself, is inappropriate for students whom it would only confuse. In The Book of the Emperor we may safely conclude that the sensual innuendo and the penis fixation — viz. the Princess, Madam Ng, Lu Wei, Chao Kao, the Emperor's statue — are those of the mutilated Imperial Historian not of the Emperor, although it was the author's lamentable decision to include them in every resubmission, perhaps due to the distracting interference of his own in-house scribe whose unrestrained loquaciousness should be assessed in this regard before she is entrusted with further employment.† Should a decision to accept The Book of the Emperor into the Imperial Archive be entertained, however, those offensive areas could be excised entirely, or obscured with illustrations.

Similar treatment could be accorded those few sections that so irritate the First Peer-Reviewer by their anti-academic tone. Again, it could charitably be argued that the hostility displayed there resides in the temperament of the intermittently insane Imperial Historian rather than in the person of the Emperor. It is agreed that, as himself a historian, the First Peer-Reviewer certainly would have performed with more literary circumspection in the matter. Should he change his vote and elect to accept the submission, however, he will get the opportunity to fill his red inkpot and do it.

It is more difficult to see the grounds upon which the Second Peer-Reviewer has reached his decision, but perhaps it has something to do with the failure of the text to achieve his own exacting standard of contemporary shamanistic scholarship. In which case, I believe, a pool of scribes dedicated to the achievement of an up-to-date checklist of academic reference already is available for hire,‡ and the necessary adjustments to the entire text could be made with several flicks of the brush.

As chair of the Peer-Review Committee, my vote cannot be cast except in the event of a tie which, given the negative assessments of the other two peer-reviewers, does not seem likely. As Imperial Curator, however, it is my prerogative to urge reconsideration. Which, in this case, I do.

Indeed, it is to my pair of learned colleagues that this, my present memorandum, is addressed in the hope that, by

---

† Upon re-reading the "Fifth Letter of the Imperial Historian," the Third Peer-Reviewer notes that this recommendation no longer is necessary.

‡ Further research indicates that just such an agency does exist. The bursar of the Imperial Archive has been instructed to place a pending order for its services, provisional upon obtaining an institutional discount.

contextualizing the situation, it will encourage them to think again. The reason? Fairness. The objective? Justice. There is also the off-chance that this particular ms., because of the very eccentricities and offences already objected to plus several others less decorous to mention, could achieve the lucrative archival status of a cult classic!

I await the reassessment and the final judgment of my esteemed colleagues.

THE THIRD PEER-REVIEW
(SECOND REPORT)

I am grateful to my colleagues of the Peer-Review Committee for their reconsideration of The Book of the Emperor and I respect their reasserted adversarial decision, although I do not share it. In view of the recent sad events, however, I have a new proposal.

The reward of an honorary archive generally is linked to a specific occasion, a notable new accomplishment by the recipient of the tribute, perhaps his especial birthday, his retirement, a desire to exalt him while he is yet able to enjoy it. Unhappily, none of the above applies with respect to the Imperial Historian. Nor is comprehensive temperamental breakdown by itself a recognized qualification. What I propose, then, is unprecedented. Which factor alone should attract some fame to the endeavour.

Other than upon the flyleaf of an inscribed presentation copy — in his present condition, the recipient probably would not notice it — gratitude for the installation of any honorary archive naturally emanates from friends, relatives, colleagues, hypocrites, and advantage seekers. Judging by the visitors' daybook at the asylum, however, the intimate circle of the Imperial Historian appears to be an unusually small one, the only regular visitor being his tongueless former scribe, though what pleasure such a visit could afford either unfortunate is beyond imagining. Consequently, the honour accruing to the Imperial Archive for its selfless gesture to the pathetic figure in this particular case would have to be noised abroad by the benefactor rather than by the beneficiary. I promise it would be.

It might be mentioned that the budget for this new project would permit the commissioning of two new essays of assessment. As in-house editor of the honorary archive, I would be inclined to give approbative consideration to the pair of peer-reviewers whose long-standing association with the submission equips them with insights unavailable to others. Quote me and we never spoke.

THE THIRD PEER-REVIEW
(THIRD REPORT)

As a final word in this protracted and painful matter, I wish to thank those associated with the history of and the hopes for The Book of the Emperor so cruelly aborted by recent events, and to assure everyone that, although guilt-motivated regret regarding its long-suffering author is natural enough, medically it remains in doubt whether the early onset of advanced senility is stress-related. The Imperial Historian's near-fatal wounding at his own trembling hand, while regrettable and disgusting, cannot be laid at the door of the Imperial Archive, though it was there that it occurred. Measures have been taken to prevent further patho-logical attempts to disgrace us.

Obviously the steam has gone out of the honorary-archive concept. In view of the bad repute we lately have received, the installation would look less like the tribute it was intended to be and more like an apology that, as pointed out above, it is unneces-sary for us to make. Never mind. We of the Imperial Archive know that our motives were pure, our intentions good, our hands clean. In the search for blame one need look no further than the victim. Not only was his medical decline self-inflicted, his professional demise will be too.

In our hearts the lamented Imperial Historian is fondly remembered as a romantic throwback to the brave days of good old archiving. Always ready with a reference or an allusion or an anecdote however peripheral to his subject and tangential to his theme, ever in search of ironies and innuendos and ambiguities and implications despite their scatology, never shy of an unending catalogue or a galloping simile or an accumulating accretion of acrostic alliteration if a little over-fond of a well-turned phrase and tediously inclined to aphorism, he was always, one might be tempted to conclude, rather in need of his own best medicine. For truly it is said there is a difference between "I never wasted a minute stroking the cat" and "Stroking the cat was never a wasted minute." The difference is editing.

In conclusion and with the commiserations noted above, I now find myself in belated accord with my colleagues of the Peer-Review Committee. Were it required, I too would cast my ballot against the soon to be posthumous applicant.

THE LAST WORDS OF THE IMPERIAL HISTORIAN

The Imperial Archive is burning because fire is what happened to the Imperial Archive, but water happens too so perhaps it will be saved, no, look at that, a flame like that, so it looks like the Imperial Archive won't be saved after all. I never imagined it would happen, not to the Imperial Archive, not fire, not that, but now that it has happened I'll find it just as hard ever to imagine it wouldn't. It didn't take much time to burn, not much more time than it would take to burn a sack of archives. It looked exactly like a museum building burning or a library building burning or any building you can imagine burning unimaginably. Someone must have wanted it to burn, someone who didn't like archives or buildings or who liked fire more. Even though I can't imagine such a person, that doesn't mean there isn't one or even that I never met him or even that he isn't me. I might have known that it would happen. It's not as if I wasn't told. I was told and told by the invisible interlocutor, which is why I was on time to watch it burn. I could have brought some water or something else. I could have thrown it at the building or somewhere else. I could have thrown it at the fire. I could have thrown it at the tinder. I could have thrown it at the spark. The Imperial Archive is gone. So are all the archives. That at least is clear.

THE ADVICE OF LI SSU
REGARDING ARCHIVES

Sire, forensic analysis of the burning of the Imperial Archive is difficult, even for those of us who attended. Naturally, ministers and courtiers were invited. Those who were not, turned up anyway. We were there because this was an intellectual and a historical event of the first magnitude.

After all, under ordinary circumstances the burning of archives is unnecessary. Concealment underground or in old walls is as effective. By the time those documents are dug up or dug out, what has not been consumed by parchment fungi has been rendered illegible by antiquation of the diction. Of course, destruction by concealment also can be accomplished by forgetfully moving house.

Furthermore, burning is essentially different from common mutilation. The mutilator actually seeks to amend, even if the operation often results in a curtailment so severe that fragments of phrases and binding alone survive. Interpolation and forgery are merely superior modes of mutilation that, if practised skillfully enough to subvert the content while retaining the form, often prove slightly more successful than outright burning, their dispersive progress through a community being comparable to the low-grade combustion of epidemic fever.

All things considered, then, the burning of the Imperial Archive was an occasion not to be missed, and certainly not by contributing historians. Not that it was an innovation. The burning of archives is as precedented as the collecting of them, which probably explains why archives, however primitive, comprise a material that burns.

Normally, conquerors destroy with zeal the archives of a conquered people. Which consideration does not apply to us. Your people, sire, have long since given up consulting their historians. Besides, when ever have historians and their emperor more completely surrendered themselves to one another?

Founders of a religion tend to burn the holy documents of the previous religion, their action often becoming enshrined as a consecrated device in the new liturgy. Many books are burned by fond relatives who do not desire that the reputation of their family be disgraced by the adding to it of literary merit. Sometimes burning is merely an occasional technique, as in the case of that patron who incinerated the collected manuscripts of a certain poet so that it would not be discovered that his own prodigy had plagiarized.

None of these instances bears the slightest relationship to this one.

There was something about this burning of these archives that made the event of more than passing interest. Traditionally, burning is confined to archives that subvert a people's stability or strike at the root of a people's thought. But in this case every archive was burned, even those in support of everyone and everything. And the question remains: who burned our Imperial Archive and why?

Consider, sire, the Imperial Historian whose own manuscript probably escaped by virtue of its rejection.

The last words of the Imperial Historian scrawled on the fragment clutched in that hand of his that remained does not entirely testify to his involvement. Are "The Last Words of the Imperial Historian" actually his? The style is less histrionic and more colloquial than usual. Nevertheless, might not a certain inelegance, a numb sincerity even, be expected to intrude upon this, his last and, perhaps, his only surviving text? Yes, it is possible to conclude that the charred note is the work of the Imperial Historian on a bad day.

Did the Imperial Historian, then, set the blaze? Did he die in a vain attempt to put it out? If the latter, how unlike him!

He above all men would have recognized that, because the fire was burning, his emperor had neglected to forbid it, and that to attempt to extinguish it was directly to disobey a manifest lack of instruction. By rushing against the flames, he certainly would have known he was committing treason and merited death. As it turned out, he died anyway, leaving us to ponder why, scant hours after the final rejection into the Imperial Archive of his own slight book, he fled the almshouse and was lurking thereabouts. The conundrum is unresolvable and inconsequent.

I thank you, sire, for allowing me to indulge myself in speculation upon this theme at greater length than usually is tolerable. I hope you do not conclude that, in doing so, I have taken undue advantage of your absence. In the confident suspicion that the news of your death and the concealment of your corpse in a vat of soured milk are merely rumours perpetrated by ambitious ministers, here is my present advice.

The burning of the archives was wrong. Even if all the archives in the empire were to be burned, that does not mean that all the archives in the empire would be destroyed. I am not referring to hidden manuscripts such as that of the Imperial Historian. Those will be ferreted out, for the burning of the archives is not one event but many, and every copy of every potential archive at last will be burned, though neither you, sire, nor I, nor those who hid them will live to see it.

I mean, rather, the transmission of archives by word of mouth. Not that archives are saved from burning in that manner. Far worse! Word of mouth results in inaccuracies. Every time an archive is transmitted by word of mouth, a new archive is born! Who will burn those? Especially if they are not transcribed? The task is endless and impossible! At that rate the empire will never die!

The burning of the archives was inadequate. I advise the burning of the historians. With the incineration of himself along with the entire Peer-Review Committee sitting in late-night session, our Imperial Historian has begun the task and shown us the way. Doubtless his manuscript eventually will be located and will achieve the destiny of its author.

THE DEATH OF LI SSU

It is not certain with which imperial catastrophe the death of Li Ssu is properly to be associated. Many commentators opt for the destruction of the Imperial Archive, though at learned colloquia and social gatherings it is not uncommon to overhear the assertion of other venues, among which: the pillage of the Great Granary at Ao, a mountain cavern so capacious it took the combined forces of the peasant rebellion fifteen years to exhaust the stores before dispersing to replant; the sacking of the Imperial Palace by the dynastic conqueror, the real burning of the archives, for it was there that resided all the proscribed material traditionally reserved for the titillation of courtiers; the burying alive of the academicians at Hsienyang, the tremors of which mound did not subside for three months.

Such conjectures will delight vengeful historians of subsequent dynasties, each with an incentive for retrospective delegitimizing and scholarly vilification. For others, it remains unclear precisely which imperial accomplishment or offence justified Li Ssu's terrible execution. Of that event itself there is little reason to doubt the authenticity of the account recorded in the famous Tale of the Saw, though its exquisite concern with the details of truncation and disembowelment and the more salacious aspects of spectator involvement do reflect the particular appetites of that bizarre era.

In any case, it is doubtful that Li Ssu outlived the machinations of Chao Kao and his league of malevolent eunuchs, nor wished to. That he seemed for one long historical moment to hesitate to agree to die probably is due to the universal uncertainty surrounding the death of his imperial master.

So long as he was not certain the Emperor was dead, Li Ssu found it difficult to die. It was to secure Li Ssu's perplexity in this matter that Chao Kao concealed the imperial corpse as long as he did. Then, when he entirely had employed the presence of Li Ssu and could see no other use for him, Chao Kao permitted the Emperor's death to be known, and Li Ssu was freed to select the manner of his own. That Li Ssu chose execution for treason doubtless reflects his depressed state of mind once he realized how entirely he had been exploited by Chao Kao. The precise mode of termination was left to the decision of the eunuch, Li Ssu's last and most excruciating tactical error.

In the final stages of Li Ssu's career, the precise abuses of him by Chao Kao are too readily available as scandal to require retelling. Many social practices and governmental procedures thereby inaugurated are manifest even today. Where else originates the inclination of our current Son of Heaven to appoint ministerial advisors of such banality as to suppress our desire to perceive them? Whence other derives the propensity of our contemporary minorities to enlarge their pitiable status by proliferation? In fact, if it were not for what happened to Li Ssu in the imperial corral and then again at the suzerain hunting lodge and then again upon the pinnacle of the palace gate, you and I should now be wearing our garments buttoned on one side and our hair drawn in plaits down our backs!

At the time, it seemed to all the world that Li Ssu voluntarily sacrificed his office and his prestige in order to shield the perfidious contrivance of a thrusting eunuch, a hateful self-seeking opportunist so blinded by his detestation of whole men that even the imminent collapse of the empire was insufficient reason to halt his intrigues.

Nowadays anyone can see that, faced with a hidden hand, one may well be blind to its manipulation though bruised by its effect. To us it is entirely conceivable that, in those primitive circumstances, even as perspicacious a statesman as Li Ssu could indeed be caused to mistake a horse for a stag, an accident for a homicide, a petition for an invasion, and might be moved to advise his adolescent imperial wards accordingly, thereby undermining their normal perceptions, terrorizing their private confidence, and guiding those impressionable juveniles along the path of incertitude into the morass of suicidal despair, and might permit himself, against his inherent nobility and natural courage and despite the humiliating allegation of optimism, to delay his own demise in the hope of the miraculous resurrection and return of his emperor, and might feel rather foolish at the end of it all.

To an elder of Li Ssu's stature, therefore, his accusation and eradication along with that of his kindred to the sixth degree must have come as something of a relief. Treason, after all, is more honourable than gullibility.

As well, apparently, he missed his friend, the Emperor.

THE LAST WORDS OF LI SSU

A man tortured for information gives the name of his friend because he is afraid to die alone. When they meet for execution, the betrayed forgives his betrayer. In whispers through the blindfold he confides that even now, if he were given the chance, he too would betray another to save himself, no, not to save himself, what is worse, he like his own betrayer would betray another only so as not to die alone.

"That," he whispers, "is the advantage the authorities possess. They are not tempted into betrayal by the possibility of companionship. It is only those who are not friendless, who are tempted and succumb and become betrayers or are betrayed which amounts to the same thing."

"That is why," he whispers through the blindfold and the hood and against the ropes that press his chest and thighs, "that is why loyalty is possible only among the authorities."

All this he whispers to his friend in the long moment before the arrows strike and both men fall alone.

XII

THE GERRHI

In the first moment of his reign, the First Emperor ordered the building of his tomb to begin. He sent word to the Gerrhi who are called "the grave people" or "those who live among the tombs."

THE GERRHI

What follows is an interpretation of the history of the Gerrhi. Wherever possible, antiquarian documents are quoted or provided. These are few. It is a well-known custom of the Gerrhi to lock away their historic script, and to double-seal the contents in hermetic colloquialisms.

There is another difficulty. Every spoken word of each spiritual head of the Gerrhi and all the tales associated with that person are recorded on fragile scrolls. These are accumulated in man-shaped ceramic bean pots that, at the moment of the death of the spiritual head, are submerged in potholes, lava-lakes, and academic libraries.

Even when a document has been obtained and has proved capable of telling, the tale yielded invariably conceals its meaning beneath information of such seamless banality that surely it must be encoded. Several times the light of day itself has proved sufficiently virulent to reduce a manuscript to dust. On one occasion a spiritual head of the Gerrhi succeeded in persuading an archivist to celebrate his deciphering of a secret scroll by immolating himself while clutching it. Indeed, the whimsicality of the Gerrhi has provoked many a scholar to inane behaviour.

THE MOTHER

The founding mother of the tribe of the Gerrhi — traditionally referred to as "the Mother" — is distinguished in antique statuary by her extraordinary round eyes and her dwarfish stature. It is written: "It was by her eyes that she communicated with the deities and by her height that they responded." Now that she has become a deity herself, jocularity with respect to her no longer is possible. Such matters as her miraculous genesis when the rod of a god divided the waters of the world, impregnating them willy-nilly, and leaving the Mother afloat from infancy until her expanding cradle beached itself and she staggered ashore amid the rushes to deliver herself simultaneously of twelve identical sons conceived inviolate and clamouring for breakfast, by now have been rendered unmentionable because of the inability of even orthodox priests to recite them without giggling.

Nevertheless, certain contemporary reports about the Mother have proved canonically irrepressible. Her famous collection of bits of string, her habit of saving little empty containers and the occasional large container to contain the little ones, her constitutional inability to throw away the merest scrap of leftover food, her treatment of domestic injuries by the topical application of hand-gathered mould, the cheerfulness of her solitary singing at high volume and the totality of her tonal deafness, her talent for childish euphemism with respect to the less entertaining bodily functions, her repertoire of moral slogans and optimistic fables that render even cosmic events unnoticeable, her delight at exchanging with neighbours information regarding the defects of absent neighbours, her ability to perceive unhappiness through the walls of the houses of the rich, her inclination to sentimental weeping at births, bankruptcies, and athletic contests, her unflagging respect for the commercial, the legal, the medical, or the theological authority of those professionally empowered to demonstrate her ignorance and to ransack her resources ... all have found a place within the vast mythology of the Mother and her liturgical celebration.

Of more pedestrian influence are her dietary and her sanitary practices. Doubtless inspired by the hellish vistas of the land of the Gerrhi, its uplands permeated with sulphurous geysers, its valleys replete with bubbling marshes and blowholes, the domestic management of the Mother historically comprised only one technique: boiling. In the preparation of meat, every bodily part however lowly its function in however repugnant a creature was rendered comestible when boiled out of recognition and spiced beyond taste. Fruits and vegetables were boiled until amorphous, then mashed to compaction and pickled for eternity. Every article of cookware was boiled before and after use, as was the clothing of those she fed and, as nearly as tolerable, their persons. The contents of her home were boiled seasonally, and from time to time the dwelling itself was purified by incineration. Her entire family was boiled internally by the periodic administration of effervescent salts that traversed their viscera with audible percolation and explosive result, and the congruence between doses and emissions was discussed with the greatest attention to detail during meals.

The Mother herself was never seen to eat. It is written that she was nurtured by the ocular satisfaction of watching her family engorge and evacuate, and was sustained osmotically by the nutritious vapours thus produced. In any case, she moved too fast to settle at table.

Certainly the Mother was the busiest of women. Try as one might to hold her in conversation, one found oneself addressing either side of her nose as it flicked about in search of olfactory dispatches that kept her aware of what was happening in her kitchen, or one was left awaiting a reply from the vacant space that had contained her little figure before it whipped around a corner to quench a catastrophe or to instigate one.

This restless manner was complemented by her propensity to adopt flowerless houseplants of woebegone demeanour and domestic pets of terminal constitution. Indeed, nothing is known of her putative husband beyond the frailty of his digestion and the duration of his demise. So careful had been her attendance upon him, so painstaking her ministrations, so sustaining her boiling, so soothing her salts, that he had outlived his fatal moment by decades. At last he vaporized entirely, and was commemorated by a pictorial representation of his silhouette that likewise vanished among the scores of reliquaries crowding her kitchen shelf.

Under the enthusiastic ministrations of the Mother, dying became an endless affair of poultices and comatose reveries during which she pacified spasms, commiserated wheezes, dissolved clots, dispersed vapours. When blessed terminality at last arrived, she sealed every aperture, fractured every joint. By ancient report the home of the Mother resembled something between a field hospital and a crypt within which she rushed from chamber to chamber, boiling furniture, dispensing homeopathic gruel, preparing ghastly tenants for interment, and screaming nasal laments that sounded to the uninitiated like happy off-key jingles.

A lifetime of attendance upon the not-yet-dead developed in the Mother her most notable characteristic: the habit of expecting the worst and, when the worst did not occur, of bringing it about so that she could continue to be of service. It is to the Mother that the traditional Gerrhi colloquial salutation "What's wrong?" may be attributed.

This inclination took the form of Matriarchal Advice, examples of which have not survived because they were never heard. That is, they were heard but they were not listened to. No, even that assertion is not entirely possible because there is evidence that the recipients of Matriarchal Advice behaved in specific contradiction to it, thereby occasioning a new piece of Matriarchal Advice.

Perhaps no Matriarchal Advice has been handed down because none actually was given? Our authority for this confusion is the sole authenticated statement of the Mother herself, to wit: "You never listen how many times have I told you not to there now maybe next time you." Despite the likelihood of textual corruption, we may thereby conclude that Matriarchal Advice comprised either a question to which there was only one answer or an apostrophic sigh addressed to a celestial auditor or a chronicle of disasters disguised as a warning against them, and it always was repeated again and again and again and again and again and again. Electing to deliver Matriarchal Advice in a variety of forms equally irritating suggests that the Mother intended it to be impossible to accept. Its incessant reiteration implies the endless succession of catastrophes guaranteeing its perpetual re-employment. Further research on the matter is too exhausting to contemplate.

It was in this spirit that the Mother of the Gerrhi guided her twelve sons into the hillocks of vicissitude and the quagmires of eventuality until she landed them, whimpering but intact, upon the wide and fertile plain of majority, whereupon they abandoned her with no thanks or a forwarding address. On the eve of their departure, the Mother disappeared for a moment into the kitchen. She emerged, her round eyes radiant, clutching scrolls: the Twelve Favourite Recipes. She distributed these among her sons, neglecting to mention that in each she had omitted an ingredient without which none would attain the precise fragrance of her own oven. Thus was assured the universal distribution of the Twelve Favourite Recipes, as well as the preservation of the eternal authority of the Mother.

How the Mother of the Gerrhi met her own end is a matter most unknowable. As she loudly predicted on innumerable occasions, the departure of her twelve sons left no one to perform upon her the intricate offices of the dying that she had inaugurated. That circumstance probably is why she disappears from history and may never have died at all. There is a legend that, in one form or another, she resides to this day in the thermal marshes of the land of the Gerrhi where the morning mist that rushes to the vortex of the sun may, in fact, be cooking steam.

TWELVE BROTHERS

Although there were twelve there may as well have been one, for each contained the identical commixture of contradictory passions. Thus it has become conventional to speak of the twelve as of one, and to name him "Twelve Brothers."

When Twelve Brothers left home, he secretly moved next door. He visited the Mother only to obtain clean underclothing and to harangue her on his need for independence. Her unrecorded replies to her multiple son elicited a series of tirades from him known to the Gerrhi as the "Thunderous Prophecies." These comprise the Prophecy of Wild Behaviour, the Prophecy of

Social Sinking, the Prophecy of Self Hurt, the Prophecy of Rancorous Music, the Prophecy of Foreign Gods, the Prophecy of Cosmetic Disfigurement, the Prophecy of Indolence, the Prophecy of Illiterate Antipensive Dis-scholasticism, the Prophecy of Bad Companions, the Prophecy of No Companions, the Prophecy of Nonproprietorial Immaterialism, the Prophecy of Theft.

The demeanour of Twelve Brothers dramatically changed with the pronouncement of each of these prophecies, as did the idiom of his invective, the repertoire of his insulting gestures, his costume, his hairstyle, his accent, his complexion, and his height. In fact, at this stage it became difficult for the Mother to recognize the particular persona of Twelve Brothers she was being required to listen to at any moment, and impossible to predict which would appear next. More often than not several guises materialized simultaneously and, by the time the Mother discerned the distinctive features of Twelve Brothers beneath them, he had departed in righteous fury to activate a homicidal intention or to fulfill a suicidal threat. The period of time occupied by the Thunderous Prophecies is impossible to specify. For the Mother it seemed aeons, for Twelve Brothers only the sum of the intervals between hairstyles.

Though Matriarchal Advice offered in response to the Thunderous Prophecies has not survived, it must have been sufficiently infuriating to provoke the several reprisals known collectively as the "Neo-Conventionalism." Those amounted to Twelve Brothers entirely belying every self-prophecy, and eventually settling into a variety of professional occupations of such stupefying orthodoxy that they rendered their practitioners interchangeable.

Not only were these jobs tediously respectable, they also were mutually causative. Specifically, the compiling of columns of figures in ledgers somehow came to govern the fortunes of mercantile enterprises that rose and fell in competitive abrasion, occasioning the fracture of contractual obligations and precipitating judicial procedures sufficiently protracted to give rise to digestive disorders necessitating homeopathic therapies, the inevitable inadequacies of which provoked the need for spiritual consolation and, eventually, for sepulchral entombment. Thus Twelve Brothers professionally progressed from accountancy through commerce, law, medicine, theology, and mortuary science without once changing clients. His ultimate employment as a funeral-director would have delighted the Mother beyond description, and that probably is why Twelve Brothers never told her of it.

How was it possible for Twelve Brothers to abide such contradictions? He did it by means of that innovation of temperament forever associated with his name: "Selective Memory." By definition the closer one scrutinizes Selective Memory, the more it recedes from definition. Its results, however, are legendary.

The practitioner of Selective Memory appears able to recall only those aspects of his behaviour that accommodate present action, and entirely to forget those that impede it. He can obliterate from his consciousness whatever torment he has inflicted upon whichever limb, organ, or sensibility of himself or another person, often believing every injury to have been perpetrated not by him but by one or several of eleven siblings who cannot be located at the moment.

Whether the practitioner of Selective Memory is wholly insane or just stupid can never be determined because he so entirely believes his own version of the recent past that he forgets to ask and neglects to answer any questions that would contradict it. Thus, domestic hatred, collegial murder, horse theft, free enterprise, amatory blackmail, and contract abuses of all kinds are rendered tolerable by the expedient of genuinely forgetting the original terms of the agreement. Even today it is only by means of the zealous application of Selective Memory that the Gerrhi as a tribe continues to outlive the Vortex, a historic event so cataclysmic that no individual son of the Gerrhi could survive being required to recall it or, if he did, to live long after accomplishing the recollection.

Collectively, this state of mind is referred to as the "Unconscious."

In the case of Twelve Brothers, Selective Memory enabled him to pass from rebellious youth to quiescent manhood without, in the face of all evidence to the contrary, perceiving any contradiction in his own behaviour.

This epoch or episode in the life or the lives of one or of twelve of its founding fathers or sons altered forever the nature of the Gerrhi. Thitherto, an unthinking obedience to the will of the Mother had been sufficient to establish tribal identity, and to prevent such important matters as class invasion, prestige error, and status pollution. Thereafter, it was deemed essential publicly to prove that an individual would survive adolescence and was destined to accomplish a successful transition into harmless maturity. Thus was devised and enshrined the single most important Gerrhi ceremonial, that famous initiation rite that establishes tribal solidarity and social stratification in a manner far more dependable than ordinary indices like arranged marriage, selective schooling, or the number of seat-holes in the family outhouse, namely, the "Ritual of the Honey Cakes."

The Ritual of the Honey Cakes is a tedious sacrament inflicted upon every male Gerrhi at the first sign of that aggressive moralizing that signals the onset of puberty. The celebration is attended by the whole tribe. The initiate youth is required to chant an antique formula learned by rote and made to sound incomprehensible by his incomprehension of it and poor pronunciation. Then, at the precise moment of the final incantation, the entire congregation formally stampedes into a backroom and proceeds to swallow honey cakes provided for the event at the expense of the youth's family.

By the time the initiate has divested himself of his ritual attire, a uniform of humiliating solemnity and unbreakable starch, there are no honey cakes left for him. His reaction at that instant determines which of the adult communities within the tribe his disposition naturally entitles him to join. Thus, righteous anger precipitates him toward the constabulary community, flexible accommodation toward the political, tearful frustration toward the priestly, bewilderment toward the military, relief toward the gastronomic, and so on. On the rare occasion that the candidate is overcome by amusement, he automatically is consigned to the artistic community where his insights can be attributed to cynicism.

The Ritual of the Honey Cakes never fails.

When it does, the delinquent is declared "Non-Gerrhi" and is erased and forgotten.

THE ORPHAN

Twelve Brothers sought wives as unlike the Mother as possible. In that era, unfortunately, squint-eyed elongated females of lethargic manner and slovenly hygiene were in short supply. Consequently most of the brothers died without issue and in abdominal discomfort. Two of the brothers succeeded in mating, but simultaneously with the same female. Each disclaimed paternity and insisted that his brother and his betrothed be executed for fornication, which in the case of the woman was accomplished twice. Her posthumous spawn was named the "Orphan," and was recognized to be the legitimate heir to the spiritual leadership of the Gerrhi and its sole surviving member.

The Orphan was an hermaphroditic creature, promiscuous by temperament and of a theatrical disposition. Addicted to auto-copulation following prolonged rehearsal in the presence of mirrors, the Orphan repeatedly impregnated itself. This entertainment accomplished two historic events: the repopulating of the tribe, and the establishment of its unbreakable heritage of intra-propagation. Dating from the era of the Orphan, no member of the Gerrhi has bred with other than another Gerrhi, and tribal marriages are celebrated with an intensity comprehensible only to those who have experienced the fervour of embracing themselves. Otherwise it is difficult to perceive the precise contribution of the Orphan to the cultural progress of the tribe.

It is said that the Orphan acquired the powers of levitation, magnetism, remote control, extraterrestrial audition, spectral discourse, and future perception, but the most that could be expected in public was a quick display of weather prediction. It is also said that it was the Orphan who invented "Parabolic Utterance." That claim presents inherent problems of authentication.

Parabolic Utterance has nothing whatever to do with the parable, a folk genre resurrected by aspiring godheads anxious to acquire the patina of historicity. Rather, the rhetorical structure of Parabolic Utterance is that of the parabola, a curve that forms an apparent solid by rotating about its own axis and running off into infinity without once meeting a line that seems to approach it. Thus, every word spoken by the practitioner of Parabolic Utterance — usually in a measured rhythm with a pronounced lilt — tends toward meaning but has none. It is as pointless to try to determine who invented Parabolic Utterance as it is to imagine why anyone would trouble to employ it. It may as well have been the Orphan, so traditionally that is whom it is taken to be.

The only other historical legacy of the Orphan is the dance. Certainly it was the Orphan who devised and named the "Dance Hut," probably for voyeuristic purposes since there is no evidence that the Orphan itself ever danced. Indeed, the only historical testament of the Orphan at recreation is a prehistoric limestone outline reclining across several hillsides in a posture of post-masturbatory languor, though the figure represented is sufficiently impressionistic or eroded to suggest that it may record the track of a dried-up mountain stream.

Perhaps such an imprecise legacy is only to be expected from an obscene monster whose descendants have every reason to try to obliterate its memory. For example, how is a tribe wishing to be taken seriously to acknowledge as a primal progenitor one who achieved a fatal paroxysm after accidentally catching sight of a reflection of itself in its bath, and expired bellowing an apocalyptic Parabolic Utterance of rampant self-love?

It is from the Mother that the Gerrhi derived a taste for suffering and from Twelve Brothers that the tribe absorbed an aptitude for compromise. It is the Orphan who bequeathed to the posterity of the tribe an obsession with the ritual re-enactment of distress.

An Orphanic strain runs through all the Gerrhi. To this day the most conventional Gerrhi family may find itself unexpectedly cursed with a flame-haired evasive-eyed inconsistency that refuses to cry or to suckle or to sleep. How such an infant survives is a mystery indecipherable even to its parents, but survive it does, lying silent on its cot and, in its vigil, seeming not so much to watch as to evaluate.

On the occasion of such a birth, the afflicted family relinquishes the normal hilarities, and formal sessions of lamentation begin. These continue until the child is old enough to be removed to the Dance Hut and abandoned there. Removal and abandonment occur as soon as the infant shows signs of commencing to dance.

The dance of an infant Orphanic begins with the eyes, or behind them. At first it seems you are being scrutinized, but no, for the infant's eyes apparently continue to move in the dark. What is it they watch? Whatever it is, it seems to flicker about the room. It hovers above the crib, beside it, beneath. It clings to the ceiling, slides down every wall, darts under the bedclothes, and emerges at the bedstead foot, vanishes up the chimney or out the window, and enters again upon your own left cheek, for it is there the gaze is fixed at the moment you light the nursery lamp. Whatever it thinks it sees, the eyes of the infant Orphanic already have taught it to dance.

Sometimes Parabolic Utterance expressed in song precedes dancing, sometimes not. Neither has anything in common with those activities practised as amusements. There is nothing amusing about the dancing or the singing of an Orphanic Gerrhi. For one thing, once an Orphanic has begun to dance or to sing it does not ever stop. No one has seen an adult Orphanic when it is not dancing. No one has seen an adult Orphanic when it is not singing.

It is not easy for an Orphanic to begin. It is, moreover, with the greatest of difficulty that an infant Orphanic commences to move, somewhat, a limb. They are heavy these limbs of an infant Orphanic, having never been moved before. But they move. They dance. And dance. The formation of the dance is not a circle. The formation seems a circle. For days, for months, the Orphanic traces the identical path round and round the floor of the Dance Hut. So it seems to those who watch only for days, for months. The Orphanic dances for decades, for generations. The Orphanic's is a lifetime of dance, and the dancer knows the dance it dances is not a circle.

Imagine an Orphanic dancing. Round it dances, round and round, not only round the Dance Hut, but round and round itself, arms raised, fingers clenched, eyes afloat, round and round it turns as round and round the floor it goes. The other Orphanics, are they not like the first? As like the first as like to like, and round and round they —

Wait! Detach yourself from the dancers! Observe the dance!

A Dance Hut full of dancers, a dance that fills the hut, yet the dancers never touch? Their orbits, see, their orbits differ, and their years. Those on the outskirts, those of the dance of the greatest arc, those of the greatest number of turns, those like the dancer we first imagined, those are the youngest Orphanics of all. Those within the peripheral arcs, those are the elders, their cycles smaller, their turnings fewer. Those within the arcs of the elders, those within the arcs of those, older and older the dancers are, slower and slower their dance, fewer and fewer their turns. And that Orphanic nearest the centre, why it hardly dances at all! Its cycles are but an arm's breadth radius. Its turns are but one or two. And its song? Ah, there it is! A murmur only, little more than an exhalation, hardly that.

Imagine again our youngest dancer, coattails flying, mouth agape, dance and dancer, song and singer, filling the hut, the hall, the air. See that same Orphanic years and years from now, years and years from then, how low its arms, how lax its fists, how soft its chant, how slow its dance, how much nearer to the centre. See it decades thence, a quiet stepper now. As you watch, it nears the point at which the floorboards join. It reaches the point.

It stops. It is no Orphanic. It is nothing, not even a Gerrhi. Its dance is done, not a circle but a spiral, a dance of death not life.

SELF-STUDY

The dispersal of the Gerrhi to every sector of the empire, the aeons of their effort to melt like rain into various regional subsoils and their perpetual re-emergence as Gerrhi, distinct and indivisible as stone, the saga of their ejection from every acre of social fertility culminating in the Vortex and their virtual annihilation at the hands of a mad land baron who believed he was responding to the imperatives of cultural husbandry by collecting the Gerrhi together and grinding to powder their every anthropological root, the grudging return to the primordial swamp of a battered remnant that hardly knew itself to be Gerrhi except for a talent at spiced cookery and an unquenchable taste for death ... those are tales too often told, and rather depressing.

This much, however, can be maintained with some degree of cheerfulness and with more Gerrhiatric evidence than is sensible. During the period of the "Evictions" there transpired the "Great Age of Self-Study."

Perhaps Self-Study began as an authentic search for comfort and for guidance among the excavated words of the tribal forebears? Perhaps, on occasion, an ancient textual revelation was accorded a practical modern application? Perhaps, once or twice, something worthwhile was made to happen? Very soon, however, the delight of the Gerrhi in the study of the Gerrhi for the sake of the delight in the study obviated any original purpose, provoking one eminent spiritual leader to conclude with a grin, "More and more is known about less and less! Eventually everything will be known about nothing, and we can begin again!" It was during the era of Self-Study that the hand mirror became the official emblem of the Gerrhi.

Of the huge and futile exercise of Self-Study examples abound. These include the following. Endless discussions of

the prohibitions to be derived from the dietary practices of the
Mother, including such provocative issues as whether it is permitted to consume a fish that was boiled in water which water
itself had not been boiled in boiled water before it was boiled
to boil the fish, a debate that produced the tradition of handing
down from generation to generation containers of pre-boiled
water, though it never resolved the problem of who boiled the
first sanctified fish and just how that marvel was accomplished.
An entire school of experimental study devoted to the attempt
to manufacture an homunculus from an agglomeration of cattle
dung. Several hundred volumes of priestly discussions concerning conflicting interpretations by various disquisitional seminars
of the significance of an edict forbidding unreasonably prolonged priestly discussions issued by a tribal ancient immediately
before he dismissed the disciples of his own disquisitional sem-
inar for failing to agree on the interpretation of an earlier edict
limiting priestly discussions issued by an ancient tribal ancient
who was throttled accidentally under several hundred volumes
of priestly discussions. And so on.

It is no historical happenstance that the Great Age of Self-
Study coincided with the Evictions. The former was caused by
the latter and, in turn, it was used to justify them. The way of it
was this.

The sons of the Mother abandoned their parent as soon
as they were mobile. Mistaking this ingratitude for a tradition,
their own children followed suit and likewise theirs. In less than
a chronicle paragraph, no community was without its contingent
of elder Gerrhi bewailing their loneliness, and younger Gerrhi
covering their ears and preparing to leave home. As a preventive
against this generational desertion, elder Gerrhi in every community developed the identical stratagem. They invented Self-Study
and inflicted it upon their children.

Certainly Self-Study had the effect of anchoring the tribe
by causing the young to carry within their nature such a ballast
of taboo, procedure, unresolved quandary, and generalized guilt

that mobility of any kind became impractical. As well, the more one studied oneself, the more of one's self there was to study, and the very selfhood of the Gerrhi swelled. Thus, by the time any Gerrhi grew old enough to think of quitting his elders, he knew too much to be able to move.

As Self-Study proliferated upon itself, however, it became more and more difficult for an individual Gerrhi to learn all that was available. And, of course, as it became harder and harder to be a Gerrhi, it also became entirely impossible to cease to be one. In effect, Self-Study became an identification device ensuring that, wherever Gerrhi dwelt, they would remain recognisable as Gerrhi, and could never be mistaken for any other. Since young and old were bound together by immobility, the Gerrhi became as easy to locate as they were to grab. It was during this period that adult Gerrhi, in pious imitation of the blessed physiognomy of the Mother, took to cultivating a naive roundness of eye, useful when pleading for mercy and in everyday commercial transactions.

The unexpected result of this entire process was that, in order to move, Gerrhi youths no longer had any need to abandon their parents. Whole families identified as Gerrhi could be evicted together. Self-Study accelerated the very process that it had been invented to arrest! Thereafter the history of the Gerrhi became a cycle of banishment, resettlement, re-banishment of families, of communities and, eventually, of the entire tribe.

The question remaining from the period of the Evictions is this: why were the Gerrhi evicted? Self-Study provides no answer. In fact, there is no anecdotal or scriptural evidence that the Gerrhi ever considered the question. Perhaps they were too busy packing?

There are several non-Gerrhi theories. Unfortunately, these are uniformly unconvincing. It has been noted, for example, that each Eviction was accompanied by a confiscation of property. Yet, had the Gerrhi been sufficiently prosperous to attract expropriation, why had they not been relieved of some of their property and required to remain to accumulate more, thereby supplying their exploiters with a regular source of income?

Other invalid hypotheses include these. The visible presence of a tribe so thoroughly matriarchal made it difficult for neighbouring tribes to restrain the dominance of their own females. The sheer irritation of beholding a tribe that resists assimilation into one's own community by means of the contemplation of itself, a phenomenon equivalent to living with an agglomeration of permanent adolescents. The widely circulated reports of clandestine meetings in closed sessions at famous unknown underground locations of a secret order of Gerrhi assassins, sea-poisoners, and pet-butchers committed to acquiring cryptic control over the destiny of the universe by the systematic extermination of non-Gerrhi, using methods too heinous to mention including discount wholesale merchandising.

Not one of these explanations satisfies. Taken together, they cancel each other. It is doubtful if the matter ever will be resolved. Whatever their cause, the Evictions did take place, and after them came the "Vortex."

VOICES FROM THE VORTEX

A man is a dying animal. A man is a builder of mirrors. Everything a man builds mirrors a dying animal.

◆

One does not wrong whom one hates; one hates whom one wrongs. Love my enemy? I may love him and love him, yet he may do me wrong. He may wrong me and wrong me, yet not because of hate. Love is not the problem. Hate is not the problem. Wrong is the problem. Were my enemy to wrong me nevermore, we should both be free of love and hate, and go about our business.

◆

Why can't non-Gerrhi tell Gerrhi jokes? With non-Gerrhi, you can't be sure they know they're joking. With Gerrhi, you can be sure they know they're not.

◆

Of course we are comedians. In the chamber of our empoisoning, we remark upon the plop and the hiss of the lethal pellet. We imagine ourselves to be the pellet, alone aware of the effect of its drop, unwilling to drop, dropping despite itself, dissolving in a giggle of effervescence. Our comedy is no evasion. It is how we see. We are as our enemy would have us: powerless and aware. We see what our enemy permits us to see: the underbelly of the world. Underbellies are hilarious. We look up and we laugh. You are pained by what we see. Underbellies are sensitive.

◆

The way of it is this. We have always signified dying. The mad land baron thinks, by killing us, he will do away with dying. He is different from those who came before him only in the magnitude of his fear of dying. Otherwise he is just like them, superstitious, hopeful. That is why we can never resemble our enemy. There is not one among us who dreams he will live forever.

◆

You will forget us, but you will not forget our eyes.

◆

Hanging on this lip of time, fully informed, bewildered.

◆

Who are the enemy? By their institutions you shall know them.

THE VORTEX

The Vortex is a period of Gerrhi history which it is difficult to contemplate. Conversation on the subject soon falls silent. Statistical evidence inflates it beyond comprehension. Eyewitness accounts erase it with particulars. Rhyming Parabolic Utterance comes nearer to the feel of it, but no one can be made to bear the hearing.

By a scrutiny of antique holy texts in a certain light, it is possible to prove the Vortex to have been prophesied, which increases one's entertainment in the scrutinising of holy texts. Likewise, the reputation of the Vortex may be invoked by descendants of its victims as a justification for the performance by them of commensurate atrocities upon others. Indeed, there is no doubt that the Vortex can be variously useful.

As in every case of widespread blaming or inbred shaming, however, the attitude of bystanders is based upon a common premise. The reality of the historical event is too enormous, its enormity too real, for it to contain no meaning. Yet there was no meaning in the Vortex, none other than the meaning of a vortex: to circle, to absorb, to absorb, to pulverize, to pulverize, to disgorge, to disgorge, to move on.

It is hard to bear that there was no meaning. Even those in the midst of it thought there was a meaning. Yet there was none, and they who vanished in the Vortex are gone forever and for no good reason in this world.

There is, of course, one way to deal with the Vortex, one way to give it cause and purpose, to learn from it, to teach. That is why the Orphanics dance, to invoke the Vortex, to relive it and to die. But, then, their grief is greater than is common, for they should never have been born.

What is more difficult to understand is why, after the Vortex, our contemporary generation of Gerrhi, that battered remnant, have claimed as their heartland the slope of an active volcano, how they came to reside there, and what, if anything, ever will dislodge them.

THE PARABLE OF THE GERRHI

Every once in a while, the earth speaks to us out of the mouth of the mountain and sends us a river of fire. It is not a happy time. It is not unexpected.

Of course we parade to the edge of the river of fire bearing holy articles, but we do not think to stop it. If the river of fire consumes our houses, that is unfortunate, but it has happened before, and always the river has cooled, and always we have built new houses and planted new crops of peppers and waited for the next river of fire.

Every one of us has been asked many times: "Why do you live here? Why not build your houses and plant your peppers where there are no rivers of fire?" Everyone asks that. Sometimes we ask it ourselves.

The answer is always the same. Yes, our peppers would grow elsewhere, though probably not with a flesh half so red and their famous taste of ash. Yes, our houses would be easier to build elsewhere, though probably not on foundations half so firm as the petrified waves of our last river of fire. Why do we live here on the shoulder of the mountain in the path of rivers of fire? We live here because it is here that the earth speaks to us.

You will not understand that reason. We do not expect you to understand it. The earth has never spoken to you.

THE IMPERIAL TOMB

It is strange that the Gerrhi are called "the grave people" and "those who live among the tombs." In their entire land there is not a single tomb and, if there are graves, they are unmarked. How could they build a tomb, how could they dig a grave in a soil that is either bog or solidified lava? What, then, do the Gerrhi do with their dead? Are the bodies dropped into the swamp or fed to the volcano? There seems no third alternative. Unless, of course, the Gerrhi never die, which certainly is the opposite of everyone's impression. The Gerrhi always die. And then, apparently, there is nothing left of them.

The reputation of the Gerrhi is due entirely to the Emperor. It was he who named them "the grave people" and "those who live among the tombs." Once the Emperor had called attention to the Gerrhi, of course, no one could fail to see them, particularly when the Emperor made it known that it was they who were conscripted to build his tomb.

After that proclamation, historians tumbled over one another to examine the Gerrhi. Theologues were driven deep into sacred texts where they discovered all manner of Gerrhi immanence. Parabolic Utterers invented prehistoric myths so as to acquire a vocabulary of rhythmic metaphor alluding to the Gerrhi. Sneak thieves and journalists and entrepreneurs of every inclination and style adopted Gerrhi turns of phrase and hand gestures. Entire schools of cookery were devolved from the recipes of the Mother, as well as new methods of dietary tract purgation, in particular among the fatally ill. Even the offspring of the mad land baron who instigated the Vortex solemnly consecrated their lives to the acquisition of personal wealth so that their descendants might afford to effect restitution for the intemperance of their forebear's mad forebear, if by that time there were any Gerrhi left to compensate and if they remembered to claim.

In fact, the people of the empire entered into the compulsive spirit of Gerrhiatric morbidity with such enthusiasm that the Emperor must have wished he never had mentioned the tribe. Especially galling was the spontaneous, empire-wide, reign-long competition to design the Emperor's tomb, the only apparent reward for which was the pleasure of knowing him to be in it. Unsolicited recommendations ranged from celestial suspension in an inter-galactic web to oceanic dispatch in a bottle. One of the most intriguing designs was discovered among the reliquary papers of Meng, the Emperor's architect and general, shortly after he misinterpreted his master's praise as an instruction to kill himself. Meng's proposal was truly imperial. It combined pacifist politics with deficit financing.

Meng suggested that, as the Emperor felt his death approach, he take up residence in his favourite palace, withdraw to his most comfortable bedchamber, and don his most pleasing pyjamas. Terminality itself, Meng recommended, should be precipitated by a self-administered fatal excess of whichever voluptuary joy the Emperor's enfeebled condition still enabled him to indulge.

Entombment would commence forthwith. A mountain would be compiled over the entire palace. To accomplish that immense work which would become the sole occupation of several subsequent generations of the imperial army, Meng suggested one concession to symbolism. At each level of earthen encrustation, life-size models of the officers of the day would be laminated in. To acquire authentic reproductions of those living gentlemen, Meng advised that each be seized while asleep, encased in modelling clay, and enkilned at sufficiently high temperature to provide ceramic fixing of the outer shell, incineration of the body within, and an individualized expression of amazement on the face.

After Meng's death and prior to the enactment of legislation posthumously protecting architectural copyright, the Emperor instructed the Gerrhi to abandon all previous designs and to build a replica of precisely such a sepulchre. This is the tomb at Mount Li about which perennially there is such a fuss, the one preceded by a vast subterranean ceramic army, the gradual excavation of which enables it to accomplish its original strategic assignment of delaying an assault by the curious upon the burial chamber.

Down the aeons, such has been the fascination of anthropologists, archaeologists, de-mythologists, tale-spinners, and other grave-robbers that their covert erosions and midnight demolitions have all but levelled Mount Li, despite the probability that it is Meng and not the Emperor who is buried there. Because of this incessant activity, the actual tomb of the Emperor — identical to the one at Mount Li but located elsewhere, perhaps not even within the land of the Gerrhi — remains undetected and unmolested. Such, the Emperor might have said of Meng, is loyalty after death.

Of course, the essential difference between Meng's proposal for the imperial sepulchre and its eventual realization is that, instead of removing to a palace and entombing it under a mountain, the Emperor lay still and pulled his empire down over him. And that historic achievement has little to do with ghastly tribes or witty suicidal architects.

XIII

THE DEATH OF THE
FIRST EMPEROR

When the First Emperor died the first of his many deaths, to mortals it seemed that he was born. Even then, at the crack of the dawn of his day among us — midwives scurrying with bedsheets, balsams, the father grasping a cue-stick but scarcely able to drop a shot without suffering a vision of his wife agape — even then the First Emperor must have been disappointed. Looking back, he saw the aperture of his awakening. Looking forward, he saw a red mist. Neither was beautiful. Neither was important. Why, the First Emperor must have wondered, why had he been wrenched by spasms too terrific to recall out of one moist receptacle into another? Unless, of course, being the First Emperor, he already knew and was waiting to inform us.

IMPERIAL GOSSIP ...

... REGARDING CHAO KAO

infamous seed of an infamous family, his father having committed a crime for which the punishment is banishment amid the barbarians, his mother was sold into slavery where she had illicit relations with various brutish masters and was punished by execution at the insistence of the wife of one of them as well as by the mandatory mutilation of her surviving bastard, who eventually parlayed his reputation as a partial castrate prized for endless copulation and supple fingers to gain access to the imperial court, where he succeeded through subterfuge and rose through betrayal until, as a minion on the final farewell imperial tour of his aged ailing master, he awaited or abetted or commissioned the Emperor's death, concealed the corpse in a cart-load of rotting fish, used the imperial seal to order the disposal of the Regent Designate (the unlucky General Meng) and the Principal Advisor (the renowned Li Ssu), and then, in conspiracy with a league of malevolent fellow eunuchs, addressed himself to the juvenile Heirs Apparent (anonymous in gender and number for reasons of security), terrifying them with theatrical apparitions, tormenting them with imagined crimes, maddening them with contrived invasions, and, upon the occasion of their collective suicide, dared to ascend the peacock throne himself only to be instantaneously torn to pieces by an unimaginative populace who could not understand how a gelding planned to establish a dynasty.

In the final days of the empire, Chao Kao wielded much power and his deeds influenced the lives of many, but no book of the Emperor contains his life. Thereafter, no matter how important a man may be, if he is wholly without admirable parts, history chooses to ignore him as much as possible.

Thus, if good is rewarded by the perpetuation of its name, then the reward for evil is oblivion, which probably is why evil so vigorously seeks its reward in the here and the now.

... REGARDING CHEN SHE

Though eventually he invented an aristocratic pedigree, he was merely an ambitious farm boy who rose from the lanes and the alleyways of the empire, squatted, used language full of peasant vituperation, and, when a member of the literati approached him in scholar's costume, snatched off the erudite's bonnet and urinated into it.

In charge of a relief detachment of forced labour conscripted to guard the Emperor's tomb, Chen She was prevented from reaching his destination on time by a heavy rain that rendered the way impassable. Remembering the legal punishment for tardiness, he reasoned thus: "Arrival means execution. Absence means revolt. Let us choose the remoter death."

Thereupon, he and his cabal of convicts raided the imperial tomb, removed the weapons from the ceramic army that no longer required them, and set forth against whatever emperor there happened to be. Thereby began the establishment of the next empire.

Thus, bad law buries its makers, and bad weather makes a hero of anyone.

... REGARDING KAO TSU

As a young soldier, he frequented the shop of the old dame Wang and the old lady Wu to buy his wine on credit and to drink it on the spot. One day while he was sleeping it off in the backroom, coloured clouds were seen in the air above him.

Thereafter, every time he came into the wine shop to drink and to sleep, customers would gather to see the wonderful clouds, and the old women would sell several times more wine than usual. At the end of the fiscal year, therefore, they would add up their accounts and forgive Kao Tsu his wine debt.

Before moving to his new capital city where, as emperor, he inevitably would be beyond reach, Kao Tsu insisted on visiting once more the wine shop of the old dame Wang and the old lady Wu. There the successor to the First Emperor and the founder of a dynasty that would last four hundred years invited all those whom he had known in former times, and he himself carried round the wine keg. He drank and he danced with everyone, laughing girls and married women, layabouts and poor wage labourers, temple boys and hardened farmers. Several days were passed telling tales.

Finally taking his leave, Kao Tsu said, "Although I must go and work in the capital city, when I am dead my spirit will return to reside at the wine shop of Wang and Wu. In the back room look for a coloured cloud!"

Thus even the mighty have lovable underbellies, for it must be remembered that this is the same Kao Tsu who, when pursued by Chen She in desperate chase, threw his children from his carriage to lighten it.

THE EMPEROR'S MADNESS

The Emperor has gone mad with failure. In fact, some say, it is his very madness that has kept him at his post so long and, since it is failure that made him mad, failure too has been a political necessity.

The Emperor, some say, is divinely mad, mad with the effort of bringing the empire to birth, and then mad again with the anguish of watching it die. For him, some say, madness was endemic, desirable even, certainly unsurprising. Without it, that spark that enabled the Emperor to father the empire would have been extinguished, might never have been ignited, for what else but madness is the will to bring to birth in this vale of dissolution and decay? It is said the Emperor often says as much, though most of us consider it further proof that he is mad.

That is the difference between us and the Emperor. We are sane or we believe ourselves to be, which perhaps is our particular madness. We have to believe that we are sane in order to explain to ourselves the obvious fact that not one of us is an emperor. Does it surprise you that we understand these things? It should not. Madness, you see, is not stupidity, not even among those whose delusion it is that they are not mad. We understand that too though, unfortunately, it marks the limit of our understanding.

It is in this respect that the Emperor has failed. He has not enabled us to understand him, which is doubtless a failure though hardly a fault since the Emperor's real task is to understand us which, of course, he does, and his work enshrines that accomplishment.

We also do not understand his work, which is unavoidable for, in that respect, we are without understanding. In fact, the Emperor says, our failure to understand his work may be proof of its success. Which is an insight, is it not? A truth? At the very least, does it not sound like something the Emperor might have said?

THE EMPEROR RESIGNS

Our emperor has resigned. He cannot do it, you say. Being the first, the Emperor cannot resign unless by death. That may be true of other emperors, even of other first emperors, but not of ours. Our emperor has resigned and not by death, for it is said that he lives and yet there is no doubt that he is no longer our emperor. He himself has told us it is so, and we are not used to doubting his word.

How did the Emperor resign? As he reigned, in response to our will. The Emperor, as you may have observed, was not an ordinary emperor. He did not, like others, become emperor by birth. No indeed, before him there was no emperor, and we were obliged to will him to become our emperor so as to save ourselves from the lack of him.

Now we are obliged to will him to resign. Why do we will him to resign? For the same reason we willed him to become our emperor in the first place. Why did we will that? You must ask him, for he is emperor or was, and only the Emperor can know why he obliges us to will anything.

AFTER THE EMPEROR

What comes after the Emperor is difficult to imagine, yet it is we who remain so there is no one else to do it. That, indeed, is the true legacy of the Emperor: now that he is no longer among us, it is difficult to imagine ourselves without him. Which makes it difficult to imagine ourselves.

It is, however, easy to imagine others. For that exercise we need only observe them. Others or their ancestors or their progeny are there before our very eyes or just behind them. The appearance of others may help us to imagine ourselves but does little to clarify the whole picture, to populate it, to establish who we are now that the Emperor is no longer ours.

Others, after all, may not have known the Emperor in life, his life or theirs, a situation that becomes ever more certain as the generations proceed. What, for example, do you, the present reader, know of him, our emperor? Having read this far, you know only that he lived, perhaps only that he lived in the words you have read which, as the authors of many of those words, is something we already knew without your assistance.

It is conventional to observe that we his people have no life after the Emperor. Such an observation is considered no more than our patriotic obligation, the debt we owe to the Emperor for his long years of dedicated service to us. We who live on pay him that duty of sincere nostalgia, though the doing brings us little comfort.

Indeed, we are inconsolable. And glad of it.

THE MUTE SCRIBE

If a deaf musician is only a poet and a blind physician is only a gardener and an imperial historian is only a castrate, where does a mute scribe seek employment? Why, where her chatter is not required! So thinking, she packed her scroll, her brush, and her ink pot, and she walked abroad to find the Emperor's tomb.

The path was clear, the direction certain. She had but to follow the course of the builders and the fame of their building to reach the destination of the tales she once had transcribed for the Imperial Historian. The distance, however, was such that it would take her remaining years to complete the journey and, perhaps, still not quite be done. And, at the end of it, would the Emperor accept her service? Well, there was no way to know before arriving, so she put her head down and carried on.

She hardly any longer thought of her former employer, the Imperial Historian. For a time she had thought of nothing else. Then she had decided it was his study and his mutilation that had made him as he was, and she resolved to have nothing more to do with history, not even her own. The past was what it said it was, out of reach and beyond repair. Only the maimed believed it not to be so. Poor man, how could he be expected to behave? A wound like that! Such a wound! She shuddered to recall it but, now that she bore her own, she seldom did. The next turning in the road was more important. And after it, the next.

Along the way she chattered to herself which required no tongue. Anyone passing would not have known her to be doing it. Anyone passing saw only a lowered head, an averted eye, a shuffling bundle that shrank as it approached, winced as it passed, shuffled on as if it knew where it was going, and vanished in the dust as if it had not yet arrived. Passersby carried on without a thought, though later they dreamt of a tiny woman, her back the curve of a crossbow cocked, her hand held taut on a drawstring bag, her eyes eclipsed in a priestly cowl, her lips alive but making no sound, and they wondered where and whether they had seen her, and why she entered their dreams at all. As she walked, she thought of the delights she was seeing along the road. Such ruts and gullies, such pools and bogs, such step-stones laid pat where footpaces fall, such shafts and shadows and flickers of leaves on the changes of soil from the blackest to red, such cascades of pebbles as carriages passed, such riots of sandals as schoolrooms let out! Who would have guessed it all? Not she who had watched tallow drip years into her lap.

As she walked, she imagined the Emperor in his tomb, and she thought of the persuasions she would use to enable him to employ her. She rehearsed them silently, which is how they would be made.

As she walked, from time to time she permitted herself the composing of tales. Not being an original nor even a historian, she had to base them upon tales she once had transcribed, and in the style and the manner of those tellers. It was not the first time she had added to their words. By now, inscribed only upon her imagination, she did not think the authors were likely to be offended. In her mind she never signed her silent tales, and to prevent plagiary she always notated the source beneath the title. Had she been a natural teller of tales, she herself would not have been offended by such a second telling. She would have been flattered.

As she walked, the dust arranged itself about her ankles, and the hem of her robes began to gather sand. She was now, she knew, in a land unlike the others and nearer to her destination. The carts that passed in her direction were full of shovels and swearing men. The ones returning held sand and soil and boulders and clay and men without shovels with mouths without breath.

As she walked, she saw that her feet had slowed. As she watched, their shuffle became a stumble and their stumble became a drag, and at last she knew that they must stop to rest, and after a bit she saw that they had. Did it mean, she wondered, that she had arrived?

After a time a workman saw a bundle in the midst of the road and used his shovel to shift it aside. Then he saw what it was, and he knelt and rose and carried it off to the comfort of the ditch to finish its dying there.

After a time, the lion of the sun was lost and the roar of the workmen ceased. After a time, a pup of a moon nosed into the ditch where the bundle of her lay. After a time, the bundle stirred and shifted and gathered and bunched and stood. After a time, it regained the road and told itself to move on. Its feet, she saw, had abandoned their shuffle and discovered a kind of a glide.

The road too had changed. What had been dust and sand was now inlaid with brick. She knew she needed to hurry before the silver of the night was swapped for the gold of the day, and the workmen returned.

And now she entered a ceramic forest where all the trees had feet. She dared not look higher than the ankles and the shanks for fear of the faces she might see. As she walked and watched, something of the sun crept in and the brick road became yellow.

And she attained the threshold.

And now she was here in a kind of a glade, though she knew it was only a room. By the curve of the wall and the echo of her steps, the vault of the chamber was vast. And there in the distance, a silver lake. And upon it, a barge and a bier.

With a boldness she had known to save for this time, she stepped into the lake and moved on. The surface below bore her little weight well, though it slipped and it slurried a bit.

The bier, she could guess, held a couch at the top and upon it the Emperor lay. Through his effigy mask and his cowl and his shroud, he smiled as she hoped that he would.

On the deck of the barge at the foot of the bier, she squatted and unrolled her scroll.

She deployed her pot and dipped her brush and nodded for him to begin.

WITHIN THE TOMB

Within his amber tomb sculpted as a physician's garden, beneath his clockwork stars and his sun and his moon that ride on rails, aboard his sarcophagus ship borne on the gravity tides of his mercury lake, his mute scribe in faithful attendance, the Emperor remembers the future and prophesies the past.

❧

"Every man fears his death so much that he will never speak of it. When he does, sometimes speaking of nothing else, it is because he reasons that, if the worst already had happened he would be in no condition to speak at all, and so perhaps it is this speaking that prevents the worst. And what is true of the death of a man is true of the death of an empire. With this exception. The death of an empire, as painful as his own and certainly more important, that death, he dreams, he himself may survive.

"Thus a man will speak unceasingly of the death of an empire when it is his own death he perceives and dares not utter. And what is true of the death of one's empire is true of the death of the empire of another. It is better to contemplate the death of the empire of another. Even wise men engaged in such a thought have been seen to smile."

❧

"Obedience is never what it seems, nor is the habit of tyranny without which obedience has no use. Of tyranny and obedience, blame is their cause. Without blame tyranny is difficult to administer, obedience is possible to resist. Once there is the need to establish blame, of the tyrant and the tyrannized neither can save the other."

"Rejection in love is the foretaste of death. It is the grievance from which one does not recover, and the anger outlives the event. He who is rejected in love can never avoid the indulgence of blame, the practice of tyranny.

"They only escape the practice of tyranny who are without grievance and anger, who are blameless and unblaming, who are accepted in love. Sometimes they are the young. To them death is an insupportable surprise, for of it they have received no warning.

"It is clear why the young bear their breasts to the soldiers. Blamelessness is the cause. Impelled by it, they require no commands. It is clear why the soldiers do not question their orders. Blame is the cause. Replete with it, they shoot.

"What is not clear is why the people fail to protect their children from obedience and tyranny. Can it be that they all are unlucky in love?"

❖

"The dying are merciless. Each holds everyone to blame and curses the nurse. For them, even massacre has a natural flavour. The order to open fire upon the young always is given by those near enough death to be familiar with the taste.

"I have left old men to rule you, the loveless, the fathers of blame, the dying. These are my true ceramic squadrons, the implacable defenders of my original tomb. Should you approach, it is they who will ignite the barricades in your path. Their fuel will be your children."

❖

"To whom do I speak these words? Why do I bother to have them transcribed? Because a word uttered and transcribed cannot be taken back. It may be unheard. It may be heard and not remembered. It may be spoken by many and read by some and understood by one or two, yet fail to achieve attribution. But it is in the world, and it awaits its hearing. It is of the world and cannot be erased. Who knows what will become of it? Who can say what it has become? It is enough to have given it breath. No emperor could ask for more."

❖

"Have you noticed that, to serious people, what can be understood is trivial and what cannot is not? I confess to you because you are serious, I have tried to be untrivial, but lately everything I say even I can understand."

◆

"I was not by nature the First Emperor. I had to work at it."

THE PARABLE OF THE DARKNESS
(AFTER THE IMPERIAL PHYSICIAN)

When the Emperor was a boy, he did not like the darkness because at night it leapt upon him too suddenly, and he banished it from his bedroom. "Darkness, vanish!" he said. And because he was the Emperor, it did.

When the Emperor was a youth, he suffered much from a faithless princess. "Ah!" sighed the Emperor, "if only the darkness would hide her from my sight!" And because he was the Emperor, it did.

As a man, the Emperor was troubled by his ministers whom he hated, and his courtiers who hated him, and his colleagues who hated one another and hated their colleagues more. "Darkness," said the Emperor, "take them all!" And because he was the Emperor, it did.

When the Emperor was an old man, he woke in the middle of a night, and he sat up in his bed, and he saw that he could not see. "Darkness?" said the Emperor.

"I am here," replied the darkness.

"I can see that!" said the Emperor, "Why are you here? Did I not banish you from my bedroom when I was a boy?"

"Indeed you did," replied the darkness, "But now that you are no longer an emperor, I have come again."

"No longer an emperor!" said the Emperor. "Who told you this?"

"Surely," replied the darkness, "surely you know that you have died?"

When the Emperor saw that the darkness was speaking the truth, he whimpered for a while, and then he said, "Darkness?"

"I am still here," answered the darkness.

"Darkness," said the Emperor, "do you think you might manage a favour for old time's sake?"

"Perhaps," said the darkness.

"The princess and my ministers and my courtiers and my colleagues and their colleagues," said the Emperor, "I feel them all around me."

"They are all around you," said the darkness.

"Darkness," said the Emperor, "please release them."

And because he had been the Emperor, it did.

And the Emperor died happily ever after.

THE EMPEROR AND THE EUNUCH
(AFTER KAO)

Lacquer bowl of incense smouldering, garnet teapot, footstool, cup,
Chessboard inlaid jade and turquoise, bed-screen inlaid jade and
    pearl,
Jade and opal headboard, footboard, velvet coverlet peacock glazed,
Washbowl, pitcher fretted ivory, rosewood commode fretted gold,
Songbird caged in bamboo, wicker, ocelot caged in travertine ...
These were carried from the bedroom, down the corridor,
Elsewhere viands, brazen pots, waxwork flowers, lacework grapes,
Settees, crockery, candelabra, heaped on tumbrels, trundled off.

When the Emperor could no longer watch his palace emptying,
He wandered through the women's quarters to the least frequented
    wing.
There in a remote pavilion miles from the imperial throne
Dwelt an immemorial eunuch, sightless, voiceless, lame, alone.
To his side the Emperor wandered, at his side the Emperor sat,
Sightless, voiceless, lame, alone ... eunuch, emperor, eunuch's cat.
When the dawn strode down the corridor, beckoned from the dusty
    floor,
Emperor shrugged and stood and followed down the corridor,
    out the door.

JACK WINTER was born in Canada, educated in Montreal and Toronto, and taught modern theatre and creative writing at several Canadian and British universities, including York (Toronto) and University of Bristol (UK). During the 1960s and 1970s he was resident playwright and dramaturg at Toronto Workshop Productions as well as a freelance playwright, producer, and director. In 1976 he moved to England, where he continues to teach and to write. The author of many stage plays, radio and television productions, and cinema films as well as academic and popular journalism, prose fiction and non-fiction, and several poetry collections, his most recent books are *The Tallis Bag* (Oberon, 2012), a literary memoir; *My TWP Plays: A Collection including Ten Lost Years* (Talonbooks, 2013), an annotated anthology; and *Tales of the Emperor* (Talonbooks, 2015), a novel. Recognition for his work includes the Telegram Theatre Award for Best New Canadian Play, the Ontario Arts Council Senior Writer's Award, the Canada Council Senior Arts Fellowship, the Canadian Film Award for Best Documentary Film, an Academy Award nomination for Best Short Subject, the C. Day-Lewis Fellowship of the Greater London Arts Association, and the Arts Council of Great Britain Creative Writing Fellowship (twice).